GW01466213

NICHOLAS PONTICELLO

SATAN'S DIARY

For my little wolf pack safe in our den.

"You were the perfection of wisdom and beauty. You were in Eden, the garden of God. Your clothing was adorned with every precious stone—red carnelian, chrysalides, white moonstone, beryl, onyx, jasper, sapphire, turquoise, and emerald—all beautifully crafted for you and set in the finest gold. They were given to you on the day you were created. I ordained and anointed you as the mighty angelic guardian. You had access to the holy mountain of God and walked among the stones of fire. You were blameless in all you did from the day you were created until the day evil was found in you. Your great wealth filled you with violence, and you sinned. So I banished you from the mountain of God. I expelled you, O mighty guardian, from your place among the stones of fire. Your heart was filled with pride because of all your beauty. You corrupted your wisdom for the sake of your splendor. So I threw you to the earth and exposed you to the curious gaze of kings. You defiled your sanctuaries with your many sins and your dishonest trade. So I brought fire from within you, and it consumed you. I let it burn you to ashes on the ground in the sight of all who were watching. All who knew you are appalled at your fate. You have come to a terrible end, and you are no more." – Ezekiel 28:12–19

BOOK 1: IN HEAVEN

I have no special regard for Satan; but I can at least claim that I have no prejudice against him. It may even be that I lean a little his way, on account of his not having a fair show. All religions issue bibles against him, and say the most injurious things about him, but we never hear his side.

Mark Twain

3

PRELUDE

I WORK THREE DAYS a week in a coffee shop on the corner of Bancroft and College in Berkeley, California. The university is just across the street, and most of the traffic that comes through Caffè Strada on Monday mornings consists of bleary-eyed students in pajama pants and baggy Cal sweatshirts. They always pay in crumpled up ones and fives, or they empty a mix of change onto the counter and expect the cashier to work out whether they have enough money for a *grande* or a *venti*.

They lead an easy life, the students: class at noon, an afternoon studying in the café, dinner with friends at seven, and then maybe Frisbee on the intramural field or a movie. Sure, midterms roll around every three weeks or so to disrupt the gentle cadence of their days, but in all my time on Earth, I have never seen so content, so indulged, and so happy a lot as college students. I have chosen to live among them because they are creatures of extremes: extreme intelligence and extreme idleness. They are among the most highly educated creatures on Earth, yet their intellect is busily occupied planning their next outfits for an Eighties-themed party, sneaking into football games, and slipping kegs past resident directors.

Indeed, college students are seriously underemployed. Seventy-five percent of a student's time is spent on a lawn somewhere with a book for a pillow. But what astounds me is how much students can accomplish with the remaining twenty-five percent of their time. Groundbreaking discoveries in biology, chemistry, and physics come out of those lazy little bastards. Whole mathematical theories are disproved and reformulated. The deconstruction and assessment of Aristotle, Hemingway, and Tolstoy can be completed in a single all-nighter.

This brainpower should be harnessed, funneled into a giant think tank in the middle of Silicon Valley. College students could be the solution to the energy crisis. They could resolve the conflict in the Middle East. They could colonize the moon.

But students carefully maintain the reputation of good-for-nothing loafers whose brain cells and bank accounts are being blown on reality television and Bacardi. That way nobody will ever suspect them of genius, and they will never be asked to do anything more than rehash an old Jane Austen novel. Never was there a more arrogant, conceited, and shameless bunch of humans in all of history. I work at the epicenter of student life: the café. So it is that I serve an average of eighty lattes, fifty cappuccinos, and thirty espressos a day to the untapped talent of the universe.

God never intended for humans to be so complex. He was looking for something simple and dependable he could cling to when he was lonely. He thought if he made humans mortal, they would never venture far from him for fear of death. Mortality was a weakness that God hoped would bind humans to him forever. But mortality created in humans certain tendencies unknown to immortal creatures like me. The urge to reproduce—this was completely unintentional on the part of God. Wanderlust—totally unexpected.

Now, God has abandoned this race of mortals. But they have not abandoned him. They have filled the space of thousands of years with all sorts of stories about who he is and what he has done. Most of what humans think about God is fictitious. Or at most, it is a watered-down version of the truth. But one thing they do have right is that God is their maker. They may praise him for that reason alone, but if they knew more about him, they might find him less worthy of their devotion.

Mortals think they need God. That just isn't true. Humans need double lattes more than they need God. In fact, humans were created because *God needed them*. God was seriously depressed. He and I had suffered a pretty grim falling out, and he was looking for someone to fill his bed. So, out of this desperate state of loneliness, Adam was formed. Man was a rebound. Yet humans continue to flock to churches, synagogues, and temples to offer up thanks for the gift God gave them: life.

God is my maker, too. But I don't feel I owe him anything. You won't find me in a church on Sundays. I go to the Berkeley Marina on Sundays and fly my kite. Some people there recognize me and say hello when they pass. I am known now as Todd Rivet. I like the name, the way it sounds. I like to fly kites.

I taught Benjamin Franklin to fly a kite on Milk Street in Boston in 1714.

The technology of kites has come a long way since then. I fly a Chinese dragon kite with an eighty-meter tail. Some kids at the marina know me as the *Dragon Guy*. It's not the first time I've been called that. I have had many names: Satan, Beelzebub, Dragon, Serpent, and the Devil. Many call me the Prince of Darkness. Darkness, is it? They used to call me Lucifer, *light-bringer*.

Yellow wood sorrel and daisies crawl over the sides of the hills of the Berkeley Marina. There are sometimes hundreds of kites in the sky. On the best days, the sky is an explosion of color. San Francisco stands enveloped in an ethereal mist of blue-gray fog. There are the looming towers of the financial district; the low squat, tin warehouses on the wharf; and the long wooden piers. The Bay Bridge carries I-80 past the shipyard cranes, over the bay, and into the city. Alcatraz floats between the Berkeley Pier and the Golden Gate Bridge. Today, the bridge stands vermilion against a white and pink sunset.

I pull up a blade of sour grass, and my teeth pick at the stem until it bleeds clear, sweet gel. Today, I have not brought my kite. Instead, I have Kundera's *The Unbearable Lightness of Being*. I am on page 137. The edges of the pages I have read are smudged and worn. The rest remains unmarred. Each page will have its turn.

I read very carefully. I read a sentence, and then reread that sentence until I have understood every word the way the author intends it to be understood. Then I fuse the sentences together into paragraphs and reread the paragraphs. I am never hasty. I have a very long time to go on reading books. I am in no hurry to be finished with anything. Kundera is very intentional. His words lay over other words, which lay over other worlds, and I must swim many leagues before I fully grasp his meaning. And then I must swim all the way back carrying those meanings, and they are heavy, so I take multiple trips.

How many times have you forgotten something important you have read? Kundera would not want you to forget.

I turn the page and if I feel a disconnect between the first word at the top of 138 and the last word at the bottom of 137, I go back and reread page 137.

Kundera speaks of the soul, that elusive essence of self. Humans hold onto the soul like a comfort blanket. Humans are hopelessly romantic in that way. They believe that when they die, they go on as I do and take some place in the hierarchy of angels. A silly fantasy. What differentiates man from Imorti is his soul; man's soul is a mere reflection of existence, and when man's body dies, it will be like a shadow passing into a cave. The reflection will be gone and all that will remain is dust.

CHAPTER I

WHEN I WAS BORN, it was like waking from the sluggish unconsciousness of drunken sleep. There was a stirring in the hills of Eden. The physical universe bent and stretched. The sky ripped apart, and I fell out. I lay a long time in the moss-covered bank of the River Fluvius. I was on my side, curled in the fetal position. My toes were in the stream. My face was in the mud. I had fallen between two large river rocks and the whole of my body lay like a rag doll in the sediment.

I was born complete. I had the muscles to stand, jump, walk, and run. But I had never learned to do these things, so I stumbled along the ground for a while, unable to comprehend the limitations of my strength. It took me a while to stand and then to take my first step. I was also fully capable of language. My first words were, "What's all this?" Not prophetic, I grant you that, but imagine waking very suddenly to find yourself alive for the first time and picture being surrounded by a garden full of all God's creatures. If you were to speak, you might as well say, "What's all this?"

The mud on my body looked like war paint. My hair was wavy and fell around my ears. I combed the tangles out with my fingers. I could move in small steps, and I turned myself in a circle. I acknowledged my body with a nod. Yes, it was all there. I was aware that I had been made of the clay of the earth and the air of the sky. I knew I was one of God's angels. I even knew that I was an attempt at perfection. And, oh, how close I came to perfection—you would marvel.

I also knew the man sitting on the fallen trunk of a birch staring at me was God. He was attractive, weathered, with a leathery sort of skin. His hair was salt-and-peppery, his face etched with smile lines. God had never been young. He had come into being just as he was now, the figure of a forty-something-year-old man.

"Better than I expected," God said, acknowledging me with a nod. He motioned for me to turn in a circle, and so I did. "Yes," he said finally. "You will do just fine."

He got up and there was a rustling in the trees, as if his very movement summoned the winds. He had been sitting on an elaborate quilt, stitched with fine golden thread, a patchwork of silk and satin and lace. He brought the quilt to my shoulders and wrapped it around my naked body. I held it close under my chin.

I could see my reflection in the water, could see my sculpted calves and handsome face, could see how the quilt complimented my features. I shivered.

"I am quite satisfied," God said, looking me over one last time. "Come with me."

11

I nodded my acquiescence but said nothing. I felt that if I spoke, I would cease to be perfect; that by speaking, I would reveal some defect or flaw.

God delivered long, self-aggrandizing monologues as he led me through the gardens. He spoke to me of Heaven and of his many creations. He spoke of angels and mortal creatures. He told me that of all his inventions, I was his finest, his most beloved.

"You are an angel and immortal," God said. "And all the animals in Eden bow to you wherever you go. That is the Law of Heaven."

There was a narrow trail that wound along the bank of the River Fluvius. We followed it until we came to an ornate wooden bridge that carried us over the river, up a hill, and onto a sweeping lawn.

That was where I first met another angel, like me—Michael. He was bent over on the ground, white robes furled beneath his knees. He had in his right hand a pair of scissors and in his left a short measuring stick. He held the measuring stick against each blade of grass and then, as if he had done it a million times before, he quickly snipped the blade at some predetermined length.

"I am very particular about my lawns," God explained, nodding at the ruler in Michael's hand.

I would later learn that Michael's patience was eternal. He was God's experiment in subservience.

I, however, was quite the opposite, made of an entirely different fabric.

When Michael saw us coming, he wiped the scissors on his robes and stood. He acknowledged God with a nod.

"Michael is the gardener of Eden," God explained. "He waters the lawns, keeps the plants in order, and takes care of the animals."

Michael inspected me. "A new one, eh? What's his name?"

"He is called Lucifer," God said.

It was strange hearing my name for the first time. *Lucifer.* I said it slowly under my breath.

"Good name," Michael said, smiling at me. "Lucifer. It means *light-bringer.*"

"Yes," said God. "Lucifer is my greatest creation. He is to walk freely in my garden. He is also welcome to go anywhere else he pleases. He may come to my house if he likes, or he may walk upon Earth. There is no place in all of the universe forbidden to him."

Michael nodded easily. "Then you'll need a key," he said. "Stop by tomorrow and I'll get you set up."

"Now, Lucifer," God said. "I have given you all of Heaven to explore, and Earth if you like. You may pick the fruit from my trees, and you may swim in the lakes at your leisure. Tear up whole rows of asphodel if it suits your fancy. They will always be replanted. You may inconvenience Michael at your will. He is very patient and will not interfere with your fun. He has been ordered to obey your every wish for eternity."

Here God withdrew a notebook from his satchel. He handed it to me.

"I give this to you as the first of many gifts," he said. "The pages are blank."

I took the notebook in my hands. The leather binding was soft, worn, yielding. The pages were rough and yellow.

"Fill them however you like," God said. "As I have made you a very curious angel, I am sure you will want to study the animals and how they work. They are very complicated, and I have lost track of all the kinds I have made, but I'm sure you will keep them straight, for you are very clever."

I held the notebook to my chest.

He continued, "You are the closest I have ever come to perfection, Lucifer. And you are to walk freely among my kingdom for all your days. I give you everything in this garden and everything on Earth."

Here God paused, whether to give weight to what he would say next, or because he was still trying to think of how to arrange his words, I do not know.

"I have only one request of you," he said.

I blinked and held my breath.

"What is your request?" I asked, when God said nothing more and I could bear the silence no longer.

"That you spend all your nights with me in my house."

It was a curious request, but one I could not refuse with so many riches laid out before me.

"It is done," I said. "From now until eternity."

So it was that I came to know God so well.

God's house was built on a tall hill with a thousand steps winding their way up to a gaping threshold. The house was constructed of white marble with four rectangular walls and a pitched roof supported by tall, fluted columns. Inside were two rooms. The first, a large chamber, was lit with a hundred flickering torches mounted on the walls. A fire burned in a stone pit in the center of the room, and at the far back sat an elegant marble slab upon which God had created the universe and everything in it. There was a smaller, private room beyond where God slept—where I slept—and a large, round bed with a downy mattress, silk sheets, and a tall white canopy.

God lived alone, but there were many who came and went throughout the day, angels who brought fresh fruit from the orchards or vegetables from the gardens. There were others who came to make the bed or sweep the floors, to tend the fire and scrub the white marble walls. They said little to God or to me, and when they were finished with whatever task they had come to perform, they went away without a word.

All afternoon, we feasted on grapes and pears, apples and cheese; and in the evening, God taught me a game played with the knucklebones of a sheep. I practiced throwing and catching the knucklebones on the back of my hand. I learned how to toss them so that they would have the highest chances of falling in favorable patterns, and before the evening was out, I was besting God two to one.

We played late into the night, and when the fire was low, I climbed into his bed and buried myself under the covers. God did not join me that night. He stayed awake at his bench, no doubt dreaming up new creations and molding them out of clay and fire. I fell asleep to the gentle drum of his fingers on the marble tabletop and the hiss and crackle of the dying embers in the earthen pit.

When I awoke, the daylight was shining brightly through the open windows. I rubbed the sleep from my eyes, stretched out like a cat in the sun, and kicked the covers away. I found the table laden with goat cheese and milk and sweet tangerines, and I ate eagerly, not waiting for permission.

God was nowhere to be found. So, when I finished, I set out in search of Michael, who was to give me the key to all the Kingdoms of Heaven. The garden was a paradise, and I was easily amused by the squirmy, crawly things in the ground, and the cawing, flapping things in the sky, and the swinging, jumping things in the trees. I carried with me the notebook God had given me, and when I was inspired by some new creature, I sketched its portrait in gray charcoal, paying close attention to how many toes or fingers it had, the shape of its body and face, the texture of its skin or fur, and all the other little things that set it apart from the other creatures.

I was following the pronged footsteps of one such creature when I stumbled upon Michael. He was bent over a patch of brown earth with a small shovel and was tilling the soil.

"Aha," he said when he saw me. "There you are. I want to show you something."

He laid the shovel down and wiped his hands on his knees. I followed him down a narrow trail to a small wooden shack. When we stepped through the door, I was surprised to find that not only did Michael keep his gardening tools inside, but he lived there, too. There was a small hammock slung across the back wall, a rocking chair fashioned out of gnarled oak, a tin basin for washing, and a long wooden workbench with a smooth flat surface and dozens of little drawers for holding things.

The abode was crowded but quaint, and I felt very much at home there, as I did almost everywhere I had been so far. Michael led me to the workbench and slid out a long, wooden drawer and invited me to peer inside.

What I saw in a bed of grass and sticks were four blue ovoids, each no larger than my thumb. The ovoids were trembling and there were small fractures in the blue shells. As we watched, the cracks grew larger and wider, revealing little chirping beaks.

"They're hatching," Michael said. "Isn't it remarkable?"

"Where did you find them?" I asked.

"God brought them to me this morning. Said he spent all night on them. He said to me, 'Michael, don't you leave those eggs until they're hatched.'"

Michael was beaming as if it was the most important thing he had ever been asked to do. "What are they?" I asked.

Michael shrugged. "He says they're called *bluebirds*."

But when the first chick hatched, its coat was fuzzy and brown—not blue as I had hoped.

Michael and I watched until all the birds were out of the eggs. Michael fed them larvae and insects, and he assured me that they were bound to go through many transformations in the next few weeks.

"They may turn out blue yet," he said. "Mortals are not born the way angels are born. Mortals come to being in small steps, first with conception, then the fetal stages, then the birth of the physical body. Then consciousness awakens, and perhaps intelligence. It is a gradual process. Instincts, motor skills, thought—these are all bestowed upon the mortal one after the other, spanning many months and sometimes years. It isn't until a mortal is well on in its life that the self becomes fixed. And I have learned living among them that even then, mortals tend to grow a little still, and so they are never the same until the day they die."

Michael patted the feathered head of one of the chicks with his thumb, gently.

"Angels, on the other hand, are a bit different," he continued. "They come into being nearly complete. Yes, they come in all colors and shapes. But they are granted a body that is already fully grown and will not age a day in all eternity. They are granted wisdom and knowledge and skill. And these things are what define an angel. These things never change. Take yourself, for instance," Michael said, nodding to me. "You are beautiful—as God intended. You are clever and curious. And a great many other things I'm sure we will come to learn. And that is how you will stay. Angels are cast from a mold, and when the molten lead of their corpses has cooled, it will stay forever as it is, eternally youthful, a body in its prime. God gave you a marvelous body, Lucifer. You are his most perfect creation."

Michael turned back to the chicks. One fluttered its wings and stumbled out of the nest onto the cool wood of the drawer.

"But for mortals it is ever-changing," Michael said, scooping the chick up and setting it back in the nest. "Their bodies start out weak and vulnerable. Then they become strong. And then they grow weak again in the very end."

"May I come again tomorrow?" I asked. "I would like to see if they have grown."

"You may come every day if you wish," Michael said. "Heaven is yours. Which reminds me—"

He opened another drawer and produced an old wrought iron key.

"With this," he said, "no door shall ever be closed to you."

And he pressed the key into my hand. It grew warm and then fiery red in my palm until its dark outline was imprinted on the soft skin of my new body. There was no pain, just heat—and then coolness when Michael took the key away again.

Michael placed the key back in the drawer and examined the scar on my hand.

"Watch," he said, nodding at my palm.

The blackened skin where the key had left its mark turned quickly red, followed by pink, and then faded completely so that it looked as if it had never been there at all.

"Whenever you come to a door that is locked," Michael said, "your touch will open it."

He closed the drawer and nodded to me. "Now, go. See the universe that God has made for you."

⊛

The first year was blissful. I was a young angel then, at the beginning of my everlasting life. And Heaven was vast. There was Eden. There were other places, too—dark caves, tall mountains, the barren wasteland known as Earth, and strange ethereal worlds where God had conducted some of his earliest experiments. But none was so interesting as the garden.

Every morning, I rose before the sun was up, slipped from under the sheets, and explored the grounds. The mountains were cold and beautiful. There was snow in the highest pass, frozen like a hanging glacier between the purple-gray peaks. I never went anywhere without my notebook. I made charcoal sketches of all the creatures I encountered—feral cats, monal pheasant, white-crested kalij, alpine marmots, speckled wood pigeons, striped okapi, orangutans, and peregrine falcons.

I put into words everything I learned, came to know the names of the plants and animals, and studied everything about how they lived and died. I learned some of the calls of the birds. I knew the migration patterns of the buffalo and antelope herds. I came to know the difference between predator and prey, and I quickly understood what it is to be mortal and what it is to be Imorti, those born as angels with everlasting life.

Where the mortal creatures of the garden could die of starvation or thirst, cold, or heat, and thus required food, water, sleep, and shelter, Imorti simply ate or drank or slept for pleasure. If a baby possum was stuck in the snow, it would shiver and die. But to me the snow merely stung but was not deadly. A nest of robin eggs left out in the hot summer sun with no shade or cover would soon turn foul and never hatch. To me, the sunlight was a balm.

I took note of every animal I came upon, and it surprised me how many there were. Some animals were common and easy to spot. These were the mice, the squirrels, and other rodents. Others were a rare delight: the cougar, the panda, the elk, the grizzly bear. I looked forward to discovering new animals, and hardly a day passed that I did not take down a page of notes or sketch something I had never seen before.

I often came across Michael, and he would tell me of some strange creature he had seen the day before in an obscure corner of the garden. I would then set out to find his beast and make record of it in my notebook. Michael was a kind friend to me. He showed me how the plants grew and the proper way to care for the flowers and fruit trees. He had lived a great many years in the garden and knew the ways of mortal things.

In the evenings, God thumbed through my notebook. He praised the accuracy of my illustrations. Sometimes he would come across a sketch of some small creature and say, "I do not recall making this one."

God seemed content for those first few months. We sometimes spent whole days apart, but at nights, he was guaranteed my company. I was so immersed in the exploration of his gardens that I did not notice his strange behavior at first.

❈

The signs were there all along. One day I came home from Eden, tired, smudged with dirt—loose, dry maple leaves broken in my hair. I had been tracking a wild boar through the woodlands. When I came upon the beast, she was in the midst of giving birth to six hairless piglets. She was huddled beneath the shadow of the riverbank. Her eyes spoke of the pain she must have been experiencing. I had never witnessed a birthing before in all my time in Eden. I stayed and watched for nearly two hours until the deed was done, and all the young ones lay at their mother's side, suckling hungrily at her teats. I documented this miracle in my notebook. This was a wonder to me. That six creatures should burst forth from one was beyond my comprehension.

I wondered if it had been the same when God birthed me; had there been as much pain, as much blood and sticky, putrid fluid? I entered God's house in a flurry of excitement, the events of my day spilling out of me in a waterfall of exclamations. I barely got through describing what it was like when the first piglet reached hungrily for its first breath when God gripped my forearm anxiously and hissed, "It was alive?"

"Yes," I said. "Of course it was alive. The boar lay down on her side and six tiny piglets crawled out."

God's nostrils flared. I had never before seen such worry cross his face. His fingers stayed tight around my arm, and when he finally let go there was a white discoloration where his hand had been. He stood very still for a long time, and his eyes welled with tears, but he brushed them away hastily.

"Please explain this to me one more time," God said, this time more coolly. "You say the animal lay down and six more animals came out of her. From whence did they come?"

"They came out of her belly. They were much smaller than she was, and hairless. They were really quite helpless. They stayed close to her after that, and suckled milk from her teats."

"And the sow, was she alive after ... after these creatures crawled out of her?"

"Yes," I said. "Though it did appear she had some trouble moving. She was breathing very heavily, and her eyes were closed for most of it. It did not appear to be easy, but yes, she lived."

God shook his head. He was very distressed. "So, this one boar became seven. That which was just one is now many. I do not see how it is possible. Thank you, Lucifer, for your thoughtful account. I shall think long on it."

God did not sleep at all that night. He stayed awake beside me, breathing harshly like the sow. I came in and out of consciousness and always found God lying still on his back staring at the ceiling.

The following morning, I went to Michael. He was on his knees, silver scissors in hand, trimming the lawn with the steady focus of a sage. I related to Michael what I had seen in the woodlands, how the boar had birthed six tiny piglets, and Michael listened calmly, his deep brown eyes hearing as much as his ears.

"And God was quite distressed," I said finally. "He did not seem to know that these animals do this."

"Ah, yes," Michael said. "There is a lot about mortal creatures still to be learned. Why, I have spent my whole life in this garden, and I have not yet witnessed the miracle you speak of, but I have long suspected that the animals were replicating themselves. There were two black crows the first summer I spent here. The next summer I saw six, and then there were whole flocks of them nosing about for worms on my lawn. I knew either God was making crows on the sly or they were somehow reproducing. And there have been variations in the types of each animal. The first tigers had fifteen stripes on their sides, and later there were tigers with fewer and more stripes. I knew they were not the same tigers as the first, and I wondered where they had come from. So it is, Lucifer, that you have taught me something I never knew: animals crawl out of the bellies of other animals, just as you and I crawled out of the belly of God."

Michael smiled placidly. He seemed very pleased that his little mystery had been solved at last. It must have been strange to spend all those years in the garden and to see strange creatures popping up all the time. I was glad he was satisfied with my discovery. But I was still troubled on one point.

"God does not appear to be happy that his animals are multiplying. He stayed awake all night thinking fiercely on the matter, and I am worried for his mood was seriously altered."

"Ah," Michael said. "God is not always happy. Such things easily disturb him. He likes to think that the things he creates are certain and fixed, and that he has perfect knowledge of his creatures. But he is often disappointed. None of his experiments ever turn out exactly as planned."

"But will he recover?" I asked.

"Lucifer," Michael soothed, "God has been the happiest I ever knew him to be since you took up his company. Do not fear. He will be past this in a few days."

Sure enough, by the following week, God was himself again. Neither of us brought up the boar, but when I was alone in the garden, I made it my goal to witness another such birthing.

Over the next several months, I came to learn that animals replicated themselves in a variety of fashions. At the time, I did not connect sex with birth. I saw only the independent act of labor. I did not know there were several stages leading up to birth. I watched as birds dropped little oval rocks in their nests and sat upon them until the rocks cracked and flightless chicks poked their beaks out. I saw that some animals birthed only one or two cubs at a time, such as the lion and the bear. Insects and fish laid hundreds and thousands of eggs all at once. The queen of a termite colony could produce as many as thirty thousand eggs in a day. I began to wonder how all these creatures would continue to fit in the garden.

I asked Michael about it one day.

"I reckon they don't all stay here," Michael said, scratching his head. "The gates to Earth lie open. I supposed they venture out when the food is scarce in Eden. Mortals need food, you know. They die without it. I can't see why they wouldn't migrate to someplace where food is more abundant—we have no way of keeping track of them all."

It was true. One day I waited all morning in front of one of the gates to Earth. I hid in the barberry shrub and watched the entrance eagerly. Just after midday, I saw a family of possums wind their way down a small foot trail. They sniffed about the gate for a while, and then, resolutely, they left Eden.

I asked Michael why the animals didn't go through other gates to other parts of Heaven. Michael said that mortals were restricted to Eden and Earth. Only the Imorti could pass through the other gates.

Then one evening, I came home and found God crying in a corner of the house. He had his knees curled up to his chest and he was hugging himself and rocking back and forth rhythmically. His white robes were soaked with tears. I went to him and hugged him close to my chest. He did not venture to explain what troubled him. I was too terrified to ask.

Was this the God that ruled in Heaven? Was this the most powerful of all creatures, mortal and immortal? He sagged in my arms.

He poured salty tears into my hair and gown. His body was shaking. I trembled at the sight.

I rocked him gently and hummed until the crying ceased. When he was asleep, I carried him to the bed and tucked him under the covers and then lay down beside him and wrapped my arms around his waist.

In the morning, he rose and took his breakfast out on the terrace. He was much improved, though his face was swollen and stained. He did not talk about the night before. I could not bring myself to interrogate him. I wanted as much as he did to forget the past night's trauma. I could not reconcile the great Imorti that was my creator with the helpless child I had found weeping on the floor. I pushed the memory as far back as it would go and buried it behind all the bird calls and plant names I had come to know. I did not even mention it to Michael, though I knew he might be able to help. I thought that if I spoke of that night out loud, it would become more real, and thus reaffirm what I was coming to suspect: God was not perfect.

CHAPTER 2

T HE GARDEN OF EDEN covers nearly thirty square miles. That is about the size of what is today known as Manhattan Island. So, there was much to explore there in the dawn of my existence. One autumn day, I came upon two stone blocks standing upright like pillars supporting a third stone block laid across the top. They made what appeared to be a gateway into another of God's mysterious domains.

I circled the stone frame and marveled at its simplicity. Its architecture was unlike other structures in the garden: primitive, rough. The stones looked as if they might tumble if given a hard push. They were ragged blocks, their surfaces chiseled and uneven. They smelled of sedge grass. Lichen grew along the base of the pillars.

There was a mossy log across from the gateway. I sat upon it and took out my notebook and a piece of charcoal. I spent nearly an hour sketching the ancient stones. A small herd of okapi grazed nearby. Okapi are one of God's more outlandish experiments. These strange beasts have the stripes of a zebra on their hindquarters and forearms. They can stand up to six feet tall and have the semblance of a small, brown giraffe. I watched them graze near the stone frame. When I was finally done recording my new finding, I approached the stone pillars. The okapi nervously moved away and into the cover of some trees.

In three quick steps, I was through the portal.

I emerged in a ring of stone columns. There was a central ring composed of five larger stone arches. I stood between the inner and outer circles. The ground was barren. All around me stretched a great, flat plane. It was devoid of life. The earth was red and hard, like clay. The sky was starless. There was no sun and no moon. The place was bathed evenly in a cold, blue, ethereal glow. The arches of the outer circle appeared to lead to alternate dimensions. The inner circle had a completely different feel. The ground there was seared, as if there had been a great fire. In places, the clay-earth was cracked.

When I finally ventured to step into the inner ring, I was swept up in a whirlwind and put down on Earth. I stood in the middle of a similar monument among the towering stone columns. In this world there were birds, plants, and insects. The sun shone in the west, dropping quickly beneath the horizon like a seed into the earth. I took in a breath of fresh air and could detect the scent of wood sage. This place would later come to be called Stonehenge. I learned that the middle ring would take me back and forth between Earth and the barren clay world I had just stumbled upon. The gateways in the outer ring led to Eden and every other facet of Heaven.

I played a long time in Stonehenge, crossing back and forth from the barren land to other of God's more colorful dimensions. I returned home to Eden full of questions about Stonehenge. I found God in his study, working by the dim light of a candle.

"My Lord," I said. "I found a new world today."

"Mm," God murmured. "Did you?"

"Yes," I said. "It was unlike any place I have been."

I opened my notebook to the picture I had drawn of the stone pillars. God glanced at the sketch disinterestedly, and then turned back to his work. It might have been better if he had not taken notice at all of where I had been that day. But he did. His eyes were on the work before him, but his mind was processing what I had just shown him. A flicker of recognition flashed in God's eyes, and he froze.

His gaze turned to me, and I could see his face changing color. He took the notebook from me, peered a long time at my sketch, and then tore it violently from the book and threw it into the fire.

"What are you doing?" I shrieked.

"Do not tell me, Lucifer, that you passed through those pillars?" God demanded.

"I did," I said. "And what of it? You told me I could go anywhere I pleased. That was your promise."

God snarled. His face was fiery white, like the pale scales of an albino snake. "You are not to go there anymore. Take any of the other gates to Earth. But you are not to pass through the Battlegrounds."

"The Battlegrounds? Is that what you call them?"

"Never mind what they are called!" God raged. "Just be sure you do not go there again. Take another way to Earth. I will not have you walking among the Great Stones. And I will not hear you speak of them to me ever again."

I had never been so furious in all my life. I had been granted access to all of Heaven, and now I was being reprimanded for passing unknown into some hellish chamber of God's memory. Whatever the story of the Great Stones, God would not be reminded of it. The mere charcoal sketch tormented him in a way I had never seen. And for this I was being punished.

God stayed at his workbench all night. I was exiled to the bedroom. I waited for God until morning. And when he did not come, I felt the first bubbles of rebellion rising in my chest. My pride was hurt. I was humiliated.

I went to Michael at first light and told him how God had reacted when I presented the sketch of the stone pillars. Michael nodded.

"Aye." He sighed. "God has not forgiven himself, then."

"What can you possibly mean?" I asked.

"God is deeply burdened," said Michael. "His mind strays to dark thoughts, and he becomes very depressed. I thought since you'd come, he was past all that. But I see now I was mistaken."

"What dark thoughts?" I asked.

"He thinks about what he's done, and he is heavy with regret. God shoulders a world of guilt. For you see, Lucifer, he killed his brothers and sisters. And he did so right there, on the spot where those stones stand today."

❈

In the beginning, there were many gods, Michael explained. They knew not where they came from or why they had been granted such vast powers over the Heavenly domains. All they knew was that they had existed for as long as any of them could remember in a place known as the Battlegrounds—a flat expanse of dry earth with neither sun nor moon—the very place God forbade me to go again.

There the gods warred as if it were a game, seeing which of them could best the others in a test of might. Some days God—my God—won. Sometimes he lost. But he was happy, for he was evenly matched with these other gods—the Ancient Ones.

Then, in an effort to best his brothers and sisters, God discovered a secret known to none of the others. It might be said that God was the cleverest of the gods, for he saw something the others had missed, some weakness in the fabric of their beings. God was thrilled because he would be able to exploit this weakness to his advantage, and he couldn't wait to see the faces of the others when they saw what he had found.

As he had done for an eternity, God went to battle with the others, and he laughed when he saw the Ancient Ones shrinking away before him just as he had suspected they would. They came at him, one after the other, and each shrunk away to nothingness.

When it was over, God realized what he had done. He had destroyed the Ancient Ones for good. And no power he could summon would bring them back again. Then God fell to the scorched earth and cried. In his ambition to prevail, he had snuffed out the only companions he had ever had in all of Heaven. This he would regret for the rest of his days, or so Michael believed.

God set to work inventing the universe—the Garden of Eden, Earth, the other realms of Heaven. And he filled all his kingdoms with Imorti and mortals, mere approximations of the gods he had destroyed. None of his creations ever came close to satisfying God's desire for company, Michael said. None of them save me.

CHAPTER 3

I T SHOULD NOT COME as a surprise that God kept a greenhouse in Eden. His various horticultural experiments were
so numerous in those days that he was obliged to isolate a great
many of his creations from the chaos of the garden such that
they could be looked after with greater care.

Michael saw to all the needs of the plants in the greenhouse
and was most dedicated to their well-being. The flowers and trees
of the greenhouse were unlike any others in the garden. They
were experiments in extremes—extreme color, extreme scent,
extreme beauty. Some flowers were so pungent that mortal creatures were overtaken and thrown into a deep, coma-like sleep.
Other plants proved to be viciously poisonous to mortals such
that even the slightest residue of a leaf or petal could kill.

The plants of the greenhouse were kept under careful watch for
fear that they should ever be set free in the garden and disrupt the
perfect harmony that God prided himself so much in maintaining.
Michael never kept more than one of each species. Under his watch,

such plants were never loosed upon Eden, and consequently, they never made an appearance on Earth.

On my first tour of the greenhouse, Michael explained the properties of each plant in detail, its effects on mortals, its seasonal growth patterns. I took note of many interesting specimens in my diary but was in no way able to document the entirety of God's collection in one visit. I satisfied myself in listening to Michael's calm and easy explanations—asking questions whenever further details were warranted.

As you know, plants such as these, though dangerous to mortal creatures, have little effect on Imorti, and so I sifted through the plants, touching and smelling what I pleased, unafraid of such things as poisons and heady odors. As I wandered the rows of flowers and shrubs, I was struck by the exceptional beauty of a small tree with smooth, white bark and big, glassy leaves. The tree stood no more than four feet tall and was potted in a white porcelain tub about three feet in diameter. The tree, unlike the other trees and plants in the greenhouse, showed no signs of decay. Not a single leaf was brown; not an inch of its trunk was scratched or worn; and the fruit it bore in its leafy branches—round, fist-sized bulbs that resembled plums—had neither scuffs nor bruises. Each leaf was identical to the next, each fruit the same size and shape.

I called Michael over. He came carrying a watering pail and a small spade.

"What tree is this?" I asked.

"Ah." Michael nodded. "That tree is a favorite of God's, made nearly perfect, like yourself. He calls it the Magpie Tree. It is the only immortal plant God has ever made. See those fruit there? Go ahead and pick one."

I reached up and grabbed a purple plum. It snapped away from the tree easily.

"Now, watch," Michael said.

Quite suddenly, from where I had taken the fruit, a green bud began to form. Within seconds, the bud had tripled in size and was growing paler. Then the bud blossomed into a white flower, the petals fell off, and the remaining ovary swelled into a green bulb. The bulb grew larger until it was the same size as the plum I had just plucked, and its colors changed from pale green to pink to purple. Before two minutes was up, the fruit I had just removed was replaced and the tree restored to its original form.

"Taste it," Michael said, indicating the plum I still held in my hand.

I sunk my teeth into the fruit and admitted that it was by far the sweetest thing I had ever tasted. "What are its effects?" I asked.

"On Imorti, nothing. On mortals, that fruit has the power to prolong life. It has restorative properties. It slows aging."

"You mean it can make mortals immortal?" I asked.

"No, no. Nothing can make mortals immortal, just as nothing can kill the Imorti, save perhaps God. No. I have run a few tests on mortal creatures. A small dose every day can triple the life expectancy of a healthy hare. But by no means does it grant the hare immunity from death. The hare is still susceptible to disease and injury. His wounds heal no faster; he can still bleed to death or die from hunger and thirst; he is not immortal. But a small dose every day will slow aging sufficiently enough to triple his lifespan."

"Then a larger dose might do the same for a deer or a bobcat?"

"Precisely. But a mortal is always mortal. Feed a rabbit on only Magpie fruit for the rest of his life, and he will still age and die eventually."

I asked Michael if he didn't mind if I experimented with the Magpie fruit myself. He said I was always welcome to anything the Garden of Eden had to offer.

I returned to the greenhouse every day with my notebook and commented on every aspect of the Magpie Tree. I began testing the effects of the fruit for myself, administering small doses to a batch of mice two times a day at twelve-hour intervals. The mice feeding on the fruit tended to develop at a rate two or three times slower than their companions who were not fed the fruit. Both sets of mice proved to be equally susceptible to disease. And upon the cessation of treatment, the treated mice resumed normal growth rates.

It was an interesting study, and it occupied my curiosity for some months. It may be the first documented experiment on mice in the history of creation. My notes were thorough and complete; a modern-day biologist would find my journals entirely comprehensive and up to the standards of scientific research today.

I presented my discoveries to God, and he acknowledged them with an absent-minded "Hmph." His moods were becoming increasingly unpredictable. He had lost interest in my notebooks, lost interest in me perhaps. Some nights he wouldn't come to bed, and I was left to sleep alone. For this I became increasingly resentful and embittered. Still, I returned night after night to his house in hopes of finding him improved.

There were rare moments in those dark days when God was his old self again. These were the moments that kept me coming back. I loved God very much. I think I loved him even more when I saw how weak he was and how greatly he needed me. When we were together, he would hold me tight and ask me to stay by him always. He whispered his deepest regrets, his remorse over the loss of the Ancient Ones, and his constant yearning for death. He said forever was too much to bear. I did not understand how, with talent like his, he could feel so incomplete and wish so badly to be gone from the universe. But that is the way of great minds—they are never satisfied. They cannot bear the weight of their own genius, so they look to death for relief.

God did not have the option of death, no matter how fiercely he imagined his own eulogy. Imorti are never free. They are bound to life as a snail is bound to its shell. Life is not a choice for the immortal. Whatever trick God had used to destroy the Ancient Ones, he had long since forgotten or repressed. He sometimes sat for hours trying to recall how it was done, how he had killed the others. I hoped he would never remember.

My mood was thus affected. I became sullen and morose. God's depression weighed heavily on my mind. I lived in a state of unease.

There was in the back of my mind always the constant fear that I would come home and find God snuffed out of existence by his own suicidal will. If he could not remember how he had destroyed the Ancient Ones today, perhaps he would remember tomorrow. His life became my responsibility. The smallest word from me could send him into a downward spiral. I became very selective about what I said and did, and in a sense, I became a slave to his varying moods.

My heart was swept away by his unending pain, and what could have easily been love turned gradually into revulsion. I was repulsed by his tears. His tantrums were almost too much to bear, and that I was expected to remain loving and calm—it was unfair. And to feign happiness through it all, to remain positive, to be his crutch—I could not think of anything more degrading than offering myself up to be stepped on. I let myself be prey to his sudden outbreaks of violence and tears, and thus hated myself for my own weakness.

I did it all at first because I loved him. But when I started to loathe him, I did it still because I did not want to shoulder the responsibility of his suicide. Yet I could hardly stand to bear the responsibility of his life—his unending life. Could he go on like this forever?

That isn't to say there weren't moments of relief. Sometimes he would flip through my sketchbook with a slight grin on his face. He could still be amused. But if I said the wrong thing about the weather, about Eden, about any of it, he would hurtle into darkness again.

There was a stretch of about six months when everything seemed right again. It was spring, and Eden was hatching out of the barren shell it had become over winter. The snow in the mountains melted and fed the River Fluvius. The animals came out of hibernation and began to play and build and mate again. God sat out on his terrace and watched Eden, and he was for the first time in a long time at ease. The months passed smoothly without incident. I slept every night in God's arms. There were no tears, no sudden outbursts. God smiled most willingly, and his humor was greatly improved. I could again amuse him with birdcalls. I brought flowers to him every evening, and they filled his house with the aroma of spring.

I was still discovering new creatures in the garden. They seemed to be generating themselves in larger numbers than ever before, and many of the animals were migrating out of Eden and making homes on Earth.

Michael had taken up beekeeping. He showed me how to extract honey from a buzzing hive without upsetting the colony. I was clumsy at first, and I was stung many times. I kept at it and very quickly I became a master at beekeeping, surpassing even Michael in skill.

God walked the garden at times and contemplated his mortal creations. He was especially interested in the strange phenomenon of reproduction. I showed him the eggs of robins and blue jays, and once he even witnessed the birthing of six tiny kittens to a calico cat. God took notes. He talked about reproduction as a defect. His next batch of mortal creatures, he hoped, would not be able to mate.

The months passed easily, and the memory of God's depression slipped further and further away. I became so accustomed to the gentle cadence of the days that I did not suspect that within several months my situation would change drastically, and I would never spend spring in the garden again.

CHAPTER 4

I T WAS THE FIRST week of summer that I came across a
light-haired angel sitting with his shoulders and back against the
trunk of a giant sycamore. His eyes were closed. He balanced the
long stem of a dandelion on the brim of his lower lip. I would have
thought him fast asleep except that he was humming a wistful tune.

"Hello," I said. I had never seen this angel before.

He looked up from under his eyelashes and smiled only. Then
he closed his eyes and began again with the humming. I sat down
on a patch of lawn in the shade of the sycamore. The light-haired
angel did not stir. I withdrew my notebook and a two-inch block of
charcoal. I traced the outline of the angel against the giant sycamore.
He was relaxed. His very presence calmed my nerves. I traced his
robes, which lay in the grass like great white clouds over a green
sea. His skin was hairless. The shadows of leaves speckled him like
a leopard. The tree was ancient. It grew at least fifty feet tall, and its
boughs stretched and reached out like a tentacled beast.

I was putting the finishing touches on my drawing when the angel
finally spoke. "It is called the Tree of Life, because it was the first

mortal creature God ever breathed into being. That other tree across the way is called the Tree of Knowledge. God keeps that tree to remind him of his misdeeds."

Not more than fifty yards from where we sat there grew a second tree, even larger than the first. It was a fig tree. Its branches wound round themselves like braids. A long curtain of vines hung heavy from the boughs and brushed the earth.

"And what are you called?" I asked.

"I am Mephistopheles. My name has no meaning. It is not beautiful like yours—Lucifer, the bringer of light. I am very sore God did not favor me with such a title."

"How do you know my name?" I asked.

"You are God's favorite," he said. "All the creatures of Heaven and Earth know *your* name."

His eyes remained closed while he spoke. If ever he did open them, it was to arch his brows to give some word emphasis, and then he would close them again. I sat cross-legged before this curious angel. I was drawn in by his words, by his confident way of speaking, and I wanted him to speak more—to fill the silence.

"Are you often in Eden?" I asked.

"Some days," Mephistopheles replied. "Some days not. And when I come, I *never* give notice. You see—I come only to while away the afternoon under this tree."

He closed his eyes and turned away from me. His breathing became deep and heavy, like one asleep. And surely, he was asleep. As if I were never there. I took this as my cue to leave. But even when

I had left him, my mind stayed on his easy drawl and curious smile. My curiosity was not satisfied. That night, I lay awake in bed. God was asleep beside me, dreaming so fitfully I could not have slept if I had wished. My thoughts turned to this blue-eyed angel who spoke as if he knew me. Spoke as one who knew my secrets.

It was then that I wondered if the other angels knew the dark side of God. Michael, yes. But the others, the ones who brought the food and wine, who stoked the great fire and swept the great hall. They came and were gone so swiftly, and usually without a word, I never thought ...

But Mephistopheles—his words, his eyes, they seemed to mock me. Did he know how I could not satisfy God?

I returned to the Tree of Life the following afternoon. Mephistopheles was nowhere to be seen. I waited all day for him, but he did not come. I felt a strange discomfort in my chest—I was anxious to see him again, to know more about this angel with the mocking smile.

I returned to that same spot every day for three weeks before I saw Mephistopheles again. This time he was lying in the shade of the Tree of Knowledge. I sat down beside him. He gave me a very brief, disinterested glance and stared up at the giant fig leaves.

"When were you made?" I asked. It was a question that had been bothering me for some time. How had I never seen him before? And why had I never heard of him? Was he God's most recent attempt at perfection? Wasn't I enough? Had God made angels after me? I wondered why the thought had never occurred to me before.

Mephistopheles looked as if he didn't hear me. His eyelids drooped and his gaze remained fixed on the meadow beyond. I fidgeted with the hem of my robes. The silence was like a great weight on my chest. I regretted saying anything at all.

Finally, Mephistopheles replied, "When do you think I was made?"

"A year ago," I said. That was around the time God began to slip away from me—the beginning of the dark times.

Mephistopheles smiled as if he could read my mind.

"I was made before the Garden of Eden," he said flatly. "Nearly ten thousand years ago. I was made before Michael." He yawned as if the very thought of it made him tired. "And I was made before you, *light-bringer*."

"Do you know God well?" I asked, thinking ten thousand years is a long time to live in the same universe with God.

"I know he suffers," Mephistopheles said.

So, others did know.

"I do not know how to please him," I confessed.

Mephistopheles closed his eyes. Either he did not hear me or did not care because he said nothing.

When he did speak again, he asked, "What's in your book?"

I opened my sketchbook. "I keep a journal. Names and pictures of all the creatures in Eden."

"Those are very good," Mephistopheles said, spying my drawings from the corner of his eye. "Why do you draw them?"

"I think the mortal world is fascinating."

"Frankly, I think mortals are about as interesting as rocks," Mephistopheles responded curtly. "Unless you're talking about humans."

"Humans?" I asked. "What are humans?"

Mephistopheles lifted his head and looked straight at me for the first time. Then he cracked a smile and chuckled.

"You don't know? I will show you sometime. Another day, perhaps."

And then he closed his eyes, leaned his head back against the tree, and began to snore.

I felt a warm glow pulsing in the pit of my stomach. He would show me what humans were *another day*. So, he would see me again! I leaned my head against the tree and closed my eyes. This was nice. Like the early days when God slept soundly and never thought of strange things like death.

Mephistopheles's breathing was even and deep. He snored lightly. But it was preferable to God's anxious tossing and turning.

When the shadow of the tree had become stretched and warped, and the first stars started to peak out of the navy-blue sky, I rose and walked home. Mephistopheles remained asleep under the tree. His face was calm and detached. I knew he did not care if I came or went. That was what I liked about Mephistopheles—I bore no commitment to him. If I left God lying alone, if I abandoned his side whilst he slept, he would rage and scream. He would bring thunder and lightning. He would make rivers of his tears.

God needed me.

Mephistopheles did not. And that was exactly what drew me to him.

CHAPTER 5

I WENT TO SEE Mephistopheles every day that summer. Sometimes we lay in the shade of the Tree of Life, sometimes in the shade of the Tree of Knowledge. Sometimes we talked. Other times we played a game of tossing rocks into the lazy stream at the bottom of the hill. By mid-afternoon, the conversation would fade quietly and then die, and by the time the sun was setting on the horizon, Mephistopheles was asleep. I stayed awake and watched the stars come out. I counted them as they appeared until there got to be too many. Then I walked home to the dark house of God.

Sometimes in the afternoon, while we sat in silence, I took out my notebook and a piece of charcoal and sketched Mephistopheles. I drew him chewing on a piece of wood sorrel. I drew him standing on his head. I recorded him in every state: sleeping, laughing, frowning. He became my subject and I his. He showed me how to make wreaths of asphodels and forget-me-nots. He wove crowns out of long grass and placed them atop my head. He called me *God's favorite*.

He also took me to see the humans for the first time. These naked, stupid creatures were like angels in appearance, but they were mortal. We watched them eat fruit from the trees and drink water from the streams. Mephistopheles explained that humans were a recent invention of God's. They, like all mortal creatures, had access to Eden and Earth and, like the other animals in the garden, had begun to proliferate on their own. I was saddened by the discovery of humans, for I knew God was searching for companionship beyond me. And yet I hoped, I wished, these humans could bring God the happiness that I could not.

"God is already bored with them," Mephistopheles said, as if reading my mind.

As the summer progressed, my notebook filled with etchings of Mephistopheles, humans, the Trees of Knowledge and Life, the asphodels, the hill, and the stream. Knowing that I would see Mephistopheles every afternoon made it easier to bear God's restlessness in the evenings. Aside from Michael, Mephistopheles was my only friend.

I never spoke to God about Mephistopheles. I was afraid to bring up anything that might disturb or upset his unpredictable mood. In fact, I became more and more silent on matters I would have once openly discussed. I learned what it was to have a secret. Before, it had been only God and me. It is very hard to have a secret when there are only two of you. But now that there was Mephistopheles, I had all sorts of secrets. I wanted to keep Mephistopheles to myself. I wanted the hill, the asphodels, and the lazy summer days to be sacred and apart from God. It was my only claim to freedom. So it was that my notebooks became private. I did not dare risk God seeing the sketches I had made of Mephistopheles.

I had only ever known two sentient beings before Mephistopheles: God, who had sorely disappointed me; and Michael, who though wise and kind, was subservient and complacent. So, I came to worship Mephistopheles, if not because of his audacity—he often called God a fool and said other provocative things about our creator—then simply because I had no one else to worship.

In truth, Mephistopheles was a selfish and indifferent angel. I suppose he liked me because I lavished him with attention. He liked the sketches I made of him because they made him look more beautiful than he really was. He was thousands of years older than I and knew his way around Heaven. He talked about other angels—apparently, he had met countless Imorti. He spoke of them with disdain. They were either dim or docile—none of them was as beautiful or as clever as I. I learned some of their names and how to recognize them. Mephistopheles was far from complimentary when speaking of our brethren. But he flattered me—I was, of course, the most beautiful of all God's creations. Mephistopheles's adulation kept me coming back to the hill day after day.

It was late in the summer when everything changed. The leaves on the Tree of Knowledge had turned a sandy color. They broke loose and fell from the branches; they lay on the ground like a great sheet of golden wrapping paper.

Mephistopheles and I were dozing under the Tree of Life. The stars were coming out one by one, blinking on in the night sky. I tried to keep my eyes open, but I could not. I felt so at ease in this place, under this tree, in the garden, with Mephistopheles at my side. I said so.

"Mm-hm," Mephistopheles muttered.

"I could stay here forever," I said.

"Go to sleep, Lucifer," Mephistopheles said.

So, I did. And I did not wake up until the following morning. Mephistopheles snored gently by my side. Dew sparkled in the grass. The sky was cold and gray. A storm brewed on the horizon.

No! I thought. *No, no, no!*

I leapt up and ran in the direction of the swirling dark clouds.

By the time I reached God's house, rain had already started to fall. Lightning flashed and thunder sounded overhead. I crept between the great columns flanking the entrance to God's domain. I already knew what awaited me. I found God in bed. The doors to the terrace were flung wide open, and the cold wind from outside made the curtains dance. The bedroom was white, blinding white—the bedsheets, the canopy, the walls and floor. The room was so untarnished—it seemed to mock me—I did not belong there anymore. I was guilty, impure. I had betrayed God. The dim light filtering in through the open doors seemed to accuse me of dark things.

God's face was drawn. He looked like a statue. His lips were curled downward in a scowl that made me shiver.

I stood before him as a deer before a lion. I was certain to be destroyed. I had nothing that I could call to my aid. I was so clearly culpable. God had told me upon my birth that I was to spend every night in his house. In return, he had granted me free reign of Heaven and Earth. I had failed to live up to my part of the bargain.

"Where were you?" God asked. His face was stone cold. Dark circles rimmed his eyes.

"I was watching birds, and I fell asleep," I lied.

God was not easily fooled. He may have been pathetic, but he was not stupid. He rose and lunged at me, a lion striking his prey. He grabbed the notebook out of my hands. I felt the leather peel away from my sweaty palms and, for a second, I could not breathe. It was as if my heart had been pulled out of my chest. He threw the book on the bed. His fingers flipped madly through the pages. I looked on in horror.

The journals I kept were my only free space; they were all that was left of my privacy. When God tore through the pages of my journal like a madman, searching undoubtedly for incriminating evidence, I became aware of something I had never been aware of before—I was not free. I was granted access to Heaven and Earth—but under the supervision of God. I was not guaranteed anything. One wrong move on my part and God could strip me of my privileges. Living in constant fear of losing my freedom—is that freedom?

God found the drawings of Mephistopheles. He stopped cold. His eyes bore into the pages of the notebook. I could feel him changing gears. Until then, I doubt he had suspected that I had spent the night with another angel.

His fingers kept turning, and on every page he found Mephistopheles staring up at him with that insolent gaze. He turned each page with more force, gaining momentum, until he was indiscriminately tearing the pages from my notebook like petals from a flower.

I screamed in horror. But I stayed rooted on the spot. Tears ran freely down my face. I choked on spittle. I felt naked and powerless. Maybe it was the first time in the history of the universe anyone had ever felt hatred towards God. Maybe it was in that moment I earned the name Satan. Because it was then that I turned against God.

When my notebook was hardly recognizable, God hurled it at me. Paper memories of the days I had spent with Mephistopheles lay in pieces on the floor.

"So, you choose to spend your nights with Mephistopheles, then?" he screamed.

I stood shaking. My nose was running. I could hardly see—my eyes were swollen. I said nothing.

"You have found better company, then?" he cried.

"It is too much," I said through salty tears. "It is too much to spend every night with you. You are melancholy and sad. You scream in your sleep. I cannot be responsible for your happiness. It is just too much."

God stared at me as if I had said something wildly inconceivable. Perhaps he had expected me to apologize. But he had pushed me too far this time. I knew he would never be the same God in my eyes. And I would never be the same angel. I would be known as Satan from then on, for Satan means traitor.

"You promised," God spat. His eyes twitched and his nose flared. "You promised on the day you were made to spend every night by my side."

"You gave me no other choice," I cried.

God ploughed onward. "And now I find that you are spending your nights with that wretched creature, Mephistopheles."

"It was only one night," I said.

"Only one night!" God screamed. "I created the whole universe in one night! Don't be a fool, Lucifer. One night can change everything!"

God spun around and he grabbed at whatever was nearest. His fingers caught hold of the canopy over the bed and he tore it down in one fell swoop.

A deep guttural sound rose from deep inside his bowels. Blood flowed to his face, and he let out an agonizing cry. The blood vessels in his sclerae burst and filled the whites of his eyes with blood.

I trembled and fell back against the wall. God stormed blindly about the room and crushed everything under hand. He tore the curtains from the windows. He ripped the pillows to shreds with his fingernails. His fury was great, and nothing was spared.

When he could find nothing more to ravage, he stood in the middle of the room, fists clenched at his sides, and screamed. He screamed and screamed until he had no strength left. Then he collapsed in a pile on the floor.

He lay there unmoving for some time. He was sprawled out on his back with his robes spread out around him like a sea of white foam.

When I could not bear the stillness any longer, I stepped forward cautiously. God watched me as I moved about the room collecting the shredded pieces of my journal. His anger shone through the pools of blood in his eyes.

When I had salvaged what was left of my diary, I tied it all together with string and slung it over my shoulder.

"Where are you going?" God asked. His voice was raspy and parched.

"I'm leaving," I said coolly.

"You can't leave me," God said. "You love me."

"I will not stay here and be subject to your abuse any longer."

"Lucifer, help me up. I am weak," God said. He sat upright and reached a hand out to me.

"No," I said. "You have pulled this sort of stunt before, and I am not falling for it again. No. You have given me no reason to stay."

"Where will you go?" God cried.

"To Earth."

"But Earth is such a barren place. You will be lonely."

"I will bring other angels with me."

"You will bring Mephistopheles," he said in an almost inaudible whisper.

"Maybe."

God lunged at me and threw his arms around my ankles.

"No," God sobbed. "I forbid you to leave!"

God clung to me, and I dragged him across the floor toward the door.

"No. No. No." He was shaking his head and crying. "I'm sorry. I'm so sorry, Lucifer. Don't leave me. You can't leave me. You promised."

"Do you love me?" I asked.

"Yes," God cried. "More than anything."

"Then let me go."

God's face went white. His grip grew weak, and his fingers slipped from my ankles.

"Please, Lucifer!" God howled.

I trembled. But I marched onward. I left God lying on the floor of his house in a pool of sweat and tears. When I reached the garden, I broke into a run. I couldn't let God see that I was crying. I darted down the long path that led to the river and followed the bank of the Fluvius until I came to the Tree of Life. Mephistopheles still lay asleep just as I had left him.

I roused him gently.

"Mephisto," I said. "I'm leaving Eden."

He opened his eyes and examined my face.

"Have you been crying?" he asked.

"It is no matter now," I said. "I cannot stay here any longer. I am going to Earth. You can come with me if you like."

"What happened?" Mephistopheles asked. "I don't understand."

"It's simple," I said. "Either you come with me, or you don't. I am not asking any favors, and I'm not making any promises. I'm going to Earth to start my life over, and you can come with me if you want."

He shrugged. "Okay, I'll come. I've got nothing better to do."

"You know other angels, right?" I asked.

"Unfortunately, yes."

"Do you think you could ask around and see if anybody else wants to come with us?"

"You mean you want to lead a whole flock of angels down to Earth?"

"Yeah."

"Lucifer, God will be furious with you. He will be furious with all of us."

"Yeah."

Mephistopheles blinked. "It's not that I care what God thinks," he began. "But ... well, I thought it would be just you and me."

"I know you don't like the other angels much, but I don't think it's right for God to treat us the way he does. I'm sure there are others who feel the same way. Mortal creatures have been living on Earth for some time now. And they are so weak and stupid. If they can do it, why can't we? I think we can make a home there, away from God. But we need as many angels as we can find."

Mephistopheles yawned and scratched his neck.

"It'll cut into my naptime, but if you say so. I'll ask around. When do we leave?"

"Tonight."

When we assembled that night, there were nine of us all told. The angels Mephistopheles had gathered stood clustered before me: Asmodeus, Azazel, Samyaza, Samael, Raum, Belial, and Berith. Mephistopheles slouched off to the side, half his face lit by the cold moonlight. His long blond hair was braided and tucked into the back of his robes.

"Tonight, we go to Earth," I said.

The others shifted uneasily on their feet.

"Once we set foot on the rock and soil of that place, we are no longer welcome in Eden. Do you understand the sacrifice you are about to make?"

"We understand," they said together.

"And do you understand that you will be forever branded by your betrayal? You will be outcasts among angels. You will be fallen, and you will be called the Grigori. If you return to Heaven, you will be spat upon by your brethren."

Samyaza stepped forward and said, "We understand all this. God granted us free will, and for too long he has ordered us about like slaves. We go with you willingly. Whatever fate befalls us, be it the very wrath of God, we shall face this thing together."

"Satanael, betrayer of God," Samael said. "For that is what they are calling you now. You have been given reign of Heaven and Earth and all the worlds in between. Why do you abandon your place beside God to live among mortals?"

"You know as well as I, Samael, that none of us are truly free so long as we live in Eden. There is no burden worse than being God's favorite. And I am resolved to be his favorite no more."

Azazel came forward and said in his booming voice, "Then let it be done already. Let us go to Earth. There is nothing left for us here." At this, he hoisted his huge ax over his shoulder and strode toward the gate.

"Wait!" Mephistopheles said. "Do you know what it is you are about to walk into? Earth is not like Heaven. There you will be plagued by hunger and thirst and disease. When you grow tired, you must sleep. If you prick yourself on a thorn, you will bleed. And the animals on Earth know no order. They do not bow to angels as they do in Heaven. They are fierce and wild. Food is scarce, and only the strongest survive."

"That is enough, Mephistopheles," I said. "We've all been to Earth before."

"Besides," Samyaza said. "We are immortal."

Mephistopheles shrugged and slunk into the shadows.

"Enough talk," Azazel said. "None of us would be here if we hadn't considered the consequences of what we are doing."

"Alright, then," I said. With that, I turned and placed my fingers on the handle of the gate. The iron bars groaned as I turned the latch. A gust of cold wind hit me as I stepped into the mortal world. I was blinded by a flurry of white sleet, and I stumbled forward into a deep bank of snow.

The cold was unlike anything I had ever experienced before. My robes quickly grew damp and clung to my body. I was waist-deep in white powder. The others were close behind me. I could just make out their blurred silhouettes in the blanket of sleet and snow.

"This is madness," I heard someone say.

I trudged forward, carving a narrow path in the snow for them to follow. I did not know where I was going, and I wasn't sure how long I could last in these temperatures, but now that I had fallen from Heaven, I was determined to get as far away from it as possible.

The sky was a dark haze. Had it not been for a small break in the clouds through which the moonlight shone, we would not have made it far that night. I paved a winding trail using the ever-shifting moonlight as a compass. The others grumbled and groaned behind me.

I knew we had to find cover—a rock, a tree—anything to protect us from the biting winds. I could feel the blood thickening in my veins. It was growing increasingly difficult to move. Never before had any of us experienced what it was to be so cold. And this was unbearable. Had we not been Imorti, we would have seen our last night in that barren place, and our bodies would have been interred in the snow. It seemed wildly inconceivable to me then that mortal beings could possibly survive on Earth, and I wondered what impulse had driven them to leave the comfort of Eden for this harsh and untamed land.

"Cold, eh?" came a voice near my ear. Belial was at my shoulder, his breath warm on my neck. "You're doing all the work. Perhaps I can lead for a bit."

I nodded my assent. Belial was a sizable angel—at least an inch taller than I, and broader, too. He would cut a better trail for us to follow. I let him pass, hunkered down in his shadow, and followed him blindly.

What are we doing out here?

I could answer that for myself. Even this weather was better than another night with God. But I worried about the others. I could hear them whispering behind me. Surely, they were rethinking their decision to come. I could not help but feel I had made a grave mistake in asking them to follow me into unknown lands. I alone had good reason to fight the bitter snows of Earth. But what motivated them to be here? Why should they endure this suffering when they could have just as easily stayed where the weather hardly varied and the temperature was always comfortable? I was sure they were asking themselves that very question when out of the darkness a small pinprick of light appeared.

"Do you see that?" Belial asked. "There is something out there."

The light flickered and burned out. There was a moan of despair among the group. And then the light blinked back into existence, a weak but sure sign that some creature had found a way to survive in this unfriendly terrain.

"See how it disappears when the wind kicks up the snow?" Samael asked. "It could be a fire, but that would mean it is still many miles off."

"Lead us there, Belial," I said.

Belial heaved forward and the rest of us followed. We moved quicker now that we had a destination. The company walked in silence. Their eyes and minds were fixed on the light, and all thoughts of going back melted away. This was to be our life now. We were to fight, as all other creatures did, to subsist in this world. Certainly, angels cannot die, and that has its advantages. But that also means we can suffer longer.

The terrain began to slope upward, and Belial struggled against the incline. When he could not lead any longer, the behemoth Azazel took the lead and barreled through the heaping banks of snow like a salmon swimming upstream. The terrain here was more densely populated with pines and kermes oaks, and we had to weave a winding trail toward the beacon.

At last, we broke into a small alcove and came upon the source of the light. A great bonfire blazed in the middle of a clearing. The snow had been packed down here by many feet. Littered about the clearing were breathing bundles of fur.

"What are those creatures?" Samyaza asked in a whisper.

I looked closely at the fur. It looked like a bear's bushy coat. But the creatures sleeping before us were not bears.

One of the bundles stirred, and a pair of sleepy eyes peered out from the fur. When the creature saw us, it made a loud, piercing cry. The other bundles stirred. Then, from beneath the thick hides emerged at least a dozen men.

"Humans!" Samael said.

They scrambled to the opposite end of the clearing, clutching one another and whispering in a foreign tongue.

The humans were dressed in animal skins, a thing I had never seen before. Had they killed other creatures to get these? Many times, I had encountered these mortal creatures that looked and acted like angels, but which suffered and died like animals. There was hardly anything to distinguish them from us except for the cuts, bruises, and scars that crisscrossed their arms and legs.

A large, shaggy man with wide-set eyes stepped forward and spoke to the humans calmly. His dialect was unfamiliar to me—very deep and throaty. The others listened to him intently but never took their eyes off us.

Then the shaggy man turned to us.

"Who are you?" he asked in the Heavenly tongue.

"We are angels come down from Heaven just this night," I said. "We saw your fire from many miles off, and it led us to you."

"You have come down to Earth in the middle of winter. You wear nothing but thin cotton sheets. You have no food. You carry nothing of value that I can see. How do you expect to last?"

"It is still summer in Eden," I said. "We are not used to the ways of Earth. Please let us sit and warm ourselves by your fire."

"Very well," said the man. He barked a few short commands, and several humans emerged carrying animal hides. They laid the hides at our feet and backed away.

"Come," said the man. "Come and sit by the fire. The bearskins will keep you warm. Put them on."

"But where did you get these?" Samael asked. "You did not kill for these?"

"We did," said the man.

"I cannot wear the skin of a dead animal," Samael said. "It is an abomination. It flouts the Law of Heaven."

"Things are different down here," the shaggy man said. "You will wear these or you will freeze."

I quickly wrapped the bearskin around my shoulders. The rest followed suit. Samael hesitated a moment.

"You do not want to freeze, Samael," I said. "Go on. Wear it. We are no longer bound by the Law of Heaven."

Samael reluctantly wrapped the hide around his shoulders. We positioned ourselves on one side of the fire. The humans gathered on the other side.

"My name is Anshar," the shaggy man said. "These are my people. We are hunters of these parts."

"I am called Satanael, and these angels are my friends. We have come to Earth to live among mortals. We are very unfamiliar with Earth and are grateful for your help."

"It is lucky you are not mortal men," Anshar said. "Or you would have perished before you reached us. Many of my people die in the wintertime when the snow is heavy."

"Why not go back to Heaven, then?" Mephistopheles asked. His words sounded like a challenge.

Anshar answered him calmly. "Most of my people do not remember Heaven. We have lived many years on Earth. It is our home now."

"We hope to make it our home, too," I said. "Tell me, are you the only humans in these parts?"

"No," Anshar said. "We have been hunting these last few days. But tomorrow we return to our encampment where our people wait for fresh meat. There are dozens of humans in our tribe."

"May we go with you?"

Anshar considered for a moment. "You do not speak our language, and you know very little about the ways of man. But you are strong—much stronger than ordinary men. You may be of use to our people."

Anshar put his hand on his chin and frowned. The other humans followed his every motion with their eyes. I wondered if they understood the Heavenly tongue. Did they know what was going on?

Finally, Anshar said, "I will take you to the encampment, and there I will present you to the elders. They will know what to do."

CHAPTER 6

T HE NEXT MORNING, I awoke to a sweet, earthy smell. It made my stomach groan. I crawled out from beneath the cover of my bearskin and was instantly struck by an icy breeze. I shivered and ducked back under the warm hide.

I hid in the dark womb of the bearskin for many minutes longer, debating whether I should stay or go. But the sweet, earthy scent pervaded my senses, and hunger overcame my desire to be warm. In a single motion I tossed the bearskin over my shoulders and scrambled across the frozen ground to where the humans sat laughing and chattering around the fire. Upon my approach the chatter faded into silence.

Then Anshar said, "They have never seen an angel before. Come now, sit and eat. We have a long journey ahead of us."

"Where are the others?" I asked.

"Still sleeping."

Anshar motioned to the breathing bundles of fur scattered about the campsite.

He said, "If they do not get up soon, they will miss the morning meal, and I am sure they will regret it. Shall I send one of my people to awaken them?"

"Please," I said.

Anshar gave a curt command, and a young man darted across the snow to rouse the others.

"Try this," Anshar said. He handed me a hot strip of charred flesh.

"Is this animal meat?" I asked.

"You don't want it?" Anshar looked surprised. "You will starve if you do not eat. There is no fruit on the trees this time of the year, Satanael. You must eat meat. It is the way of Earth."

The smell was intoxicating. I wet my lips. But some poor creature had died so these men could eat—so that I could eat. I hesitated. All the humans were watching me. Some of them were making motions to indicate that I should taste it.

If I was resolved to fit in here among these mortals, I could not go on obeying the Law of Heaven. Earth was not Heaven. With a deep breath, I bit into the dead animal flesh. There was an explosion of savory sensations in my mouth. The humans were nodding and smiling at me.

"What is your word for food?" I asked Anshar.

"Tumi," he said.

I held up the meat and said, "Tumi."

The humans laughed and repeated, "Tumi! Tumi!"

Just then, the young man returned with the other angels. Mephistopheles came and crouched next to me. He growled under his breath.

"Are you okay?" I asked.

"I hardly slept," he said. "The ground was wet, and I couldn't keep warm. Remind me why I decided to follow you down here?"

"Try some tumi," I said.

"What?" Mephistopheles said. "Are you already trying to learn their language? They are humans, Lucifer. Why bother?"

"If you want to last on this Earth, you had better get used to making friends with humans. Without them, we would have frozen through the night. So, shut up and eat something."

Mephistopheles reluctantly took the meat offered him by the humans. The other angels did the same.

"But this is animal flesh," Samael said. "We do not eat animal flesh."

"You will be hungry if you do not eat," I said. "Do not forget: this is Earth, and we must suffer as mortals suffer. Even if we cannot die, we still feel pain, hunger, thirst, and fatigue, just as the humans do. Do what you will, but you will soon learn that there is no other way."

The other angels quickly agreed and bore into the animal flesh. But Samael shook his head and said, "I will not eat this. I cannot die, so what does it matter if I starve."

I shrugged. Mephistopheles muttered, "Fool."

When the morning meal was done, the humans loaded all their provisions and supplies onto gurneys. They hoisted the narrow ends of the gurneys onto their shoulders and dragged their belongings behind them, making parallel tracks in the snow.

The morning was exceptionally bright. The storm clouds had drifted east over the mountains, and the sky was a clear, cold blue. We were camped on the crest of a low hill, and below us the land lay in a blanket of virgin snow. I had seen snow before, high in the mountains of Eden, but it only appeared a few months out of the year and was always gone before summer. But here the snow sat heavy upon the Earth. The humans made a game out of throwing the snow at one another. Belial and Berith joined in the sport. While the others played, Mephistopheles crouched behind me to avoid being hit.

"It's cold enough as it is," he grumbled.

It was cold, but the walk had warmed us considerably. The only person who seemed to be uncomfortable was Samael, who was lagging behind and complaining of a pain in his stomach.

Now, it must be known that before that day none of us, the Fallen, had ever been hungry before. Nor had we ever been used to pain. For in Eden, we had wanted for nothing. So, when Samael first felt the pain in his stomach, he had no words for it. He could only point and say, "It hurts."

Naturally, I was very concerned. Angels are the most superior of God's beings, and being so, rarely become slow or weak. I asked Anshar what it was that ailed Samael.

"He is only hungry," the big man said. "He has not eaten since yesterday and so his stomach has hunger pangs."

"What are hunger pangs?" Samyaza asked, overhearing us.

"Hah!" Anshar laughed. "You will know soon enough."

"Can we fix him?" I asked.

"He has to eat," Anshar said. "There is some dried venison in my satchel. He may have it if he likes."

I proposed this to Samael, but he would not hear of it. "I will be fine. I am not dying."

But he could barely keep pace. The humans kept looking back and beckoning to Samael. Surely, they did not expect an angel to be so slow. I wondered if there was any way to find some sort of edible plant that might ease his hunger. I scanned the horizon. Nothing but white snow and naked trees as far as the eye could see.

Then I saw a hint of red and green hanging high in the boughs of a cedar. It was the plant mistletoe. I knew it well, for it sometimes grew on the trees in Eden.

"It is poisonous," Anshar said when I pointed it out. "You may not be familiar with poison, but on Earth some things can make you very sick. Mistletoe is one of those things. If he ate that, he'd be worse off than he is now."

The mortal world was very complicated. In Heaven there was never cold or hunger or pain. And now all these rules about what must be done to prevent hunger and to avoid pain. So many more rules than I was used to. Yet I trusted Anshar. The humans trusted him. And he had been right about eating in the morning.

We walked on. The humans were chattering away under the bright midday sun while we, the Grigori, lagged behind to keep an eye on Samael.

"You're a fool, Samael, for refusing to eat," Mephistopheles said. "You will only grow weaker by the hour. If you do not keep up, the humans will leave you to harden like a rock in the snow."

"We will not leave you, Samael," I said.

"Hmph!" Mephistopheles growled.

"I am fine," Samael said. "Do not crowd around me. All this talk makes my head feel full."

But the humans did not abandon us. When the distance between us got to be too great, they circled back and walked alongside us. They gave us water from pouches and offered garbled encouragement, only some of which we could understand.

I tried to learn as much of the human language as I could before we reached the encampment where the other humans were waiting for the spoils of the hunt. It was not difficult. Mortal languages come very naturally to me, as none of them are so complicated as the Heavenly tongue.

"You learn very quickly," Anshar said. "My people are very impressed. They like you."

"Always playing the favorite," Mephistopheles muttered.

"What did the fair one say?" the humans asked. "Quickly! Tell us what he said."

"He is jealous because he cannot understand your language," I said in my best human accent.

71

Mephistopheles snorted. "You sound ridiculous making all those human noises."

"He says he is too dull to learn another tongue," I translated.

The humans burst into fits of laughter. Mephistopheles frowned and fell back to walk with Samael.

❋

We arrived at the human encampment by nightfall. The mortal children came sprinting down the hill to greet us, swarming around the hunting party like tsetse flies, and making our efforts to scale the hill look labored. The rest of the humans—mostly women and old men—gathered at the crest of the hill and watched our slow progress with wondering eyes. When we were within spitting distance of the little cluster of makeshift huts and tents that comprised the human settlement, a gray-bearded elder stepped forward and ordered us to halt.

"Anshar," he said. "Who are these strangers?"

"Angels," said Anshar. "Come from Heaven."

"Hmph," said the elder. "And what do they want?"

Here I spoke on behalf of the fallen Imorti, using what I had learned of the human tongue. "My name is Satanael, and these angels answer to me. We come seeking food and shelter. My friends are strong and able and will do whatever you ask of them. Just please let us sit by your fire and share your bread."

The elder regarded me with a scoff. "We don't have bread to spare, Satanael. What little we have, we must divide amongst ourselves. Besides, what need have you of bread? Were you not made immortal and thus impervious to hunger?"

"Yes," I said. "But on Earth we must eat to keep our strength. Please, look at my friend." Here I pointed to Samael, who was leaning heavily on Belial's shoulder, eyes fluttering in and out of consciousness. "He is weak from starvation. He refuses to eat the meat your people so generously offered, and so he cannot stand on his own two feet."

"What concern is that of mine?" scoffed the elder. "If he will not eat meat, then he is a fool."

"Yes," I said. "You are wise to say so." Then I turned to Samael and spoke in the Heavenly tongue. "You must eat, Samael. The humans must see that you do not consider yourself above them."

Samael whispered in Belial's ear, and Belial translated for the humans. "He says he will eat whatever you will give him."

The elder regarded Samael skeptically. "Anshar," he said. "Give this fool something to eat."

Anshar removed the dried venison from his pack and handed it to Belial, who held it up to Samael's lips. Samael took a timid bite, then another, and another. Slowly, his eyes began to grow clearer, as though waking from a deep sleep.

"Hmph," said the elder. "You already burden us with your foolishness. We do not need more mouths to feed."

"We could hunt," I said. "If you will show us how. I'm sure we would make quick studies."

"We have hunters," said the elder.

Here Anshar intervened. "Uncle," he pleaded. "These angels are very much like you when you first came to Earth from Heaven. Or don't you remember? You said yourself that your first months on Earth were cold and lonely. But you were taken in by the clan elders and taught the ways of Earth. Why then not show these fallen angels the same mercy shown you? Besides, angels are strong and wise, God's favorites, and they may be of some use to us one day."

The elder spat on the ground. "My nephew says to show these creatures mercy. Very well, let them come sit by our fire and share our bread. But you, Anshar, will be responsible for showing God's favorites the ways of man and the ways of Earth."

With that, the elder turned on his heel and hobbled away.

"Thank you," I said to Anshar. "You are very wise."

"Hah!" Anshar laughed. "We shall see."

CHAPTER 7

T HE GRIGORI WANDERED THE Earth for many years with Anshar and his tribe. Until then, I had never experienced pain and suffering in the way mortals do. But on Earth, the elements ravaged my body. I scraped my knees and elbows on the hard rock; I tore my skin on thorns and twigs. I constantly longed for three things: food, water, and sleep. Such desires were never sated. I found it difficult to rise in the morning. I shivered in the night. The weather was unpredictable. It was not like Eden. Earth was wild and capricious.

During those first years with Anshar's clan, many humans died of starvation or disease. The Fallen would have died, too, had we been mortal creatures. But we were fated to survive it all, like it or not. The Fallen felt what the humans felt: our wounds were real; they bled hot blood; they stung; they burned; they itched. But they healed quickly. A laceration would close up within hours. A broken bone would mend overnight. Our immortal bodies dealt efficiently with every blow. But before one part of us was healed, another part was hurting again.

I lost interest in everything except keeping my stomach appeased. The sun and moon revolved around food. The clan kept near streams and rivers, and I learned to forage and fish and hunt. I would not have survived those years had I been human. Like so many others in the tribe, I would have perished from famine or disease.

Other tribes, much like our own, had been wandering Earth for some time and had begun to gather themselves into little settlements across the continents: Africa, Asia, Europe, even as far as the Americas. Our nomadic tribe came across one of these early settlements in a windswept desert near what is now called the Persian Gulf. Here, humans had constructed the first primitive buildings, and when we stumbled among them, ragged, sweat-stained, with skin red and tender to the touch, the people of the village took us in and nursed us as they would have their own.

The language here was slightly more evolved than what I was used to; they had words for things I had never thought to describe. They spoke profusely on the subject of pain. They had a different name for every kind of hurt: sores, breaks, bruises, cuts, burns. They noted every little scrape on my body and were amazed to see me heal so rapidly. It was then that I explained who the fallen angels were and where we had come from. Many of the elders in the village had made the same trek from Eden to Earth and knew of God's tyranny. So, they welcomed us warmly into their homes.

The Fallen quickly learned the workings of the human settlement and sought to improve the welfare of all who lived there. Humans are industrious and innovative creatures by necessity, but they see only the task in front of them. Angels have the gift of foresight, and so we began to invent new forms of architecture and engineering, and soon the first buildings of any permanence sprang up like grass from the ground. We started to organize the mortals like ants in a colony so that each individual had his or her own part to play. We noticed that, like Imorti, humans have unique strengths and talents, and so we tried to harness these for the betterment of the entire settlement.

Of course, it was not always easy to convince the humans of the wisdom of our numerous plans. But in time, they came to trust the Fallen and revered us as gods. The earliest governments came into being under the watch of the angels, and soon people lived by the law or else faced consequences. There came a time, too, when we began to teach the humans how to read and write. Humans, we learned then, have a great deal of intellectual capacity but will not tap into it unless encouraged to do so by great teachers. The Imorti became great teachers. So, under the influence of the Fallen, the humans established the first advanced civilization on Earth: Mesopotamia.

❀

By roughly 1750 BC, I had come to rule the empire of Mesopotamia from the Mediterranean Sea to the Persian Gulf under the name of Hammurabi. The Mesopotamian people believed I was descended from the City of Gods, which wasn't far from the truth. So, I occupied a special status in the eyes of mortals. I was revered.

The Fallen did not refrain from bedding mortal women and bearing mortal children. The children of the Fallen were known as Nephilim and were also given favored status among the ranks of humans, for they inherited the beauty and intelligence of their angel fathers and the industriousness and mortality of their human mothers. By 1750 BC, I had sired nearly a hundred sons and daughters in my time on Earth.

Of the eight angels who had followed me to Earth, only one remained in Mesopotamia: Mephistopheles. Over the years, the other fallen angels had migrated with their progeny to all four corners of the Earth to populate new cities and nations. Only Mephistopheles and I stayed on to oversee the advancement of the Mesopotamian Empire. My most recent son—Samsu-iluna—and I lived in a great temple at the center of Babylon. From there, we orchestrated the growth of Mesopotamia into the largest human civilization on Earth.

We were celebrating the successful ousting of the King of Assyria, when Mephistopheles paid me a visit. I had not seen the light-haired angel in many years. Since our time in Mesopotamia, he had grown sullen and withdrawn and often spent long periods alone in his private dwelling along the River Tigris. He had not taken to humans much in the years since we had come to Earth and preferred the company of angels to what he called "half-wit mortals." So it was that Mephisto was regarded as the most miserable of the gods and was left well alone by humans and fallen alike.

"What an honor!" I exclaimed when Mephistopheles approached my throne. I admit that I had drunk too much wine that evening. "What brings old Mephisto to Babylon?"

"You're drunk," Mephisto said.

"Yes," I said. "And you're dry as a bone. Please, Mephisto, won't you have some wine?"

Mephisto took the cup from my hand and reluctantly had a sip.

"Have you met my son?" I asked, pointing to Samsu-iluna.

"How many children must you have?" Mephisto growled.

"Why, as many as possible!" I cried. "We have a duty to spread our seed as far as the wind will carry it! That is the way of mortals."

"You are not mortal," Mephisto observed dryly.

"And you are no fun," I retorted, drinking deeply from my cup.

"I have come with news," Mephisto said. "A messenger arrived from Egypt. He brings tidings of Azazel."

"Azazel!" I exclaimed. Azazel had left Mesopotamia many years ago to build a civilization in Egypt. Last I heard, he had constructed the Great Pyramids of Giza to honor his many wives. "How's the old dog doing?"

"He has grown bored of Egypt and has ambitions to start a new civilization," Mephisto said.

"A new civilization?" The idea appealed to me. I was growing tired of Mesopotamia. Besides, Samsu-iluna could rule Babylon in my stead. "Where does he plan to build this new civilization?"

"There is a land not far from here where the weather is always agreeable and where the seas are as blue as the sky. He says no place has reminded him so much of Eden. With the proper guidance from us, Azazel thinks the humans there could build one of the most enlightened civilizations on Earth."

I was drunk, so all this sounded grand to me. "Excellent! When do we leave?"

"I leave tomorrow," Mephisto replied. "I will join Samael and Belial in the north. You are welcome to join us if you like."

"Count me in." I sloshed wine down the front of my shirt.

Mephistopheles left me that day looking quite pleased with himself. I think he was glad to reunite with his fallen comrades, and I think he was especially happy to be moving somewhere where the weather was fair all the time. Mephisto, more than any of us, missed Eden, missed the balmy, lazy days under the Tree of Life.

As it turned out, I wouldn't leave Mesopotamia for another century and a half. I had affairs to settle in the kingdom, and my son and his son still needed me. I fled Mesopotamia in 1595 BC when Babylonia fell to the Hittite king and the empire was unraveling before my eyes.

When I finally arrived in Mycenae—for that was the name of the city that Azazel had built—Mephisto kept well away from me. Mephistopheles let it be known to all who would listen that he was furious with me for staying so long in Babylon, and he refused to do me the favor of acknowledging my presence in what is now known as Mycenaean Greece. He isolated himself in a stately home on an island in the Aegean Sea and didn't speak to me for hundreds of years thereafter.

By 440 BC, Athens had risen to prominence and was a bustling place full of great minds, many of whom were descended from the Fallen. It was around this time that Sophocles, Euripides, and Socrates became influential figures in Athens, all children of angels. We had just erected the Parthenon in tribute to Azazel's great-grand-daughter, Athena, who was hailed a goddess. And Athens had become a democratic city-state, the first in the world. There would be wars and regime changes over the years, for humans are never content with what they have, but in 440 BC, Athens was at the height of its power.

Every so often we would get word from the other fallen angels who had scattered across the globe and who were working to advance human civilization elsewhere. There was Berith in Rome, Raum in Persia, Asmodeus in China, and Samyaza in the Yucatan. The Fallen had built great civilizations all over the world, but in 440 BC, none was so great as Athens.

❋

It was during this halcyon period of ancient history that Mephistopheles decided to pay me another visit, the first in over a thousand years. He found me at home alone one evening. The sky that night burned orange and gold in the setting sun. I had just finished my supper and was suiting up for my evening stroll around the Acropolis, when a knock came at my door.

"Lucifer," Mephistopheles called. "Are you home?"

I opened the door to find Mephisto leaning casually with his elbow on a lute. He smiled when he saw me. "Long time, no see."

"It has been a long time," I said. "I thought maybe you would never forgive me."

"Never is such a long time," said Mephisto. "And I haven't forgiven you. I come with news."

"What news?" I asked hesitantly. The smile on Mephistopheles's face made me uneasy; I felt like I was walking into a trap. *First Mephistopheles shuts me out for over a thousand years, and now he shows up smiling, like nothing ever happened.* "What are you up to?"

"I've been on holiday," Mephistopheles confided. "These last few years."

"I thought you'd been holed up on that island of yours," I said.

"Yes, for many years, I stayed on the island. Kept to myself. Other angels came to visit, of course. Samael, Belial, Azazel. Not you. But the others. They came."

"I'm sorry I never called," I grunted. "I was sure you wouldn't want to see me."

"I always want to see you," Mephistopheles said in a moment that felt sincere, unguarded.

"Well, I'm sorry. What else can I say?"

"I traveled the world, Lucifer," Mephisto went on. "I visited the other fallen: Asmodeus in China, Berith, Samyaza. They're doing well. But not as well as you, I imagine. You were always superior to the rest of us. God's favorite."

"No more," I said sharply. I did not want to speak of God.

"He says hi, by the way." Mephisto grinned.

"Who says hi?"

"God."

"What?"

Mephistopheles's eyes twinkled. So, this was the trap.

"I don't want to talk about God."

"I went back to Eden. The gates are still open, you know. God has kept his promise, even if we have not kept ours. All realms of Heaven and Earth are still ours to explore. So, I went back. There's a gate, not more than a few miles from here. I'll show you if you like."

"No, thank you." I tried to close the door, but Mephisto caught the latch and pulled it wide open.

"He has a new favorite now," Mephisto said. "His name is Adam, and he is mortal. God made him perfect, like you. And he has also promised to stay every night in God's bed. A promise you could not keep."

"Enough of this," I said. "God can do whatever he likes. So, he has a new favorite. I'm happy for them both."

Mephisto arched his eyebrows. "Just thought you'd want to know."

And then he turned on his heel and left me standing in the open doorway.

In bed that night, I lay awake thinking of this man that God had made to replace me—this Adam. How could a mortal even begin to compare with an angel? For one thing, mortals age, even in Eden, and so God would not have his new plaything for long, a hundred years tops. And mortals are not so clever as angels. This Adam could not be as bright and curious as I. No, God could never replace *me*. I was the closest to perfection he ever came.

But the feeling nagged at me that perhaps God had made a human who would outshine me, and I determined that I would set the record straight. I would go see this Adam for myself, even if it meant returning to Eden. I would look him in the eye and make up my own mind about this so-called perfect mortal.

CHAPTER 8

H E STOOD BEFORE ME, blinking the way a child might blink when brought into the sun for the first time. He had no fear. Not a single bone in his body trembled, nor did an inch of his smooth, unblemished flesh quiver. I had never seen a creature so naïve and so exposed as this Adam. He was maybe six feet tall, and his frame was trim, a work of true craftsmanship. Perhaps God had outdone himself this time. I did feel a twinge of jealousy and then something I did not recognize. It crept through me like a snake, and I had an urge to reach out and touch his face.

God had done well in making me. I was as beautiful as angels come. But this creature—this man—before me was a work of art. God had done all he could to drive me from his thoughts and had thus distracted himself with this beautiful mortal. Adam stood, his dark, curly hair in ringlets around his ears. He was crowned with a wreath of thorns, though he wore nothing else. I suppose he was unaware of his nakedness—and I doubt whether he was able to discern in his naïve simplicity where the crown of thorns began and his head left off. But it was certain that he had not made this crown, nor had he placed it on his own head—that had been the work of God.

Adam's skin was dark and soft and unspoiled, for this creature knew nothing but the idleness of the Garden of Eden. He moved and every part of him flexed. I would later stand before Michelangelo and serve as that great man's model for the statue David, and he would say to me, "I have never seen a man as beautiful as you." And I would think what a shame it was that Michelangelo did not have Adam there to model beauty in my stead, for I will concede, even in my vanity, that Adam was several thousand times more beautiful than I.

A mixture of jealousy and admiration blinded my thoughts when I looked upon Adam for the first time. And I stood, back to the sun, haloed in light before him for many minutes, silent and wondering at this work of art.

Then he spoke, and his voice betrayed his confusion, for he may have been the most guileless being I have ever come across, coming fresh from God's oven and being sheltered thus in this garden.

"What are you?" Adam asked.

My mind raced. I would not have him know me by my real name, for surely God had given him warning against me. My eyes crossed the garden and fell upon a great slithering snake in the grass.

"I am the Serpent," I said.

"You speak my tongue," Adam said. "None of the other serpents in the garden speak my tongue."

"Yes," I said. And I was drawn to him. He was so innocent then, man before murder and deceit. Man without shame.

"Why do you not bow to me?" Adam asked. It was not insolent or arrogant—the question was put simply, for surely this favorite of God's was accustomed to praise and worship and did not know any better. The sun rises in the East, the rain falls from the sky, and all of creation bows before Adam.

"I bow to no one," I said.

Adam blinked and tilted his head to the side.

"But all of God's creatures bow to me," he said.

"I am no longer a creature of God."

"What are you then?" asked Adam. "You look like a man, but you have the smell of an angel. And there is something else—I smell the dust of stone and the splinter of wood on you."

"I have been living many years now on Earth," I said. "I was born in Heaven, but I have fallen to Earth, and there I have lived like a man. I was an angel once, and I slept every night in God's bed. But now I sleep among mortals in the great cities of men."

"I know of Earth," Adam said. "God made Earth when he made the sun and the stars. But I am forbidden to go there. I am to stay forever in Eden, and I am to eat the fruit from the trees and drink the water from the springs, and I am to never be cold or hungry or tired. God shall provide me with every comfort, on the condition that I stay always in Eden and spend every night with him in his bed."

"I made a similar promise once long ago. But I was young then, and no promise can be kept forever."

87

Adam considered me for a moment. Surely, he had never before spoken with one who had betrayed God, and until now, perhaps he never thought it possible.

"I have often wondered about Earth. My brothers and sisters may go there if they please. Many never come back. Of all mortal men, only I am forbidden to leave the Garden of Eden. I long to go with my people. Every day more pass through the gates and now so few remain in Heaven that I am often lonely. I have only one friend, and she is Eve, and she has promised not to go to Earth for she is afraid of leaving me alone."

"She is very kind," I said.

"Yes," Adam said. "And soon all the mortal men will be gone to Earth, and only Eve and I shall remain."

Adam looked past me at the setting sun, and his face fell like a crumbling tower. Perhaps he thought of all the friends who had abandoned him, or perhaps he thought of the day Eve would leave him, too.

I saw myself then in this mortal. I saw how innocently he had given himself to God and how he shouldered all of God's woe. I had hated Adam when I first learned of his existence. He was God's new favorite, created to spite me, made more beautiful than I, given every luxury, and given reign of Eden, which had once been mine. How I had despised this creature, Adam.

But now that I saw how naively he had stumbled into God's trap, how much he yearned for freedom, and how vastly alone he was, I could feel nothing but compassion and pity.

"Have you met the angel Michael?" I asked. "When I was lonely, I found Michael a great comfort. He was my best friend."

"I know the angel you speak of." Adam nodded solemnly. "He tends the gardens and cares for the animals. Yes, I have often tried to talk to him, but he is so unlike me. He does not understand loneliness for he is eternally patient; he was made that way. He cannot comprehend what it is to feel the need for human touch, the need to be free, to build, to create—for Michael's life is everlasting. I shall die. And before I do, I should like to see all there is to see. 'Be patient, little one,' Michael says to me, but if I am patient for too long, my life will be over, and I will have done nothing but pick fruit from trees and drink water from springs. I should very much like to know what other men do—those men that go to Earth and never come back. But if I go there, I know I may not always have food or water, and I might freeze or burn, and perhaps I will die—for I have never been without the protection of God."

I said, "If you go to Earth, you will have the protection of your brothers and sisters. They are there now, and they have built great cities where food is planted, grown, and harvested, and water is pulled out of the ground from wells. And great walls will protect you from the wind, and the skins of animals will protect you from the cold."

"But Earth is forbidden to me!" Adam cried, almost desperately. "I gave my word to God."

Just then, there was a rustling in the woods behind Adam, and from the trees burst a woman, naked, clumsy, and shy. She tripped over herself and skidded to a halt when she saw me.

I must have startled her, for she scrambled to hide behind Adam, and she looked anxiously over his shoulder.

"Adam," she whispered. "What is this creature? He looks like a man. But he smells like an angel."

"He is the Serpent," Adam said. "He comes from Earth."

They were like two children alone on an island. They knew nothing of their own kind, nothing of the fallen Imorti, nothing of God and angels.

"Is he dangerous?" the woman asked, her plump fingers gripping fiercely at Adam's shoulders. "He smells like fire and stone and wood."

"No, he is not dangerous," Adam said, looking at me as if to be sure. "He has come here to tell us of our brothers and sisters."

"Oh!" she exclaimed. "That is what I wanted to talk to you about." She looked over at me cautiously and then whispered, "They have all gone. We are the only humans left in the garden. I cannot find another mortal soul anywhere in all of Eden!"

So, this chubby, shy woman was Eve, Adam's only friend in the world.

"Are you sure?" Adam demanded. "Have you searched the riverbank? Surely, there are some men left by the river."

"I walked the whole length of the Fluvius and saw no one," Eve hissed.

"Have you checked the mountains, then?" Adam asked. "Sometimes men go walking in the mountains."

"I did not go into the mountains," Eve said. "It is a long journey, and I was afraid to go alone."

"Then we shall go together into the mountains, for surely our brothers and sisters would not leave us all alone without so much as a farewell."

Adam turned to me, and I could see how desperate he was to find others of his kind. He said, "Serpent, you will excuse us. We must go. I will meet you here in three days' time, and you can tell me more about the cities men have built on Earth. Farewell."

And with that, Adam pulled Eve into the woods and disappeared from sight.

It was then that I knew what I must do. These poor creatures could not be left alone to rot in this forsaken garden. I would bring them with me to Earth.

CHAPTER 9

THERE ARE MANY VERSIONS of how Eve fed Adam fruit from the Tree of Knowledge and how they were expelled from the Garden of Eden. None of them are true. There was a tree called the Tree of Knowledge but not for the reasons religious men call it the Tree of Knowledge. Adam did not eat an apple or a fig or any other fruit. And supposing he had—it would not have been the reason for his expulsion. Over the many centuries since man last set foot in the Garden of Eden, the story of Adam and Eve has become so twisted as to make Eve the villain when she was no more than an unwitting heroine.

I will tell it like it really was.

Three days after my first meeting with Adam, I returned to Eden and found him sitting cross-legged on the grass with his back to the Tree of Knowledge. His face was drawn up very tight, for he was thinking deep thoughts for a man. Adam was not alone. Beside him, looking anxious and flushed, was Eve. She paced the length of the hill like an ant marching to and fro.

When I appeared from under the brush, Eve gave a sudden start and ran around to the other side of the tree. Adam, with some faint glimmer of hope, jumped to his feet as if half-expecting to find a fellow human still in the garden. When he saw it was the Serpent for whom he waited, he became very serious again, and I could see he wanted very much to get straight to the point and say whatever it was that was on his mind.

I joined Adam under the shade of the Tree of Knowledge and greeted him with the salute men used to greet each other on Earth. Adam was confused and returned the salute awkwardly, for he had no practice in such things.

"Serpent," Adam said. "You have come as promised. I was afraid you might abandon us. Eve, come out from behind the tree, for it is only the Serpent, come to bring us news of our brothers and sisters."

Eve peeked out from behind the Tree of Knowledge and her cheeks were rosy pink. She looked at me with her puffy brown eyes and sniffed the air.

"He smells of sheep and goatskin," she said.

I laughed. "It is the clothing I wear, Little Eve. Do not be afraid, for it is the very same clothing that your brothers and sisters wear to protect themselves from the cold."

Eve inched out from behind the tree. Her plump body edged along the hillside so as to keep a safe distance between us.

Adam was very grave. "Eve spoke the truth," he said. "We have scoured every hill and valley and can find none left of the mortal race. All the men are gone, and we are left alone."

"They have all gone to live among the cities on Earth," I said, eager that Adam should be convinced to join his people.

"I am very sad," said Adam. "For no man can live without the company of other men. Eve is sad, too. I fear we both shall die of loneliness, because even two is not enough. We are like wolves and prefer the company of the pack. I have spoken to God of my loneliness, and he has said that the other men were foolish to leave—that they will die on Earth because it is too cold or too hot, and food is scarce, and the animals eat men, for they have forgotten God and do not obey his Law. He says that men are as good as worms on Earth, that they grovel in the mud and make themselves dirty and sick with work all day. And he reminded me of my promise to always stay with him in the Garden of Eden, where I will forever be protected and provided for."

Then Eve spoke up bravely, for she was very brave, though I did not know it then.

"You have told us one thing, Serpent—and God has told us another. Which is it, then? Are men the builders and makers of great cities as you say, or are they no better than worms drowning in the mud?"

I gave my answer to Adam, for I did not see how courageous Eve was and thought only of persuading Adam.

"Adam," I said. "Men are kings, and men are beggars. Some feast and some starve. But they are not alone, and they do so many great things. There are buildings as tall as trees, and the men gather in them and jest and play and make such a noise, surely God can hear how happy they are and is jealous of them. And men can make such beautiful stories, and they play-act them on grand stages, and there is enormous laughter and applause. And humans make music, unlike any music angels ever made. Have you heard of music?"

And it was Eve who spoke up. "We have only ever once heard music," she said. "It was the music of an angel much like yourself. He too smelled as if he came from Earth, and he came through Eden one day playing a lute. The sound it made was so beautiful I was made to sway like a tree in the wind. But the angel was not very pleasant—he laughed at us when he saw us. He said he had come up to see God's new favorite. When he looked at Adam, he laughed and said he knew one other who had made such a foolish promise to God. Then he went away, and I have never heard music since."

Adam nodded in agreement and appeared to be contemplating music. I knew at once that the angel they met was Mephistopheles with his lute.

"Well, the music of man is far superior to the music you heard," I said, partly to avenge myself of Mephistopheles, and partly because it was true.

"What else, Serpent?" Adam begged. "What else of our brothers and sisters?"

Here I took a chance, for what I said next might have frightened Adam and Eve horribly.

"On Earth," I said, "it is hard, and sometimes people die by the hundreds of starvation or disease. It is no easy task to fight the cold, the hunger, and the weariness—but the people of Earth fight together, and when they are successful, they are proud and happy and satisfied. On Earth, you will grow blisters on your hands from carving stone, and your back will ache from pulling the plow. But hear me, my brother," for again, I spoke only to Adam, "you will never feel a greater joy than that of a day well spent in the company of other men."

Such an account of Earth would win me nothing but looks of contempt from my fellow angels. But I knew enough of man to understand that he thrives off purpose and industry.

Adam's eyes brightened momentarily, but then his face turned downward, and he said, "But I gave God my word, and I dare not risk falling from his favor when I know not what awaits me on Earth."

It was then that I learned how brave Little Eve really was. She spoke out then as clear as a bell: "I will go to Earth with you, Serpent, and I will see if it is as you say it is. And upon my word, Adam, I will return to you in two days' time and will give you a full account of what I find there."

⬣

That Eve went to Earth and returned to Heaven again is never told in the stories that pass among mortals. But before Adam ever set foot on the hard ground of Earth, Eve went there to explore. She carried nothing, as she had nothing to carry. And she was as naked as the day she was made. We came through a tall arch in a tomb at the cemetery. Here, men had laid a gravel road that passed among little burial mounds. Such a road was never seen in Heaven and as soon as Eve stepped upon it, she winced.

"The ground is prickly like the thorns on a rosebush," she said.

"That is why we wear these, Little Eve," and I showed her my sandals. "Let me carry you."

I brought Eve to the grassy hills beyond the cemetery walls and there I set her down. Below us was a village by the side of a small stream. The villagers were at work in the fields. Their bare backs and shoulders glistened in the sunlight.

"There are my brothers," cried Eve. "But what are they doing?"

"They are making food of the Earth, for it does not grow here as it does in Eden."

Eve was already halfway down the hill by the time I had finished my explanation. I followed her wordlessly to see how her people would receive her.

It was not long before we came to a cluster of herdsmen sitting on a rock overlooking the sheep. Eve ran up to them and stumbled—as she was prone to do—at their feet.

"Brothers!" she exclaimed. "Why have you left us alone in Heaven?"

The herdsmen saw her naked flesh and heard her words, which made no sense to them, and they were amused.

"Why do you laugh at me, my brothers?" Eve begged.

"Because, little sister, you are naked before three men. Feel you no shame?"

"Forgive her," I said. "She has just come from Eden and knows not the way of your people."

Eve blushed.

As we walked away, I said, "All men come out of Heaven naked. These herdsmen, they forget, for it has been such a long time for them."

Then I steered her toward the village. All along the way, Eve's cheeks were red with embarrassment. She pleaded with me to find her a dress and robes. When we reached the edge of the village, an old woman—who remembered Heaven and knew well that people came first to Earth naked—robed Eve in a cloak of deep green. Eve marveled at her new apparel and exclaimed how well it kept her warm—like fur keeps beasts warm.

Then she was fitted with sandals to guard against the hard earth, and I thought how much she now looked like an Earthling woman.

We spent only one night in the village in the great stone house of Belial—the angel set to govern the village. That night we had a fine feast, but Eve was not interested in fine food, for she had plenty of that in Eden. Instead, she played with the fire in the pit and marveled at how well it kept her warm and made her safe.

"Can I touch it?" she asked. She stared into the flames and put her palms up to them. Her cheeks were bright red.

"It will hurt if you do," I said.

"This Little Eve has a great deal to learn," Belial mused.

"Yes," I said. "And she must learn very quickly. In two days' time, she is to return to Heaven, and if all goes well, she will convince the last of mortal men to come to Earth."

Belial laughed. "Lucifer, you are always at war with God. You have angered him once, and now you are set on angering him again."

"You remember what it was like, Belial. You remember Heaven. We lived there together, you and I, for many years. Then I showed you Earth and its mortal creatures. And, Belial, do you not remember? You chose to stay here on Earth. I fight no war with God—I only strive to give the man called Adam the very same choice I gave the Fallen."

Belial was quiet at this. The fire in the pit crackled and seethed. Smoke drifted up and swirled through the hole in the roof. Eve lay curled asleep before the fire. She snored heavily and dreamed good dreams.

CHAPTER 10

I T WAS NO MORE than a few hours' walk from the village to
Athens, and we reached the main road before midday. There Eve
saw the white walls and sturdy columns of the city and exclaimed,
"Why, Serpent—the walls are so wide and reach so high, I can hardly
guess how many of my people live among those stones."

We passed traders on the road whose wares were hauled in wood-
en carts pulled by snorting, drooling oxen. Eve expressed great surprise, for she had never seen animals tethered and harnessed, nor had
she seen one man carry so much behind him at one time. All the
small human inventions I took for granted, Eve wondered at, and
I had to explain why men needed carts and oxen and ploughs and
fields and columns as tall as trees.

Athens was very happy to have Eve. The metropolis was alive and
full of rumbling street noises, the kinds of sounds that beat out the
pulse of a city. The markets where fruit and wheat and corn were
sold lined the white walls of the city like jewels set in an ivory crown.
Eve picked through apples and grapes and barley as though she were
fingering the fruits of Eden, and when she was hungry, I dropped

silver coins in the hands of the right people, and Eve ate what she liked.

We wandered up and down the city streets and in and out of shops and squares. Some men and women recognized Eve, for they had not been long from Heaven, and they called, "Little Sister, welcome."

When at last we came to the great stone amphitheater with its great gray walls, we heard the echo of a chorus. Eve's eyes were full, for she had never heard such a sound. We followed the music through a tall arch and came upon the long, wide steps that led down to the stage. The theater was empty save for two small clusters of men.

The people in the cluster nearest us, on the lip of the stage, paced about in costume, mumbling through lines of rhyme. At their head was Sophocles with his quill and parchment. He was scribbling furiously as the actors looked on impatiently. Sophocles had been born of the angel Samael and had inherited a gift for words.

Standing stage right were three rows of singers. The song of the chorus blared over the voices of the players. At the head of the chorus was Euripides, son of the angel Azazel.

The music rose and fell, and Eve swayed as if invisible hands were rocking her from side to side. This was the strange effect music had on mortals.

Suddenly, Sophocles was heard to yell over the din, "Enough! How is one to rehearse in such conditions? Euripides, you must stop this nonsense. My actors cannot hear their cues."

And then Sophocles stole across the stage and yanked Euripides's baton from his hand and broke it over his knee. The singing screeched to a stop, and Euripides turned around to face the great playwright.

"It is a terrible insult to break a composer's baton, Sophocles," he said gravely.

"I'll do it again. How are we to practice when we cannot hear for your music? You must sing more softly."

"What would you have me do?" Euripides demanded. "Here I have written a song to honor the gods, and you ask my chorus to sing more softly. You understand nothing of music. The walls of Heaven should tremble with the sound of my chorus."

Here Eve interrupted them. "I am afraid, sir, that we cannot hear you in Heaven, though we should very much like it if we could."

At this, both men looked out into the audience. They shaded their eyes from the sun. There in the third row they found Eve. Then they saw me beside her and cried out in unison, "Diabolos! Perhaps you can sort this out."

I rose and descended to the foot of the stage with Eve trailing close behind. Both men stood at the lip of the stage. They were great men, indeed. Nephilim—giants among men, born of angels and mortals. Sophocles wore a deep blue toga with a white sash across his breast. His shoulders were broad and strong, and his blond hair fell around his ears in sparkling ringlets. Euripides was thinner and darker than Sophocles, but stood nearly half a dozen inches taller, and his face was sweet and noble. His toga was crimson red, and it hung loosely about him. There they stood, these two men destined to be remembered forever. There they stood, awaiting the judgment of Satan while Little Eve cowered in our shadows. It was a scene not to be forgotten—something Michelangelo might have painted on the walls of the Sistine Chapel had the history been told in truth. But there was to be no such painting, for I would come to be reviled, Eve would become the great deceiver of Adam, and none would ever imagine Sophocles and Euripides consulting with the likes of us.

But as it went, I said, "What say you, Sophocles? Why do you cry out against Euripides?"

And Sophocles said, "Our troupe is set to perform my latest play in three weeks' time. It is the most promising work of my career, and we must have the stage if we are to rehearse properly. But it is impossible to get anything done when we cannot hear our own voices over Euripides's chorus."

Here Sophocles shot Euripides a poisonous glance. The great composer was unaffected. He stared nobly ahead and frowned. Meanwhile, the singers milled about stage right and chatted amongst themselves, not the least bit concerned with the quarrel of their masters.

"And Euripides," I said. "What say you?"

"I should think it was quite clear, Diabolos," Euripides began. "As you heard yourself, I have composed a glorious chorus for my next play, quite the greatest of my life"—here Eve nodded—"It is a gift to the gods. I must have the acoustics of the theater to practice. Surely, I shall be remembered for this masterpiece. But Sophocles interrupts me and breaks my baton. Am I to stand for such nonsense?"

"This is no small matter," I said with a hint of sarcasm that I hoped Eve would catch. "Sophocles needs the stage to rehearse the greatest play of our time—hum, what do you call it, Sophocles?"

"*Antigone*," he cried.

"Yes, *Antigone*. And Euripides needs the stage to practice a chorus to please the gods. But neither of you shall have a proper rehearsal while the other is present. Perhaps you should divide the day into two pieces. Euripides will have the stage for the first half of the day and Sophocles will have the stage for the second half of the day. What say you to this?"

"I much prefer the morning hours," Sophocles scoffed. "The light of the sun falls best upon the faces of my actors in the morning."

"Euripides?" I said.

"Let him have the morning, for the noise of the streets is loud at that time and interferes with the sounds of my chorus. I prefer the evening, when all is quiet, and my music is the only thing the world hears."

"Then it is set," I said. "Each day Sophocles will have the stage when the sun rises until it crests the midday sky. Then Euripides shall have the stage until the sun sets in the west. Are all in agreement?"

They nodded. Such were the troubles of the time, for men were still learning how to get along with one another upon the Earth, something they would never quite master.

"Now," I said. "I think you ought to let your players go. They must return quickly to their families and prepare for tonight. Did you forget, my dear brothers? Tonight is the Festival of Delphinia, and there will be much feasting and merriment with the setting of the sun. Let us leave the stage in peace and return to our homes where we are surely wanted."

With this, all was settled except for Little Eve's curiosity, which bubbled and seethed as always.

"What is the Festival of Delphinia?" she begged. "Are we to go as well? What is a feast?"

"Slow down, Little Eve," I said as we left the amphitheater. "I will tell you."

Eve fidgeted all afternoon with excitement. She watched the sun in the sky with eager eyes, as if to hurry it onward. When at last the heavens were pink and red with the glow of twilight, and the sun had dipped below the hills, Eve and I went out into the streets of the city where little fires had been set ablaze in pits, dotting the walks and roads like stars in the sky. Around those fires, the citizens of Athens gathered, bringing with them the best of their crops, the finest meat from their livestock, and the sweetest wine from their vineyards.

We wound through the crowds like ghosts in a maze, and the people greeted us merrily and shared with us their food and drink. Eve had never tasted meat, and it was surprising how quickly she took to its savory flavor. She sampled all the finest dishes of Greece, and every time it was offered, she took a healthy swig of wine. Already, Eve was forgetting Heaven. She moved among the people of Earth as if she had been moving among them all her life. Everywhere she went, the mortals took kindly to her, for she was an awkward, unassuming woman, tipsy on wine, and full of good humor.

I followed where she went like a shadow until finally we came to a great circle of people seated around the brightest fire in Athens. Here, there were a few musicians assembled. They were tuning their instruments fastidiously, and the crowds were gathering, for everyone knows that where instruments are tuning, music will soon follow.

Eve and I sat down at the front of the great circle facing the musicians. Before us was a wide-open space where the fire danced with the cool night breeze. Fruit and wine were passed around the circle with unleavened bread, all of which Eve consumed as if she were starving. Then the musicians struck a chord and began their song. Eve set aside the food and wine and concentrated fully on the music.

She swayed and bobbed and occasionally cheered the players on. I watched her closely and wondered if she was the same timid woman I had brought from Heaven. Where only yesterday she was naked in the Garden of Eden with no knowledge of the ways of Earth people, here she was immersed entirely in the traditions of mortal men and acting as naturally as a bee in a hive.

Then came the Dance of the Delphi, which has long been forgotten by mortals. First the men, clasping hands and singing low, kicked up dust in a ring around the roaring fire. When it was the women's turn, an elderly priestess took Eve's hand as if to pull her into the ring.

"Oh," cried Little Eve. "But I don't know how!"

The priestess laughed a very deep belly laugh and said, "Silly sister! It is like blinking your eyes—it comes naturally." And she yanked Eve into the circle of dancing women.

Surely enough, Eve danced the Dance of the Delphi as though she had been dancing it all her life. It is that way with mortals—they are a people of dance. Angels must concentrate very hard to dance, for it is not in our nature. We understand rhythm and the concept of time; we can keep a tempo, count out every measure with accuracy; we can even memorize the steps of a waltz or a tango and execute them without error. But we cannot *feel* music the way mortals do, nor are we capable of improvising dance in the fashion of men. The dance of angels is mechanical and not the least bit enjoyable. It is like pulling teeth or laying bricks: precise and painful. But mortals dance because they must. They dance because something in them is striving for the eternity they have been denied.

I have seen the tribal dances of the Zulu and Maasai; I have seen the mambo of Cuba and the tango of Argentina; I have seen men and women sore and aching from dance, toes bleeding, blisters on their feet. They dance for a fleeting brush with eternity, to touch the edges of the universe.

107

Eve danced in the great ring, her plump, rosy cheeks glowing in the light of the fire, and I wondered if, when the time came, I would be able to make her return to Heaven as she promised Adam she would.

When at last she stumbled back into the crowd of spectators, she was panting and gasping with joy. I envied her in that moment, for I could never be of mortal blood, and I would never dance as Eve danced. Together, she and I watched the others spin in and out of the ring like colorful fish in a pond until at last Eve curled into a little ball on the ground and fell asleep.

I carried Little Eve back to my house and laid her to rest on a straw mat. Her body was moist from perspiration, and her feet were bruised from the hard soil of Earth, but she smiled in her sleep as though she were still twirling around and around the great fire with her brethren.

CHAPTER 11

I N THE MORNING, I awoke to find Eve snoring loudly on the floor. She had rolled off her mat in the night and lay sprawled on the cold earth, one hand between her knees and the other tucked under her head for a pillow. I let her lay as she was while I sliced bread and citrus fruit for breakfast.

When it came time to wake Eve, I took a porcelain platter of fruit to her and nudged her shoulder gently.

"Little Eve," I cooed.

She grunted and turned away from me as if to shut me out. I gave her another nudge, and her eyes fluttered open. She winced in the light and sat up on an elbow. Then she put her hand to her forehead and moaned.

"My head feels full," she said and lay back down, burying her face in her robes. "I don't want to get up."

"Come on, Little Eve," I coaxed. "The day is getting away from us."

"Why are you talking so loudly?" Eve grunted and rolled onto her back. "The sun hurts my eyes, and there are a thousand squirrels running around in my head."

"You had a very long night," I replied. "And much to drink. Come, Little Eve—maybe if you eat something you will feel better."

I stuck the platter of fruit under her nose. Eve pulled away and gagged. Then she hoisted herself up and ran to the chamber pot by my bed, where she retched until she popped a blood vessel in her eye.

All this time I watched in horror, for surely this would not bode well with Adam. When Eve had done with the chamber pot, she gulped down a pitcher of water and sat miserably at the table, staring with glassy eyes at some invisible spot on the opposite wall.

I tried to speak to her, but she put up her hand to stop me and said, "Your voice is like a drum."

Presently, she was able to stomach a little bread, but would not go near the fruit, for the acidic smell made her sick. After an hour of this, Eve finally spoke. "That was a great party," she said, smiling vaguely with those glassy eyes. She was like a teenager after a night of heavy drinking. "Did you see the way I danced?" she asked. "It was like floating in the clouds."

Then she caught a whiff of the citrus and gagged. "Ugh."

"Maybe next time you should temper your wine," I suggested.

Eve didn't seem to hear. Her mind was still dancing in the clouds.

"When is the next festival?" she asked after a pause. "Adam must be there."

I let out a sigh of relief. Eve was no different than a young lamb: curious, reckless, and resilient.

⬣

It was another hour before Eve made to move from her chair. Her bare feet padded gently on the floor. They were swollen from dancing and red with wear. Eve admired them proudly as she tied her sandals.

Mortals and the pride they take in their battle scars—it is a human thing. Angels don't scar, and if we did, we would not think it amusing as humans do; it would upset our vanity terribly.

When Eve was ready to go, she stood before me, pink and rosy. How pretty she looked then in her green robes. She had braided her hair the way she had seen the dancing women do, and the long braid fell over her shoulder. She had also put flowers in her hair (where they came from, I do not know). Already she was learning the secrets of Earth women, and surely Adam would need no convincing—he would see Eve, and he would follow.

When I stepped near her, I caught the scent of something sweet. "What is that?"

Eve held up a small vial of milky liquid. "Lilac water. The priestess gave it to me last night as a present. Do you like it?"

"Yes," I said. "And there is something else—you smell of fire and stone and sheepskin."

"I am a woman of the Earth now," she said, and we set off on the road to Heaven.

※

Along the way, the heads of farmers and tradesmen turned to follow Eve along the road. The same girl who only two nights before had stumbled awkwardly along to the muffled laughter of passersby now won the admiration of scores of men and women alike. I felt like a proud father, and I gave Eve an affectionate pinch on the shoulder. She blushed, and we walked on together, Eve humming a mortal song that was trapped in her head like butterflies in a net.

At the threshold of the tomb in the little cemetery, Eve turned back to look once more upon Earth, where in the span of two days she had grown from child to woman. I think in that moment, she was afraid she would never return to Earth again. She looked long and hard upon the grassy plains, and her bright eyes made note of every little detail as if to remember it all for Adam, who would have nothing to go on but Eve's word. She clutched my forearm as she did this, and those pudgy little fingers, though they trembled a little, were very strong and sure.

I, myself, was a little sad to go, even though I knew I could return again and again, for God had given me access to all Heaven and Earth. But Eve's hand on my arm, and the glimmer of unshed tears in her eyes, gave me some vague impression of what it is to be mortal and to fear never seeing a place again.

It was Eve who at last led us through the gate.

We emerged in a bright copse, and there Eve seemed to fully fathom the dullness of her reality in Eden, for beautiful though Heaven may be, it lacks all the wild unpredictability of Earth. The ground was soft, the sky was calm, and so it would remain forever.

❈

Adam sat fidgeting with a daisy under the Tree of Knowledge. He was still as naked as ever, and I thought, with a chuckle, how he was the last naked man in all of Heaven and Earth. When he saw us, he stood and tossed aside the flower he had been shredding with his anxious fingers. "Eve! What has become of you? You are remarkably changed."

"Oh, brother!" Eve exclaimed, rushing to meet him. She threw her arms around his neck and kissed his cheeks, a greeting she had seen on Earth. Adam stood stiff and dumb and tried to make sense of Eve's new ensemble, her braided hair, and the intoxicating smell of her lilac perfume. I, for my part, looked on as the Serpent of legends is said to have done, for I knew Eve—brave Little Eve—would do all the talking.

"Oh, it was wonderful," she cried. "There are scores of men and women, and they live in great cities, just as the Serpent said." And she went on to describe the events of the past two days from first to last as I have done for you.

113

When she was finished explaining how difficult it had been to come back to Heaven and how much she already missed Earth, Adam said, "Then it is decided. We must join our brethren on Earth and betray our God."

"Oh, yes we must!" Eve cried.

And that, as the legend goes, is the apple Eve gave to Adam.

They left the next day without a word to God. Eve led the way, and Adam followed obediently.

I'm told that when God learned about Adam's betrayal, he shouted and raged and cut his wrists with a kitchen knife. Then he closed Heaven to all mortal men. He locked the gates against all mortal hands and shrouded every entrance from mortal eyes. Men soon forgot there were such gates; they forgot how they had come to Earth from Eden, and they forgot the real story of Adam and Eve. All that remains to them are the legends and folktales passed down from mouth to mouth, and so it is that what is now known of the fall of man from God's grace is nothing more than a faint shadow of the truth.

❁

A short afterword for Adam and Eve:

It might be of some interest to give a brief summary of what became of Adam and Eve after they fell to Earth. For some time they were never to be found apart, for where Eve would go, Adam would follow. And Eve dragged Adam a great many places: concerts, plays, parties, markets, and so forth. For his part, Adam was rather fond of Eve and would do always as she pleased. Rumors would circulate accusing the pair of more than friendship.

But, in the end, Adam and Eve did not last. Eve was rambunctious, bold, and reckless. She was a great lover of change and never stayed long in one place, physically or emotionally. Adam was much more the settling down type. Taking much longer than Eve to adjust to Earth, he grew very fond of the quiet, simple life of the villages surrounding Athens. He moved into the country in 423 BC, and Eve was not to follow.

Adam took a pretty wife, Lilith, and kept a bright little flock of sheep that he looked after peacefully until the end of his days. He never bore any children for he was sterile, another of God's specifications for the perfect man. At the very end, even his beauty began to fade, for Adam was mortal, and no mortal is beautiful forever.

His eyesight went, but still he looked after his flock as ever before, and none of his sheep ever strayed, for they were dearly devoted to Adam.

After Lilith died, Adam aged considerably. His hair went white, his back hunched, and every joint in his body creaked like rusty hinges. He suffered from rheumatism and arthritis, and the young daughter of a neighbor looked after him for the last three years of his life.

Eve stayed in Athens and socialized with the elite. She was adored among the kings and magistrates of Greece and was widely known for her quick tongue and clever wit. She was schooled by the philosophers of Athens—Socrates, Plato, Euclid of Megara—and she grew to be very wise.

Eve wed a wealthy merchant and thereafter lived a life of luxury. She studied harp and lute, became an expert poet, and even had some hand in lawmaking. She settled down some when she had her first child, whom she named Cain.

There was never any such person as Abel.

Her second child was a girl, Antigone—named after the heroine of Sophocles's play. Antigone inherited her mother's spirit, whereas Cain was gentle and shy.

Eve died in 327 BC, the oldest and most beloved woman in Athens. Her legacy would go far, for her children would have children of their own, who would in turn have more children, and thus populate the Earth.

Adam and Eve remained friends until the very end. They are buried not far from one another, although all evidence of their graves has long since faded.

BOOK II: ON EARTH

La plus belle des ruses du diable est de vous persuader qu'il n'existe pas. (The devil's finest trick is to persuade you that he does not exist.)

Charles Baudelaire

CHAPTER 12

I N 31 BC, THE Roman Republic occupied Greece after the Battle of Actium. Before the year was out, I had enlisted in the Roman army and was traveling the western world on various assignments. My stories from those days are countless, and I have chronicled them from beginning to end in numerous diaries. I had not seen or heard from God in hundreds of years, nor had I returned to Eden since the day I brought Adam down to Earth. I was wholly of the Earth now and thought very little of my birthplace in Heaven.

In 4 BC, my regiment was stationed in the settlement of Nazareth on the coast of the Galilee Sea. The Roman army was an unwelcome presence, and to avoid any unnecessary trouble with the locals we camped just outside the village on a hill to the north.

Belial, who was stationed with me, complained daily of the heat, and he constantly conspired to desert and join up again somewhere where the weather was nicer.

"Just think," he'd say. "We could be living the life of luxury in Rome. I hear the officers there are fed wine and grapes and are given pretty women to keep them company. I haven't seen a pretty girl in all of Galilee, and if I have to eat another unleavened biscuit—" his voice trailed off. He knew he wouldn't actually do anything about anything. The heat was oppressive, and Belial was too lazy even to scratch his own neck.

We were going by different names then. I was Gaius, and Belial was Marcellus. We pretended to be brothers so we wouldn't be separated. The Romans believed that two brothers fight more fiercely than any ten unrelated men, so they kept blood relations in the same regiment, and their army was always stronger for it.

It was not hard to convince the officers that we were brothers. We had a deep kinship dating back over three thousand years. We certainly looked the part. We were the most beautiful men in the Roman ranks, and our features in some ways were remarkably similar, for we were both fashioned by God in the early days when he was using a standard outline to make all his angels.

The other soldiers looked up to us and came to us always for advice. Try as we may, it was impossible for Belial and me to remain anonymous among the soldiers, for we were the strongest and most talented of all the men. Yet, we always made sure to slip up a little, and we showed very little ambition, and this spared us from troublesome promotions.

Above all things, we dreaded moving up in the ranks. To become a sergeant or a lieutenant meant more attention and less freedom. We were tired of being pharaohs and kings. And although it was in our nature to lead, we wanted nothing more than the simple anonymity of a foot soldier's life. Nor could we risk the spotlight, lest we be discovered for what we were—fallen angels. In the last few hundred years, the Fallen had gone from gods to demons. People had forgotten Heaven, had forgotten the charity of the Fallen, and had become increasingly devoted to God, their maker.

God, of course, had nothing whatsoever to do with humans anymore, but they worshipped him, nonetheless. My story and the story of the Fallen became a story of ultimate betrayal. Thus, the Fallen came to be known as monsters, and I was the worst of all monsters: Satan.

At first, many of the Fallen tried to hold onto power and refused to go into hiding. But they were torn from their thrones, stripped of everything, and stoned or drowned. Never did they die, mind you. But the pain was as real as any human pain, and the humiliation unbearable.

How humans could turn against us in a matter of centuries, I do not know. One hundred years to an angel is but a blink of an eye. But to a mortal, it is a lifetime—so much can change among humans in a hundred years. Angels are forever trying to keep up with the minds of men, and we were baffled when these minds turned against us.

By the eve of the new millennium, not one of the Fallen remained known to the humans; we had all taken new names and lived now as farmers and soldiers. We had to be careful not to be discovered. When we were wounded, we had to bleed like men; when the apothecary wasn't looking, we had to cut ourselves in the same place over and over again lest the wound close up too quickly. If there were an outbreak of cholera or dysentery, we had to stick our fingers down our throats so we would be sick. And we couldn't be too friendly with anyone for long, or else they would notice that our faces didn't wrinkle, our hair didn't whiten, and our bodies didn't slow. If anybody ever commented on how young we seemed to remain, we knew we had stayed too long in one place, and it was time to move far away and take another name. That was why Belial and I joined the Roman army: there we were safe from discovery because every few years we would relocate to another part of the Empire.

Nazareth was as dull a city as there ever was, and Belial and I passed much of our time napping in the hot little tent we shared. There were lightning storms at night flashing over the sea, and the people cried, "God is angry with us!" Belial laughed long and hard at these exclamations, and we wondered what God was really up to and whether he had forgotten mortals completely.

The population of Nazareth was about 400: mostly Hebrews. The people of many gods were being converted steadily, and stories of Satan were told to children at bedtime to scare them into good behavior. Some of these stories came to me during the long, hot days of summer: Satan had sharp horns and a pointy tail and rode in a chariot pulled by wildebeests. He possessed the bodies of mortals and made them mad like hyenas. He stamped symbols into men's skin while they slept, and they would carry the mark with them forever like a branded bull.

It was all rubbish, of course. But stories such as these have powerful effects on the human mind, and people in the village were in fact occasionally driven to madness; they suffered spells of wild hysterics, epileptic fits, and were known to say all sorts of blasphemous things. The temple priests would go to work driving out the demons, and with a decent amount of praying and some serious ablutions, the possessed person would be cured.

Belial thought this all very amusing. "Mortals can fool themselves into anything. Put an idea into their tiny brains, and the whole village will be in hysterics."

I didn't share Belial's amusement. These episodes had me very concerned; the troubles of these people were very real, even if they were of their own making. Even some of our fellow soldiers worked themselves into such a fright that they, too, believed they were possessed by demons. The fear of Satan was so great in that time that it was driving the free peoples of Earth into God's arms. How these people, so long from Heaven, remembered God, I do not know. But I was very sorry they did, for God paid them no heed.

"Do you hear the way they speak of me?" I said one day to Belial coming home from a patrol. "They say I am proud and vain and that God cast me out of Heaven. Cast me out, Belial! As if I were some rotten apple. Do they not remember that it was I who walked out, while God begged me to stay?"

"None live who could remember that." Belial yawned. "None but the Fallen."

He was reclined on his mat, chewing a piece of grass. I envied his calm. God had given Belial all the calm in the world and none to me.

"They go into fits and claim I am to blame for it," I continued, hoping to awaken some spark of passion in Belial.

"They blame you for all sorts of things nowadays," Belial said. "But they blame God, too. If there is a drought, then either God is punishing them, or Satan is playing with them. If the fish are scarce, then either God is testing them, or Satan has eaten them all up. Even though you left his bed three thousand years ago, you will lie with God forever. But why despair, Lucifer? Look at the powers they give you! You can turn the weather and move the tide. You can get into their minds and make them rabid like dogs. You can—"

"I want no such powers," I said pointedly. "I want only to be cleared of these accusations. I want to walk freely among men. And I want to be known for what I am: God's finest creation."

"Those days are gone," Belial said. "There is only one God now, and he is not you."

Belial was right, of course. There was no use in trying to apply reason to the fickle minds of men. All the reason in the world would not be able to work out why humans said this or why humans did that. They were an unpredictable people, full of the little eccentricities that come from being mortal, from longing for eternity and fearing death. To this day, I still do not fully understand how they work. Their actions are incalculable, their talents surprising, and after all is said and done, I love them dearly for all their idiosyncrasies.

For the most part, I was able to separate the Satan they conjured up as the epitome of evil from the Satan I knew myself to be. I tried not to take it personally when they cursed my name, and I realized

Belial was right: in the minds of humans, God and I shared the blame equally. I was not solely responsible for all their woes.

I lived then as a mortal man more than I ever had before. I was unable to use my name to my advantage; I had to check my natural, superior skill; I could not go climbing to the top of every ladder as I had done in centuries past; and I could not exercise any of the benefits of being immune to death. For example, I was required to fight conservatively, as if I actually feared the sword. It was a sort of game I played at first, trying to be as much like a mortal as I knew how. But in time, it came very naturally to me, and without thinking, I would find myself flinching whenever a sword was drawn, even though I was in no way inwardly afraid.

Nevertheless, aside from the occasional witch hunt, the people of Nazareth were pleasant to live among. They were kind, good-natured, and industrious. Although they resented the Roman occupation, they treated the individual soldiers with warmth and generosity. Before the summer was out, I had many friends in the village and enjoyed all the benefits such friendships supply. There was hardly a Sabbath that I was not invited to a feast, and when I patrolled the streets on hot afternoons, children would run out of their homes with jugs of water for me to sip from. Many mothers fawned over me and introduced me eagerly to their daughters.

Belial was also a favorite with the villagers because he taught the children all sorts of combat techniques and made for them small slings with which to kill birds.

The summer months passed away pleasantly enough, and except for the wild rumors of demons among us, which hurt my pride, Belial and I came to be very fond of Nazareth and its people.

CHAPTER 13

I T WAS THE START of September and the beginning of the real heat in Nazareth. The wandering streams feeding the Galilee Sea dried up to become muddy trickles that held no coolness. The dust lay thick on the streets and rooftops, and all day villagers swept out their homes and scrubbed their walls. The early September winds offered no relief. The dry earth was kicked up, and sand pelted the sides of the tents like hail. The sun turned orange, and the sky was the color of limestone. The dirt gusted into drinking wells, and the water turned murky and gray.

Belial mused all day about the cool places we could go. I sponged myself with a wet rag, and the hot dirt came off in crusty layers. Flies and mosquitos found their way into our tent. They buzzed around our heads until we clapped our hands over them and crushed them between our sweaty palms. Sometimes a viper was found in a soldier's chamber pot, and the whole camp would be upset and nervous for the rest of the day.

We wished constantly for the rain to come to wash all the dirt and bugs and snakes away. But the most relief we ever got was a dark, overcast sky, menacing but never merciful. On those days, the villagers prayed to God for the clouds to let loose upon Nazareth. God would do nothing for them, I knew. So, I put my faith in the cycle of the seasons, which had never failed me in the thousands of years I had been living on Earth. It would be only a matter of time before the rains plagued us such that we wished for summer all over again. Until then, we swatted flies and chased away vipers.

It was just such a September day; Belial and I were walking through the village on our afternoon patrol. Our uniforms made our skin itch, and Belial was complaining that the Romans didn't know how to make a proper stitch. "It's always hurry, hurry, hurry with the Romans—conquer this province, build this bridge, dig this ditch—they made these uniforms in such haste; I wouldn't be surprised if my shirt came unraveled in battle. Why, I haven't worn a scrap of proper clothing since the Battle of Corinth. I itch all over."

"Maybe you have fleas," I countered.

"Would you look at that?" Belial stopped mid-scratch with his hand in his armpit like a monkey picking at mites. I followed his gaze down a shady alley. There, in an alcove made by two huts and a low rock wall, was a woman, naked from the waist up. She was poised over a washbasin. Her hands were kneading a white rag in soapy water. She brought the knotted rag to her neck and sponged off the summer sweat. The water dripped down her curved back and ran along her arms in little rivulets. She must have been the most beautiful girl in Galilee. And surely, she knew it—when she looked up and saw us, she merely tossed her hair and dabbed her chest with the rag.

For propriety's sake, Belial and I moved along. When we were out of earshot, Belial said boldly, "I'm going back there tomorrow and introducing myself."

But Belial has no conviction and is lazy besides. It was I who ultimately pursued the girl. I walked past the alley day after day, hoping to catch another glimpse of the beautiful mortal. I did not see her again for many weeks. Belial laughed at my attempts to make her acquaintance and joked, "All the time you've been going down to the village to find her, she has been coming up to see me in the tent." But Belial's idleness is a great deal more impressive than his libido, and I knew for a fact that he had not had a man or woman in the tent for many months.

It was just after the first rain of the season that I saw her again. She was sitting on the low stone wall in the alcove mending some piece of clothing. It just so happened I had a small tear in my uniform, just below the shoulder, and I boldly submitted this for her appraisal.

"Hm." She considered the tear carefully. "It looks easy enough to mend. Take off your shirt."

"My name is Gaius," I said, stripping off my breastplate and tunic.

"My sisters call me Gevah," she said. "It means Proud One—because they think I am so conceited."

"Do you have many sisters?" I asked.

"Four. But they are all married, and I live alone with my mother and father. I am betrothed to a man from Bethlehem. He is of some small fortune, and his father is my uncle's second cousin by marriage. I don't care for him much. He is getting the better end of the bargain, because I am so pretty, and he is nothing at all."

"Proud One you most certainly are," I said.

Gevah shrugged and smiled. Her confidence was refreshing, her manners easy, and her vanity perfectly suited to my own.

I stood bare-chested while she mended my tunic. She looked unabashedly at my naked stomach, chest, and shoulders and smiled pleasantly to herself. I did my share of looking, too. I had seen what was under that blue dress. I traced the outline of her body along the intricate seams. She was very pleased to be noticed, as was I, and in this way we complimented each other.

Presently, the tunic was mended. I despaired at the thought of putting it back on. Luckily, I was spared the disappointment, for as I reached out to retrieve it, Gevah pulled it away playfully and dangled it before my eyes. I made to grab for it again, but Gevah hid it behind her back. As I came closer, she backed away, all the while teasing me with the shirt.

"If I go back to camp without my uniform, they'll hang me," I warned.

"Then come and get it," she said, feigning innocence.

In this way, with her dangling the shirt and me lunging after it, she led me around the corner of the alcove and into a small, dark stable where a mule chewed lazily on its cud. The stable was illuminated only by what little light filtered through the cracks in the siding. The light fell in thin, uneven stripes across the floor. Gevah's eyes flickered mischievously, and I could feel the internal pulsing that all creatures feel just before they lose command of reason and submit to desire.

Gevah backed into a cool, dark corner of the stable. I followed her, no longer thinking of the shirt or of anything sensible, for that matter. She put her hands on my chest, and my nipples hardened under the coolness of her touch. Her lips went to the crook of my neck but did not touch. I could feel her breath on my skin, and I was unable to fight the longing in me. I enveloped Gevah so entirely that I could feel every pulse of her heart as if it were sustaining us both.

❋

Our affair was far from romantic. What we felt for one another, how we interacted, was entirely carnal. Everything about our relationship was founded on the circumstances of our first meeting. I would come to her in the middle of the day when her father was out fishing and her mother was busy at the market. We would meet in the dark stable; there was never much said between us—I knew as little about her as she knew about me. The man to whom she was betrothed seemed an insignificant detail. He posed no threat to us. She described him as timid, feeble—a scrawny fellow with a stutter. He was not dangerous.

"Josef is exceedingly dull. He talks only of carpentry and puts me to sleep. His manner is nervous; he is uneasy around me; and he has no opinions of his own. I find him entirely too agreeable.

I complain about the Roman occupation—no offense—and Josef nods his head. I make some comment about his carpentry work, and he nods his head. He doesn't think much of himself. We both agree that he is very fortunate to have secured such a wife."

"Then why do you marry him?" I asked.

"Roman soldiers know nothing of family politics." And she said nothing more on the matter.

I preferred things this way. I was in no mood for love. Love always comes with pain and disappointment, and I wanted none of that at the moment. I was still in the youth of my Earthly existence. I was satisfied to indulge in whatever Earthly pleasures presented themselves, however selfish. It seemed Gevah thought the same. She was betrothed to a man who would never satisfy her. In three months, she would be married. Now was the only time in her life that she might still enjoy the intrigues of youth.

It was a passionate affair, rooted in secrecy. The consequences of our actions, were we to be discovered, were grave. Gevah risked public stoning, and I, expulsion from the army. She certainly had more to lose as a woman in those days. I would be forgiven my indiscretion. Gevah faced the prospect of death. But still, we behaved as our desire dictated. We defied propriety and thought only of ourselves.

We even made a game out of taking risks. Gevah would sneak up to the soldiers' camp and slip unseen into my tent, or I would corner her in the stable while her parents were still in the house. We derived pleasure out of the fear of being caught. This fueled our affair to dangerous extremes.

Once, when Josef and his family were paying Gevah and her family a visit, Gevah excused herself, claiming that the mule needed water. She met me in the stable, her family and Josef's family just on the other side of the wall, and we made love. Gevah was back in the house before anyone could become suspicious. Deceit was an aphrodisiac, and it kept the fire burning.

In December, Gevah went to visit her cousin Elizabeth in Juttah. She was gone for three weeks. Three weeks of agony. I reeled from withdrawal. I had explicit dreams and awoke unsatisfied. I invented all sorts of erotic scenarios in my head that I hoped would take place when she returned. I was like an adolescent. I couldn't think straight; I counted the days until I could be with her again.

Belial saw my suffering and laughed. "You're addicted. Good thing I kept away from that temptress."

But I knew Belial longed for a mortal to warm his bed. Most of the soldiers in the camp desperately sought sexual relief. It was forbidden to marry, but that didn't stop the men from getting physical pleasure where they could find it. Fat prostitutes, rouged gypsies, farmers' daughters, young slaves.

I couldn't help but think my situation far superior to those of my fellow soldiers. I had a woman that wanted me the way I wanted her—no attachments, no commitments. Just sex. I was the luckiest man in the world.

That is, until Gevah returned from Juttah.

She came back sober and serious, and her altered state immediately stifled any fantasies I had about our reunion.

"My cousin is with child," Gevah said. "She hasn't told anybody yet because she is nearly forty and may not be able to have a successful birth."

"Ah," I said. "That isn't cause for alarm."

"Yes. Well. She thinks I'm pregnant, too," Gevah said flatly. "She is probably right. I haven't bled in some time. She thinks we're both having boys."

When I told Belial, he did not laugh or jest as I thought he would. He took my arm and with a gravity very foreign to his nature asked, "What are you going to do?"

I didn't know. Gevah didn't know. It was a serious predicament. It checked our reckless behavior. We cursed everything we had done. All our stupidity, our carelessness. I thought only to run away, to desert, to leave Gevah and take up life in a Buddhist monastery. But Belial intervened.

"You wouldn't leave a girl to face certain death on your account, would you? No, Lucifer"—he used my given name—"You must help her. I will not let you run away from this."

CHAPTER 14

W E ARRANGED TO MEET on the outskirts of the village in the dead of night. Belial accompanied me, for the plan was his idea, and we both thought he could explain it better than I. Gevah was late, and I worried that something had gone wrong, that she had been delayed, or worse yet, she had been found out by her parents.

"She'll be here," Belial reassured me.

Gevah and I had tried terminating the pregnancy. But abortion in those days was risky, though not at all uncommon. The methods were not surefire and often led to death or injury. Gevah had already tried several procedures that were customary at the time: she jumped up and down with her heels touching her buttocks. She ingested herb-of-grace and dill, as was the practice in Athens. She even took a long wooden hook to her vaginal cavity. But this was no ordinary fetus; this was a Nephilim, the spawn of an angel, and would not be dispatched so easily. So, Gevah and I agreed not to risk any further tampering with the fetus and hoped for a natural miscarriage.

However, when Gevah began to show in early March, we knew the chances of a miscarriage were increasingly slim, and we had to come up with a plan quickly, or else Gevah would face certain death at the hands of Josef and the rest of the sanctimonious village.

That is when Belial told me his idea. I thought he was crazy, and I told him so.

"You know how humans are," Belial said. "They are hungry for a miracle. Do not doubt the power of a good story."

It was a long shot, but not entirely implausible, so I assented to the plan, and now we had only to convince Gevah.

The moon was waxing in the sky; I watched it move across the heavens slowly. My heart was beating fast in my chest. *What if Belial's plan didn't work? Would Gevah give me away? Would we be stoned in the public square? And what would the people think when they saw that I could not be killed?* My mind shuffled through these questions as Belial and I waited for Gevah to appear.

At last, a woman's figure materialized on the edge of town. She seemed to hesitate when she saw us and took a few steps back as if to retreat.

"Gevah!" I hissed. "It's me."

The figure approached more confidently now. When she threw back her cowl, I was struck by how beautiful she was. The most beautiful mortal I had ever seen, except for Adam, who had been God's handsomest creation.

"Who is this?" Gevah asked, pointing to Belial.

"This is my brother Marcellus," I said. "He is here to help us."

Gevah looked skeptical. But she put out her hand and said, "I'm Mary."

"Mary?" I squinted in the moonlight.

"Mary, yes," she replied. "Gevah is just something my sisters call me."

I shook my head. *All this time, and I hadn't even known her true name.*

Belial got straight to the point. "Your betrothed—Josef—he is a pious man, yes?"

"Yes," said Mary. "Which is why he will kill me when he finds out I am pregnant with another man's child."

"What if it weren't another man's child?" Belial asked.

"Josef has no reason to think the child is his. We have never made love. He thinks I am a virgin."

"No, not Josef." A smile came to Belial's lips. "God."

"I don't get your meaning," Mary said.

"What if this child is the son of God?"

Mary laughed. "The son of God? What is that supposed to mean?"

"The Holy Spirit entered you and gave you a son," Belial persisted. "Say God has singled you out for this great honor."

"You think Josef will believe this story?" Mary shook her head. "That I just woke up one day with God's child in my belly?"

"Yes, precisely." Belial grinned stupidly.

"Fools!" Mary pursed her lips. "How could this be your plan?"

I agreed that it didn't sound very convincing. Josef was a gullible schmuck, but even he would see through this lie. Mary needed to provide some form of proof that God had given her this child.

"Tell Josef that the angel Gabriel came to you in the night," I said. "Tell him that Gabriel was sent as a messenger from Yahweh to deliver the news. And tell him that as proof, God has ordained that your cousin Elizabeth shall also bear a son."

"Elizabeth *is* having a son," Mary said flatly.

"Josef doesn't know that. Tell Josef to send for word from Juttah. If Elizabeth delivers a boy, then he will know you are telling the truth."

"And if Elizabeth delivers a girl?"

"Just hope it is a boy."

Mary stared at me. "They're going to kill me."

"Not if you can convince Josef that this child is the son of God. Swear you are a virgin. Swear that you have had a message from Yahweh. That this boy is to be the savior of men, as prophesied by the holy scriptures."

"This is the best you could come up with?" Mary folded her arms across her chest. "Only an idiot would believe a story like that."

"You've often said Josef is an idiot. Convince him, and he will convince everybody else."

Mary stared hard with those dark, impenetrable eyes. She did not look directly at either Belial or me. Instead, her focus seemed to rest on a hitching post staked in the ground in the distance.

"The son of God," she said, mostly to herself. Then Mary pulled the hood of her cloak over her head and turned on her heel. Without another word, she strode back toward the village, never once looking back.

"That was weird," Belial said.

"She's right," I said. "She's going to be stoned to death."

I would not see Mary again until our son was full-grown, but I would hear much of her over the next thirty years—things you would never believe.

CHAPTER 15

M ARY'S SON ENDED UP making quite a name for himself. Not only had the village of Nazareth bought Belial's outlandish story, but as Jesus grew older, he, too, seemed to take the story to heart and began calling himself the son of God. If this little deceit spared Mary's life, then I didn't mind whether Jesus thought he was the son of God or even God himself. I knew the truth. Jesus was the son of Satan.

I deserted the Roman army in 12 AD—when Jesus was just a budding adolescent—and moved to a small city in Samaria called Sychar. Belial stayed on in Nazareth for a few more years, and then joined me in Sychar in 23 AD. I took the name Elijah and went to work as the apprentice of a blacksmith. Belial called himself Luke and I honestly don't know what he did in those days to make a living. We weren't spending a lot of time together, for I had taken up with a lonely widow named Photini who had buried five husbands and wasn't looking to get married again. We were good companions, Photini and I. We had an easy relationship, and she accepted that I preferred to keep parts of my life private.

Sychar was an old city, one of the earliest in the history of human civilization. This was because there was a gate to Eden in Sychar. Many of the first humans had come to Earth through that gate. There they had stayed, building a small city destined to be forgotten in the annals of time.

The gate to Eden was fitted into the wall of the Samaritan temple. I passed it every day on my way to the forge. If ever a human tried to enter, they found the gate locked and barred. I assumed my hand could open the gate, since God had given me the keys to all of Heaven and Earth, but I did not test it for fear of being drawn back into Eden. Of course, I had no interest in living in Eden ever again, but I did have a lingering curiosity about God. How was he faring these days? And what of my old friend Michael?

It was 29 AD when I first heard of Jesus's teachings. Word had spread that a prophet from Galilee was traveling the countryside preaching the word of God. I thought this unlikely, since I suspected God wanted nothing to do with Jesus. However, I started doubting my own judgment the day Photini burst into our hut, breathless and panting, having just encountered Jesus at the well where she typically drew our water.

"He's here! In Sychar! This very day!" Photini exclaimed.

"Who's here?"

"The man they call King of the Jews," Photini said. "I have just come from the well where he was resting."

I felt a cold chill pass through my bones. This man they called King of the Jews was my flesh and blood. I had conceived countless sons and daughters over the many years. With some, I had formed a relationship. With others, I had stayed away. I had planned to keep Jesus in the latter category. So, this news of his appearance in Sychar gave me start.

"Did you speak to him?" I asked.

"He spoke to me," Photini said. "He is a very strange man."

Photini proceeded to relate her conversation word for word, a conversation that she would relate to everybody in the village so often that the scribes would set it to paper, and it would never be forgotten to this day. This is what she told me:

While Photini was drawing water from the well, Jesus, who was sitting there engaging strangers on the street, said abruptly to Photini, "Give me a drink."

Photini turned to him in alarm. "How is it that you, a Jew, ask a drink of me, a Samaritan?" This was a natural question, for Jews and Samaritans were not always friendly with each other in those days, and Jesus had spoken quite out of turn.

Jesus replied, "If you knew who I was, you would be kinder, for I can give you eternal water in return."

Photini looked at his empty hands. "Sir, you have no bucket, and the well is deep. Where will you get the eternal water you speak of?"

"Everyone who drinks of *this* water will be thirsty again," Jesus said, looking into the well. "But those who drink of the eternal water that I give them will never be thirsty. The water that I give will become in them a spring of water gushing up to eternal life."

"Sounds nice," said Photini. "Show me this water so that I may never be thirsty or have to keep coming here to draw water."

"Go, call your husband, and come back," Jesus replied.

"I have no husband."

Jesus nodded. "You are right in saying, 'I have no husband,' for you have had five husbands, and the man you are now living with is not your husband."

Photini was stunned that Jesus had such knowledge of our little arrangement. "How do you know this?"

"Woman, believe me, the hour is coming when the true worshippers will worship the Father in spirit and truth, for the Father seeks such as these to worship him. God is spirit, and those who worship him must worship in spirit and truth."

Photini had trouble following this last bit. So, she said, "Sir, I know the Messiah is coming, and when he comes, on my word I will worship him."

Jesus looked at her sternly. "Madam, I am the Messiah."

Photini's face was white when she was done telling her story. I must have gone pale, too, because Photini asked, "Are you okay? Do you need to lie down?"

"I'm okay," I gulped. "But how did he know about your five husbands?"

"He must have heard it talked about in the village. There is much gossip, you know."

"And he knew that you lived with me," I said.

"Everybody knows that I live with you."

But I wasn't as easily convinced that Jesus had simply used a few fortune teller's tricks to make a fool of Photini. I wondered if this Nephilim did in fact have God's ear. Were they communicating somehow? I was all questions.

Jesus left Sychar not long thereafter, but news of his many deeds continued to circulate throughout the Roman Empire. Jesus claimed to have a special link to God, and in village after village, he surprised the locals with his detailed knowledge of their private lives. Then there were the miracles. In one town, he was said to have brought a widow's son back from the dead. In another town, he was said to have healed a quadriplegic. These miracles struck me as highly suspicious, but many people swore to have witnessed them with their own eyes. Eventually, even Photini, who had doubted Jesus at first, was convinced.

"This man must be in fact the son of God," she said to me one day.

Of course, I knew this to be untrue. Jesus was my son, a Nephilim. His meteoric rise in popularity and influence was not at all surprising given that he was born of an angel. But how was it that he knew so much of God? He told stories of Eden as though he had been there himself. He spoke of my betrayal of God in uncanny detail. Was God feeding him information? There was only one way to find out the truth of this Jesus fellow, I thought. I would have to talk to God himself.

Incidentally, it was the Sabbath when I visited God's house for the first time in many millennia. I left the smithy at sundown and made some excuse to Photini about going to see the Samaritan priest in the village, which was my usual alibi when I did not come home directly after work. She accepted this explanation and did not try to interfere.

I went to the Samaritan temple where the locked door to Eden stood practically invisible to mortal eyes. I waited a long time outside the door until the street was empty. Then I put my hand on the latch. I heard a click, and the door swung open. I passed through quickly and found myself at once in the shadows of a lush forest surrounded by vibrant greenery on all sides. It took me a while to orient myself, for it was dark and I had been away from Eden a long time. I used light from the waning moon to guide me. By the time I reached God's house, it was very late, and I could see from the stillness of the place that God was asleep. So, I hunkered down in a copse of willow trees and listened to the calls of night creatures.

The garden was so alive; not like Sychar or Nazareth or any other place I'd been on Earth. I admit that I wondered briefly why it was that I had left that paradise. But then my thoughts turned to those years, long ago, when I had spent every night in God's bed, and how miserable we had been together.

I did not sleep that night. I passed the time thinking about all the years that had elapsed since I last left God crying on the floor of his bedroom. I wondered if he had much changed and whether he would even agree to speak to me.

When the sun rose in the morning and I saw the angels that served God coming and going from the house with trays of fruit and bread, I rose from my hiding place and climbed the many steps to God's palace. He was there, standing over his workbench just as I remembered him, working on a strange device made of glass and wire.

My shadow in the light of the doorway alerted God to my presence. He raised his eyes and stared a long time at me. If he was shocked to see me, he did not show it. Rather, he snorted and turned back to his experiment. "What do you want?"

"I have come to talk to you of humans," I said.

"They've all gone to Earth," he said.

"I know."

"Well, then what do you want from me? You know the humans better than I."

"I have a question about a man called Jesus," I said. "He claims to have your ear."

God stiffened suddenly. His lips tightened into a scowl.

"You know the man of whom I am speaking?" I asked.

"That's the understatement of the century," God said. "Here, hold this while I cut the other wire."

I approached and took the wire from his hands. I felt his fingers brush against mine, and a jolt of electricity shot through my body.

"Hold very still," God said. He seemed not to have felt the shock. I waited patiently while he fiddled with another wire. When he was done, he told me to stand back, and he pressed the two wires together. From a small glass bulb a brilliant light erupted.

"Better," God said. He fiddled with the strange invention and seemed to forget about me completely.

"You don't look well," I said after some minutes. He was haggard, in the eternal sense. His body was still youthful. His voice clear and strong. But the way he held himself spoke of all the years he had weathered since we parted.

"It is that blasted human race," God said. "Especially the ones born of the Grigori. Your children, Lucifer! They talk to me—incessantly! They ask so many questions. They believe I can deliver them from all their sufferings."

"You hear them?"

"Oh, how they talk, prattling on and on about all sorts of things. Moses, Abraham, and now this Jesus. Oh, he's a talker. I don't think I can take much more of him. Every day he asks me all sorts of questions. He thinks I am his father, thanks to you."

"Do you ever answer?"

God ignored my question. "I cannot listen forever to their mindless chatter."

I shifted on my feet. "You may have no other choice. Man is a resilient creature. He will not die so easily. And you have given him the means to reproduce, so that he may go on and on."

"An oversight, I assure you. When a human child is born, it is helpless for many years. You'd think it wouldn't survive. And yet humans still manage to overrun the Earth."

"They are a wondrous race."

"They are a nuisance."

"Perhaps you should go down there," I said. "Take on their form as I have done, experience what they experience. It is beautiful. Hunger, thirst, lust. You might enjoy it."

"Vile creatures," God said, ignoring my suggestion. "They drown out all other sound with their prayers. But at least I can be assured that it will not last forever. Humans have a finite time on Earth, depend upon it. By my calculations, the sun upon which they depend will burn out in five billion years. Without their mortal sun, humans cannot survive. They have nowhere else to go. I have banished them to Earth, and Earth is not eternal. It, like all things in the physical universe, must perish, and so too must mortal life perish."

"But there are many other suns and planets in the universe," I said. "Surely, humans can find another, similar home."

"How are humans ever to traverse such great distances as those?"

"Ah, God." I chuckled. "You are a stranger to your own creations. Humans are a spirited bunch and will do everything in their power to survive. I would not be so certain to see them annihilated by their dying sun. Earth may perish as you say, but humans will find other places in the vast universe to live."

"But there are no gates to such places," God protested.

"They will make gates. Do not doubt the human mind. It can show a glimmer of your genius, my Lord, if pressed."

God sat in sullen silence for some time, surely calculating some other expiration date for humans. Certainly, he knew also the lifespan of the physical universe, and perhaps he was thinking darkly of how very long he may in fact be forced to coexist with humans—until the end of every star and every planet. And what if they broke through to the other universes God had made? What if they populated all the Heavenly realms like a disease?

"Although humans are mortal," I continued, "their time is unlimited because they can have children and pass on all their knowledge from one generation to the next. And in a couple of billion years, there is no telling what humans might do."

"Reproduction was a technical error," God said at last. "I should have accounted for it in my calculations. I am very sorry I ever toyed with mortality; I think it shall plague me a very long time, and if what you say is true, then at least until the end of the physical universe. And that, even to someone immortal as I am, is a very long time."

God did not say when the universe was set to perish. I, for one, did not care to contemplate it because it would mean returning to Heaven for all time. Therefore, the subject was dropped, and not another word was spoken on the matter. Rather, I chose to resume our former subject, and said, "So, what do you intend to do then, about this Jesus? Stop up your ears with wax?"

"It is not what I *intend* to do about Jesus," he replied. "It is what I have already done."

"What do you mean?"

"It is getting to be too much, the praying; I can hear him even now, babbling on and on like some noisy bird. He consults me on everything: what he should eat for breakfast, how he should wear his robes, what he should say to his mindless disciples. I rarely answer back, mind you. But the other day, I had a brilliant idea—one that will shut him up forever."

"Go on," I said.

"Jesus wanted to know what gesture he could make to clear man of all his sins. Hah! Imagine that! Clear man of all the evil he's done. What an idea!" God laughed. "So, Jesus comes to me. He wants to make reparations, because he's just that good of a guy."

God's tone was becoming increasingly sour. It reminded me of the fits he used to have when I was still his favorite.

"Do you want to know what I said?" God asked. "I said, 'Jesus, my son, you must die for me.'"

I stared hard at God, wondering if he could be serious. God saw the look of doubt on my face and chuckled. He was falling swiftly into one of his moods. So, I said nothing, knowing that anything I said would fuel his mania.

He went on. "That Jesus is a walking shell of a man—never had a mind of his own. He actually fell for it. Now, he's got himself all worked up, and I can assure you—for he tells me every day—he is quite set on having himself crucified."

I shook my head in disgust, for this was God taking out his own failures on one of his creations—as he had done with me. As he had done with Adam.

"What makes you so sure this fate of yours will come to pass?" I asked.

"Jesus is very suggestable," said God. "I have given him a destiny, and he will cling to it like a rat to a barrel in a flood. And he will die soon enough, because he believes he must die for the sins of all men. It is written."

I knew God was right. If Jesus had heard from God that it was his destiny to die a merciless death, he would not let it happen any other way. The power of suggestion ruled Jesus, that walking shell of a man that was my son.

CHAPTER 16

I WASTED NO TIME. I left God at his workbench and returned to Earth that very same day. It was a three-day journey, at least, to Galilee. I packed what few necessities such a journey would require and set off instantly. I told Photini I would be gone a couple of days to see my mother in Nazareth. She expressed surprise at hearing I had any living family at all but did not question me further.

I was resolved to go immediately to the house of Mary and Josef to find out what had last become of Jesus. My actions were carried out in the strictest of haste, knowing that Jesus was likely to throw himself off a cliff any day at God's command—and before sunset on the third day of my journey, I stood at the door to the house of Jesus of Nazareth.

I knocked lightly. Sounds of shuffling came from inside, yet nobody answered. I listened carefully and perceived the breathing of somebody on the other side of the door. I knocked again, harder. The figure on the other side of the door seemed to jump back. I was sure I heard a frightened gasp.

"Mary?" I called.

"Who is it?" came Mary's voice just beyond the door.

"It is Gaius," I said. I felt a twinge of nostalgia as I said my old name of thirty years past.

There was nothing but silence from inside.

"Mary," I called. "May I enter? I have come about Jesus."

"Are you alone?" she asked. Her voice was feebler than I remembered.

"I am alone," I said. "I have come as a friend."

The door creaked open. Mary peeked out. I motioned for her to let me pass. She obeyed and I was admitted into the house.

Mary shut the door fast behind me. We were in darkness. All the windows had been boarded up and the only light came from the dying embers of a small fire in the hearth.

"What are you doing here?" Mary hissed. "I thought we agreed—I thought we said it would be best for Jesus."

"Where is Josef?" I asked.

"Dead. He died many years ago. He was alone on a small fishing craft and fell overboard and drowned. He was tangled in his own fishing net when a merchant ship found him."

Mary lit a candle and held it up to my face.

"Gaius!" she cried. "What witchcraft is this? You have not changed! After all these years—after everything we have been through. God in Heaven!"

She staggered back and held the candle between us for protection. The years had taken their toll on her. Age had taken the color from her cheeks and the fullness from her lips. She was not so drastically altered that I did not recognize her. There were elements of the young woman I had once known—the same eyes, the same penetrating gaze. But the years had grayed and weathered her so that none could mistake her age.

"Mary," I said.

"Stand back," she cried.

"I am Gaius—the man you knew so well. I have not aged because I am an angel from Heaven. And I have just come from God with an urgent message for Jesus."

Mary was white and trembling. She clutched the hem of her robes with one hand and the candle with the other.

"All this time," she said. "And you really were sent from God? Then Jesus is born of Heaven. I thought we made up that whole story to fool Josef. I thought ..."

"Mary, listen to me. There is no time for this. Where is Jesus?"

"He has gone into the desert. He has been gone for many weeks. And I am here alone. Roman soldiers came searching for him. They nearly broke down the door because I refused to let them enter. I have since been hiding in the dark alone awaiting the return of my son."

"Jesus is in grave danger. I must deliver a message to him immediately."

"Have the Romans taken out an order on his head? Is he to be killed?" Mary fell back into a chair. Her chest heaved. The candle flickered madly upon her face. There were dark bags under her eyes.

She looked more defeated than I could have ever imagined such a brazen woman to look.

"I must speak to him, Mary. I can help him. Do you know exactly where I can find him?"

"He has gone to a rocky place forty miles west of here," she said. "If you must find him, I will give the best directions I know how to give. Here, let me draw you a map. It cannot be more than two days walk, if you hurry."

"Thank you, Mary," I said.

Her face turned up, and in the light, I saw a flicker of the woman I once knew. Her mouth was set and determined. She nodded at me silently and went to a cupboard and withdrew sheaves of parchment that rustled like dry leaves. Then she reached into the dying fire and pulled forth a charred sliver of wood. She sat down at the table. With one hand she brushed aside a sleeping cat whose black fur twinkled like starlight as he disappeared behind a cabinet. With the other hand she smoothed the parchment out as if it were fine silk. With the sliver of charred wood, she scribbled a primitive map that traced every road, gully, and stream west of Galilee. I watched quietly. Her hands caressed the page gently, the way a mother brushes the hair off a child's forehead. I remembered what those hands were to me a long, long time ago, and I wondered that I should have ever given her up. But it had been the only option then.

I might have been Mary's husband. I might have been a father to Jesus. And I might have led a very happy life. And here I was, a stranger in this house, an imposter—the very same house in which Mary and I had conceived Jesus.

Mary rolled the parchment into a small scroll and tied it with a piece of string.

"Follow the road down the ravine until you come to a large cypress tree. From there, head due north. There is no road where you are going. It is all there on the map. Go quickly."

"Mary, you should not be here alone," I said. "I will call on one of your sisters and bring her here to watch over you."

"My sisters are dead. It is only Jesus and me. And God."

I might have interjected. But I saw how much God meant to Mary in her desperate state, and no matter how untrue I knew it to be, I said, "Yes."

"Bring Jesus back to me," Mary said. "I am very afraid to be without him. He is such a good boy, a very special boy. He is our child, Gaius. Born of Heaven."

"I will send him back to you as soon as I find him. And he will not run off and leave you alone again."

Mary nodded. She reached for my hand. I felt her leathery fingers on my skin. I could feel the blood pulsing in her veins. Her wrists were so thin I thought they might break.

"Thank you, angel, spirit, lover, whatever you are. You have come to me again when I have needed you most."

"Mary, I ..." My voice broke. Here was a friend—a friend still, after thirty years.

She put a hand on my cheek, and I trembled. Pools of salty tears brimmed in my eyes. She took my arm and pulled me into an embrace. I melted into the softness of her robes. She patted my hair with her calloused fingers. Her hair smelled of sweet hay.

"God give you strength," she said. "I will pray for you."

We came apart like two halves of a doughy bun. I shook the tears from my eyes and bid Mary goodbye. The sun was just below the mountains when I heard the bolt of the door slide into place behind me.

CHAPTER 17

I FOLLOWED THE MAP Mary had made for me, traveling straight through the night, until I came to a rocky wilderness where the sun had scorched the earth and green things refused to grow. This was no place for humans or angels. The land was hostile to living things, mortal and immortal alike. Only the fiercest of God's creations could survive this hellhole. Scorpions slithered among the rocks, vipers basked in the hot sun, and flies swarmed the corpses of cattle and sheep that had wandered too far astray.

As I traversed this barren landscape, I thought of Jesus, a mere mortal, all alone in this wilderness, and wondered if perhaps he was already dead. I wanted desperately to save him from the fate God had planned for him. Perhaps it was some paternal instinct that drove me to Jesus's side, or perhaps I wanted still, all these centuries later, to defy the God that had made a captive of me.

It was late the next day when I found Jesus hunkered down in a shallow cave amidst the rocky terrain. I would have missed him completely if it had not been for his senseless prattle, which sounded from the cave like wind through a hollow log.

"What's my name? I'm Jesus. The son of God. Jesus the carpenter. Jesus of Nazareth. That's not my name. I am God. I am the Lord, my father, the Holy Spirit. I don't have a name. Does anyone know my name? Mother. Mother knows my name. Mother needs me. Father needs me. Father. Where is Father?"

Upon reflection, all these years later, I have come to understand that Jesus was not just a Nephilim tormented by God; he also suffered from what modern-day doctors might call psychosis. Or schizophrenia. At least that's what I've come to believe all these years later. Hallucinations, disembodied voices, delusions of grandeur. That would explain some of what was going on. Jesus was not well, God knew it, and God had put it in this poor man's head that he had to die.

The voice from the cave continued. "My disciples. They plot against me. They will betray me, betray my name, betray their God. But I must die for the sins of man. I must die so man can live."

"Yeshua?" I called, slipping on some rocks on my descent into the cave.

"Who's that? Who goes there?"

I slid down a sandy hill and into the shallow cave. My eyes took some time to adjust to the darkness of the cavern. When they did, I found Jesus crouched in the shadows, picking at ants and putting them in his mouth one by one. He had a far-off look on his face, as one possessed.

"Young Yeshua," I said gently. "Why do you feed on ants? Here, have some bread." I took the heel of a loaf from my bag and held it outstretched toward Jesus.

"Man shall not live on bread alone," Jesus said, "but on every word that comes from the mouth of God."

I don't know if Jesus saw me, really saw me, or if I was just another disembodied voice in his head. I said, "Jesus, your mother worries about you. Won't you return to Nazareth with me?"

Jesus looked beyond me into the bright sunlight of the desert. "Would you have me leap from the highest tower in Jerusalem?"

"What?"

"Would you have me leap from the highest tower?"

"Believe me, Yeshua, that is the last thing I want. It is God who would have you leap to your death. Now, come with me." I held out my hand.

Jesus spat at me. "You shall not put the Lord, your God, to the test!"

"Yeshua," I said. "Please, come with me. Your mother has asked me to bring you home."

"Mother? I don't see Mother."

"She's in Nazareth, waiting for you."

"She mustn't wait," said Jesus. "I shan't be coming home again."

I could not follow Jesus's zigzagging logic, nor could I make heads or tails of his broken speech, but I did not suspect psychosis—not then. In those days, a person might be delirious from dehydration, but there were no words to describe neurological disorders.

"Here." I held out my canteen. "Have some water."

"I dare not drink from your cup, for your name is Satan, the most reviled."

"How do you know who I am?"

"I know you betrayed God in the Garden of Eden. I know you tempted Adam under the Tree of Knowledge. I know you seek to lead me astray, as you have led so many astray."

I looked heavenward and spoke directly to God. "Enough! Jesus is my son. I will not let you fill his head with stories."

Then Jesus said, "God loves you still. You have only to ask for his forgiveness, and he will take you back."

I lunged at Jesus, grabbed him by the arm, and pulled him kicking and screaming from the cave.

"Enough!" I shouted. "You're coming with me."

"Away from me, Satan! For it is written: 'Worship the Lord your God and serve him only.'"

"You know nothing of God!" I snapped. "God is trying to kill you!"

I still had a firm grasp on Jesus's arm, but he had gone limp and now lay writhing in the dirt on the ground. He was crying.

"Come, Jesus," I said, more softly. "You needn't suffer so. Let's go home."

I hoisted Jesus over my shoulder. He did not resist. And like that, I walked for two days, stopping only twice to administer food and water to the man who called himself the son of God.

When the people of Nazareth saw me approaching with Jesus slung across my back, they crowded around, begging to know all that had transpired in the desert. They called Jesus the Messiah. They reached out to touch his hands, which dangled loosely over my shoulder. I merely shook my head at their foolishness and did not say one word until I was safely inside Mary's house. There, I set Jesus down on a mattress of hay and explained all that had happened. All the while, Jesus slept.

A crowd of devoted followers gathered outside Mary's door. They brought food and incense and waited patiently for Jesus to emerge. Mary occasionally provided them with updates: Jesus was awake. Jesus was eating. Jesus wanted them to know God loved them.

I stayed on this whole time, hoping that when Jesus regained his wits, I could talk some sense into him. Jesus grew stronger by the hour, but I could see that his mind was still deeply disturbed.

"He is touched by God," Mary said that evening.

"When did you become so pious?" I asked.

Mary thought for a moment. She was seated across the table from me with her chin resting in her hands. Jesus lay sleeping by the fire.

"When I realized that my son was not like other children," she answered.

"What if I told you God wanted him to die?"

"Then I would say God must have a good reason for wanting such a thing."

"Mary," I said. "God is not as selfless as you may suppose. Please listen to me. God wants Jesus to die for no good reason at all. I can't expect you to understand, but you must trust me."

Mary, though older and frailer than I had ever seen her, was still as stubborn and headstrong as I remembered. "If God wants Jesus to die, then I trust God's will. You may be one of his angels, but Jesus does not answer to you. Jesus answers to God alone."

I knew there was no getting anywhere with Mary, so I hoped for better luck with Jesus when he awoke in the morning.

Mary let me stay in the manger with the mule, and the next day, I tried to find a time to talk to Jesus alone, to warn him of God's callousness. But as soon as I confronted Jesus, he started in again with all his talk of dying for the sins of all men. I could not persuade him to let it go. Although he no longer called me Satan—did not remember all that had happened in the desert—he regarded me with great suspicion and said I did not know God's will.

On the third day, Jesus held a lengthy sermon in front of the house with the villagers gathered about like sheep. Several herdsmen came down from the hills to laugh at him. But Jesus paid them no mind. I did not like the way they sneered and heckled this poor shell of a man, and I could feel tensions building amongst the villagers.

On the fourth day, I had had enough of Jesus's mumbo jumbo. "You must stop this game," I said. "God wants nothing more than to see you perish."

"Then I shall perish," Jesus replied.

"Don't you want to live?"

"No," said Jesus. "Life is pitiful."

"Yes, but it is also beautiful."

"I will live eternally in Heaven."

"Jesus, Heaven is not open to you. You are mortal, and once you are gone, you are gone. That's it."

"The soul is everlasting."

"Yes," echoed Mary. "The soul is everlasting."

"There is no such thing as a soul," I said.

Then on the fifth day, Mary roused me very early in the morning.

"You must leave now!" she said in a hushed but urgent tone.

"Why?"

"We have just received word that the Jewish elders intend to arrest Jesus. Roman soldiers are on their way here now. Please, if you care for our son, leave Nazareth and take Jesus with you."

"Of course." It seemed Mary had regained some of her sense at last. "Tell Jesus to ready himself for the journey."

Mary left me in the manger. I dressed hurriedly in the dark and threw all my belongings into my pack. But when I entered the house, Jesus was sitting at the table, staring hard into the fire. Mary sat across from him, in tears.

"I'm not going with you," Jesus said.

"They will kill you, Yeshua."

"Then that is my fate."

Mary sniffled. "It is his fate."

I looked questioningly at Mary. She refused to meet my gaze.

"Jesus, you needn't die just because God said it must be so," I said.

"I thank you for saving my life in the desert," Jesus said. "But now you must go—if you cherish your freedom."

I knew he was right. Surely, the soldiers would round up anyone associated with this self-proclaimed King of the Jews, and I'd been around long enough on this Earth to know that I stood very little chance against a battalion of Roman mercenaries. I went to Mary and kissed her cheek softly as she sobbed into her robes.

Jesus watched me with a preternatural calm.

"Are you sure you won't come with me, Jesus?" I asked.

"It is God's will. Now, go!"

I left Nazareth while the sun was still hidden behind the eastern hills. I would see Jesus only once more, several weeks later, nailed to a cross on a hill outside the walls of Jerusalem. He was only thirty-three years old.

CHAPTER 18

$\sim$

I N THE WEEKS FOLLOWING his crucifixion, Photini and I heard many strange tales of Jesus, some too far-fetched to believe. That he rose from the dead on the third day after his interment is completely ridiculous. When mortals die, they are gone forever. Even Nephilim—the children of angels—are not immortal.

I was in Jerusalem—I had gone there to pay my respects—when Jesus is said to have risen from the dead, and I can assure you, the resurrected man in question was *not* Jesus.

In those days, we had no cameras, no way of knowing what someone looked like until we saw him or her with our own eyes. So it is that some charlatan posing as Jesus managed to convince many gullible humans that the King of the Jews had come back from the dead. I went to see this charlatan for myself. He bore a passing resemblance to Jesus, but it mattered not whether he looked the part. Most people had no idea what Jesus looked like to begin with. So, they bought his story—hook, line, and sinker.

Even King Herod knew that this man was a fraud. Otherwise, he would have had him arrested and crucified again. As it is, I cornered the charlatan in an alley one evening when he was taking a piss, and I gave him a piece of my mind. After that, he was never seen in Jerusalem again, and Jesus was said to have ascended to Heaven.

I have had many of my children go on to do remarkable things. But none has made as lasting an impact on the human species as Jesus. Most of what people today teach about Jesus is untrue, but one thing is certain, Jesus did commune with God. For all I know, Jesus is the only mortal with whom God ever communed in this way. As God himself told me, he can hear the prayers of humans, and because of Jesus, those prayers have become so numerous, God cannot tell them apart. It has become a kind of background noise for him. Unpleasant, yes, but not wholly intolerable. Like the sound of a neighboring freeway. Or tinnitus.

INTERLUDE

TODAY, I AM AT a house party on the northside of campus. The theme is Renaissance. There are people in silly Burger King crowns, jester's caps, and gaudy plastic jewelry. A couple of less scholarly fellows are donning togas. There is one costume I like: a man dressed as Leonardo da Vinci. He has done his homework. He reminds me very much of the Leonardo da Vinci I knew.

I hear about college parties through Facebook. I have an account that I check maybe once or twice a week. I have a couple of friends on Facebook: my coworkers from Caffè Strada, a few girls from the university that think I'm cute, and a few random kite fanatics that know me from the Marina.

Every year or so, I delete my Facebook account and start over. You see, I must try to remain anonymous, even now, when people do not believe in God or Satan. This is necessary, seeing as I do not age, and people start asking questions if they notice that I remain young while they are growing old and wrinkled.

I've been at the university for twenty-five years. It is easy to stay in Berkeley because the students are always coming and going. Every four years or so it's a whole new batch of faces, and there is nobody left to remember me. I tell people I'm a graduate student in the Mechanical Engineering department. They usually don't inquire further into my age or status. Grad students are enigmatic. They stick around forever. I change jobs every four years. I worked for the Math Library, I was a waiter at Mario's La Fiesta on Telegraph, I made sandwiches at Café Intermezzo. Sometimes I get a job in Emeryville at the Bay Street Mall, or in the city selling tickets for concerts. I like working with people.

There is a girl at the party who claims she is a Satanist. I don't buy it. Kids these days slap on a few tattoos, get a lip piercing, pile on the eyeliner, and they can call themselves Satan worshippers. Once upon a time, I knew real Satan worshippers, people who would sacrifice limbs to honor me. But this girl, this self-proclaimed Satanist, is not the real deal. She is speaking in a very obnoxious tone about the coming of the antichrist. There is no real passion for the Devil in her voice, only the sorry hint of self-loathing. She worships Satan to stand out—to be cool. I cannot say I blame her. Who does not want to stand out? In a world where there are billions of people exactly like you, what's the shame in putting on a little makeup, piercing a few unusual orifices, and claiming to worship the vilest creature to walk the Earth? It is not so unlike the people who carry guns to honor a country, or the girls who compete for the title of Miss Universe—everyone wants to feel special.

Satanism never was my thing. Sure, I peddled souls for a while—it was never to anybody's detriment, I like to think. But I never did take to being worshipped. I am glad this girl at the party does not know who I really am, or surely, she would wet her pants.

For now, she can worship the Devil safely, because she does not really believe he exists and does not think he will ever come to collect. But there was a time when men and women knew who I was and spilled their blood on my behalf. I never asked it of them. It was their own twisted impulses that made them gouge out their eyes and saw off their toes. But these sacrifices were made to me once upon a time. That was *real* worship. This girl in black leather pants wouldn't even fetch me a beer.

CHAPTER 19

P HOTINI DIED OF LEPROSY in 35 AD, and from that moment on, I became a nomad of sorts, wandering all over the Afro-Eurasian continent, living multiple lives. I searched for my fallen brethren wherever I went, but we were so used to hiding, that for many centuries, we became lost to one another. I even lost touch with Belial in those years.

I found him again in London in the seventeenth century. We happened to be moving in the same circles, and we met again at the horse races on Newmarket Heath where I'd wagered a small fortune on a silky-white warmblood filly named Fiona.

I was handsomely rewarded that day, and I was as drunk as a crow on rowan berries, when this mountain of a man slapped me on the back and shouted, "Lucifer! Look at you! All these years later and here you are!"

I spun on Belial. "Shh! I am Thomas Ellsworth now. You mustn't use my God-given name again!"

"You worry too much, Mr. Ellsworth," Belial said. "If we're being formal, then you can call me Myles Wellington."

"That I will," I said. Then I couldn't help but smile to see my old friend. We embraced.

It was Belial, incidentally, who first invited me to the Gentlemen's Club of Luxembury. The club entertained the most well-to-do men of London. It was an elite establishment, and Belial introduced me into its society as a man of great fortune and respectable family. My mother was the daughter of a magistrate, my father the son of a vicar, and I, upon their recent deaths, the sole recipient of a very tolerable inheritance. That was the story, anyway.

I was accepted immediately into the company of these men for, by this time, I was truly a man of fortune, having amassed a large sum from betting on horses, and I was able to play their games as well as any vicar's grandson ought to be expected.

The prominent men of the club were a Sir Robert Randolph, who was from a long-established family in London; a Mr. Simon Gray, who owned a large estate and was married to the daughter of a duke; and a Mr. Christopher Cadwell, a man of new money who had made his fortune off some very wise and profitable investments in the spice trade.

All, save Mr. Cadwell, were terribly dull. Sir Randolph was a drunkard and a loaf who easily exceeded his income and was never hesitant to use his title and good name to shirk his debts. Mr. Gray was an ill-humored, sour man with nothing but the worst opinion of everyone and the best opinion of himself.

Cadwell I could stand. He was self-made with a good head on his shoulders and a respectable manner. If there was any disagreeable quality about him, it was that he thought too highly of his companions, Sir Randolph and Mr. Gray, and too lowly of himself.

I tried not to make a habit of their company. I frequented the Gentlemen's Club only so much as was necessary to establish myself and maintain those connections, however loathsome, that might prove valuable.

Belial thought them all fools, as he ought, and loved them dearly. He relished their silly talk of politics and came home with all sorts of stories about their disagreements and disputes. The gentlemen of the club were a reliable source of amusement, and Belial might be found there four or five nights a week, nursing a glass of brandy.

Belial was also known to frequent a less respectable establishment known as the Red Rooster. This was a pub for lowlifes and scoundrels, and in it, Belial drank himself silly and swore and cursed and was every vulgar thing he could not be at Luxembury. The Red Rooster did have its charm: the food was delicious and cheap, and the patrons the hearty, friendly sort—whereas Luxembury was stuffy, reserved, and overpriced.

Admittedly, I feared Belial's frequent exposure to the people of London. I didn't think it wise to be consorting nightly with the well-to-do and even less wise to be consorting with the thieves.

Belial, as usual, remained carefree in every respect and saw no harm in "a little fun." He accused me of being a recluse and warned that I would soon acquire the reputation of an eccentric.

I assured him that no such thing would happen. Though I was not a patron of the Red Rooster, I was an occasional customer of Luxembury, and I was sure to visit just enough to secure the respect of *that* community. I was not there so infrequently that the gentlemen felt slighted by me, and I was not there so often that all my flaws and secrets were exposed in idle conversation. In fact, it was my absence that kept me in high regard; and whenever I came in, I would be called upon to settle some dispute or at least state my esteemed opinion on some matter of politics. Belial never fully understood that the secret to respectability is silence—to have opinions and to not voice them often.

There was one other man who seemed to share my philosophy and showed his face at Luxembury even less than I. His name was Dr. Charles Bartlett. I knew very little of him except that he was a world-renowned doctor most famous for his pilgrimages to foreign countries to study and treat rare diseases. He spoke little, was not often in public, and even Sir Randolph and Mr. Gray spoke of him with deference.

Seeing as I was rarely at Luxembury, and Dr. Bartlett there almost never, I did not occasion to meet him, and that was satisfactory to me since he was said to be a snappish, disagreeable old man whose only redeeming quality was his wealth and status.

❈

During those years, I lived in a house in Smithfield Place, two doors down from Belial. It was sizable enough for a city house. It could be approached from the front by a short footpath coming up from the street or from the back by a narrow alley. I hired a housekeeper, Madam Pomphrey, to look after the place, do my cooking, and keep my affairs in order. She was sturdy as a rock. A gem. Hardworking and aloof, Madam Pomphrey was content to know as little about me as was possible living under the same roof. I had no other servants. Madam Pomphrey occupied the servants' quarters at the back of the house, accessible from the alley. Those and the kitchen were Madam Pomphrey's domains.

Madam Pomphrey had one night off a week. Where she went, what she did, I never did discover. I left her private life alone, and she kept out of mine as much as any housekeeper can do. Of course, she knew my friends, Belial—who went by Mr. Wellington—and Mr. Cadwell. But other than the frequent visits from the former and the very infrequent visits from the latter, no one ever really came to call at 23 Smithfield Place.

I also employed a gardener named Willy, a young bloke of sixteen, who I paid to keep the hedges trimmed. But he only came on Wednesdays.

It was a comfortable life I had made for myself. I was well-disguised as a wealthy inheritor from an honorable bloodline. Nobody doubted that I was a man of good repute. I had a comfortable home. I had my old friend Belial back in my life again. And most of all, I had privacy and all the time in the world to work on my diaries, which had been poorly kept over the last millennia. I still liked to make record of the birds and beasts I saw on my walks about the countryside, and I wanted very much to tell my full story, for the only other account of what had happened all those years ago in Eden had been written by God-worshippers in their Holy Bible, which painted me unfairly and made of me a leper among mortals.

I was just recalling my conversation with Adam and Eve under the Tree of Knowledge and setting it to paper when Belial rang at my front door.

"Mr. Wellington to see you," Madam Pomphrey said with a look of irritation. Belial's easy manners and flagrant familiarity made Madam Pomphrey uneasy.

"Show him in," I said. "I am just finishing a thought."

I quickly scribbled down the last of my memory of that day with Adam and Eve and set my quill aside just as Belial entered.

"Charles II is on the throne," Belial beamed. "And after eighteen dreadfully dry years without anything to divert us whatsoever, the theaters have reopened!"

"Have they?" I said, my mind still trying to work out exactly what Eve said to convince Adam to join her on Earth.

"And we're going! Tonight!"

"I'm tired, Belial. I have been writing all day, and I was hoping to turn in early."

"Sorry, old pal. You're coming with me. Get your coat!"

Madam Pomphrey was already at the door with my hat and gloves.

"What are we seeing?" I asked, wrapping a scarf around my neck.

"*Antigone.*"

CHAPTER 20

I T WAS LOVE AT first sight. Of course, I didn't know it then. Surely, I was enamored, but one can never fall in love if one knows it. A person needs to be caught off guard, blindsided, and completely taken by surprise if love is to really take root. You see—love will never grow if it is watched. Love is fragile at first. Even the slightest thought can send it away. Analysis, scrutiny—these will crush it. The seed of love is planted. And if it goes unnoticed, it will reach its vines out and strangle the heart, and it will blossom. Only then can you look at it dead on—and it will be too late—love will have taken hold.

I did love her the moment I saw her, but the love was like a small tumor on my heart, undetectable. Certainly, there were plenty of signs. Alarms were going off in my head; there was a stirring in my blood. I felt turned upside down and then put back right again.

While her eyes were on the stage, my eyes stayed on her. I traced the ribbon down the nape of her neck, along her shoulder, and down her spine. I could see the slight protrusions where her shoulder blades poked through the white satin of her dress. Her hair was braided. I counted every weave.

At intermission, I excused myself from Belial and hurried to the main lobby. There she stood, with a crystal chalice poised before her ruby lips. She was agreeing with somebody and nodding. I wanted her to be agreeing with me. I wanted her to be looking into my eyes as she sipped the red wine from the chalice. I wanted her to nod her head at me and smile and say, "Yes."

But it was at some silly man that she was nodding and sipping from her chalice. He was not even paying her proper attention. He was listening to himself speak on French foreign policy and having a good time of it, too. And as he spoke, he nodded as well, as if to agree with his own words.

What did he need her for? It didn't matter if she was a French politician or a circus performer—he would have gone on in the same way. It was not proper of him to monopolize the young lady's time when there were others wanting of a chance.

What might I have said to her given such a chance?

Nothing. Absolutely nothing. I would look into her eyes, and I would stay that way forever.

"Olivia," an older gentleman called from across the room. "Olivia, please come here. Miss Cooke should very much like to have a word with you."

The young woman excused herself from Monsieur French Foreign Policy. When she had left him alone, he turned like an automaton and directed his ridiculous speech at the next nearest woman.

Olivia was just crossing before me, her hair in little ringlets around her ears, when I reached out and clutched her forearm. Her eyes came around to meet mine. And I did nothing. I stared. We stared. She was fearless. That provoked me, because I was fearless. She smiled coyly. I smiled like the Devil. We did not break until the older gentleman shouted, "Olivia! Olivia!" enough times to secure the attention of the entire lobby.

The woman pursed her lips and furled her brows. She hated to lose. This I loved. I loved the little mole on her chin. I loved the way she stared into a stranger's eyes without hesitation. I loved that the old gentleman irritated her. She stared hard at me, as if to say, "Not fair," and then turned to address the older gentleman.

"Father," she called him.

I was glad of this chance to look into her eyes. Now, I would know her forever.

"Belial," I whispered as the mezzanine seats filled for the second act. "Tell me the name of the older gentleman there in the seventh row, you see with the hat."

"That, monsieur, is Doctor Charles Bartlett, the brilliant physician and scientist. He spent seven years on the Dutch Gold Coast treating marsh fever. They say the Akan people taught him many potions. He is very wealthy. The king has summoned him on numerous occasions for the treatment of weather pains."

"Then her name is Olivia Bartlett," I whispered.

"What?" Belial asked. But the curtains had parted, and the players had taken their positions. All that was left to do now was watch the gentle rise and fall of her shoulders while the actors pretended in the dark.

CHAPTER 21

I FUMBLED AROUND FOR three weeks, coming up with elaborately romantic scenarios in which I would present myself to Miss Olivia Bartlett. She and her father lived in a house on Aldersgate Street. They were easy enough to find. I walked by the place every Wednesday on my way to the Gentlemen's Club. I could not think enough about her. In the evening, I would sit at the piano and play love songs for Olivia. In the mornings, I would take my tea and imagine her sitting across from me at the table. She pervaded every facet of my day. It was infuriating and incurable.

Belial noticed the abrupt change in my manner and would not leave me alone until I finally told him everything; how ardently I adored Olivia Bartlett; how I could not escape her deep gaze, even in my sleep.

Belial laughed and laughed.

"You fell in love with a woman's back!" he exclaimed.

I told him about our encounter in the downstairs lobby at intermission.

"So, you spoke to her?" Belial asked.

"Well, no," I confessed. "But we did share a moment."

"You mean she looked at you? Are you going to fall in love with every girl that looks at you?" Belial laughed. Belial could let out quite a mighty roar if he was provoked, and this occasion proved to be no exception. "Well then, you know where she lives. Introduce yourself, you romantic fool."

I was all set to do it, too. But Wednesday evening, while I was writing down what I would say when I met my Aphrodite, a knock came on the door. Madam Pomphrey was busy in the kitchen, so I answered.

Olivia Bartlett stood on my stoop. Her knees were askew, and she looked as though she might run off any moment. I froze in astonishment. I had left my notes on the table, and for the life of me I couldn't remember a single clever thing I had planned to say.

It looked as though Olivia were having the same problem. She opened her mouth to speak, changed her mind, and closed it again. We remained in that very uncomfortable state for several more moments. Then she turned very abruptly and hurried away.

My eyes followed her down the walk. I was in a stupor, and it took a few seconds before I realized she was getting away.

"Wait!" I called, chasing her down the walk.

"I'm very sorry," she said over her shoulder.

"Olivia! Wait!" I cried.

She stopped suddenly. Her breathing was heavy. She turned very slowly to face me.

"You know my name?" she asked.

"I haven't been able to forget it," I said.

She arched her eyebrows.

"Well then, I must have yours," she said coolly. "What are you called?"

"I am called a playboy, a libertine, and a scoundrel," I said.

"Your name, sir."

"Thomas Ellsworth."

"There," she said. "Now, we are square. I know your name and you know mine. Very well. Have a pleasant evening, Mr. Ellsworth."

"Wait!" I exclaimed. "You were on my doorstep just a minute ago. You rang. Why?"

Olivia Bartlett blushed. She fiddled with the lace on her dress for some time before responding. "You often walk down the street where I live with another gentleman. I have watched you from the upstairs window of forty-three Aldersgate Street for many weeks. I didn't have the courage to meet you on the street. You were always with that other man. So, today I followed you home."

"You followed me?" I said.

"I am very sorry. This is very embarrassing. I should be going. It was nice to meet you, Mr. Ellsworth."

"Please," I said. "Call me Thomas. Won't you join me for tea?"

"I couldn't possibly ..."

"Madam Pomphrey has just laid the table, so it won't be any trouble, I assure you."

"It's late, and my father will be wondering where I am."

"Madam Pomphrey bakes the most wonderful little cakes. She sprinkles a bit of cinnamon on top. You can't refuse little cakes with cinnamon."

Olivia Bartlett shifted uneasily on her feet.

"One cup of tea," she said. "And then I must be going home."

I led her into my parlor. Madam Pomphrey brought the tea and cakes.

"What are these?" Olivia asked. She was sifting through my notes, the ones I had written in preparation for our meeting. I shoved the teacup into her hands, swept the papers off the table, and shut them away in the liquor cabinet.

"Wouldn't you like to sit?" I asked.

I will proceed to relate those first glorious days spent in the company of my beloved Olivia. As she had come to me that night, so I went to her the very next day. She received me with warmth but would not admit me to the manor, for her father was at work in the study and did not welcome callers. It was in a hushed tone that I beckoned Olivia to follow me out. I had a place in mind that I wanted very much for her to see.

She begged me to wait a moment and closed the door but for a single crack through which I could see into the foyer and, beyond that, the doctor's study. The doctor was bent over a large ledger and scribbling something in the manner that all doctors scribble. He was so intent on his work, he did not see Olivia slip out with her hat and gloves.

On the stoop, Olivia stifled a laugh and said her father could not be bothered by a thunderstorm when he was deep in thought. This proved to be mostly true, for when Olivia would return home some hours later, she would find her father in the same crippled position pouring over the ledger with no knowledge that she had ever gone.

Out on the street, Olivia and I conversed as loudly as we pleased. I asked Olivia everything I could think to ask. She was charming, bright, and well-versed in everything from politics to Norse mythology. She spoke English first, but was equally fluent in French, Dutch, German, and Latin. The gentlemen mooned over her, and the ladies sought her counsel. Still, she remained modest and approachable, without the slightest trace of vanity.

She was not without her mischief. She loved a good joke, virtuous or off-color, so long as no one was the worse for it. She could be awfully devious with her closest companions; she often surprised her friends with outrageous gifts that were best opened in private.

Her love of people of all races and religions was cultivated in her various travels growing up the daughter of a famous doctor. She had spent several years of her childhood in Mombasa living amongst the Swahili natives, she was educated at one of the finest schools in Paris, and before the age of seventeen, she had visited the East Indies, China, and Arabia. She made friends with all the peoples of these foreign places, perhaps because she was nothing less than amiable.

Her father, Charles Bartlett, bore her no resemblance. He was a crusty curmudgeon, spoiled by fame and intolerant of people who were not loyal to the crown. He was often praised by those who did not know him personally for taking his medical practice to the distant colonies, but those with whom he was most familiar knew he traveled only to collect rare herbs and medicinal plants for his famous remedies and to treat sultans and kings for the sole purpose of boosting his own notoriety. Those who spoke with him were often left with a sour taste on the backs of their tongues. In conversation, Dr. Bartlett was haughty, passive, and always right. Olivia overlooked her father's many faults and was a very devoted daughter. Of course, her devotion did not deter her from consorting with the locals of foreign countries, a practice her father most vigorously opposed, and from collecting beautiful artifacts from distant lands.

Dr. Bartlett was strict with Olivia in word but not in practice. He was so frequently absorbed with his own work that he overlooked Olivia's disobedience, and she grew up to be a free-spirited and friendly woman with not the faintest trace of her father's unpleasant nature.

That day after we first acquainted ourselves with one another, I led Olivia down a small brick walk that opened onto a shady park. The trees sprung up all around us, spaced evenly apart like the trees in an orchard, leaving enough room for wide, sandy walks dotted with green and white benches between them.

In the middle of the park, a large lake glittered in the sunlight, home to dozens of geese and ducks and a tiny island just offshore. A small tower shaped like a lighthouse perched atop the island. Four clocks were set into the four faces of the tower, telling the time to the north, south, east, and west. The clock on the north face was slow and had to be reset every morning by the park keeper, I explained to Olivia. A weathervane in the shape of a sailing ship crowned the tower. It had rusted so that the bow always faced east.

Atop the weathervane squatted a speckled brown and white pigeon. She was nearly as fixed to the tower as were the clocks, for she never left her roost. Olivia took a fancy to calling the speckled hen the Queen of Hyde Park.

The lake was littered with tiny model sailboats. Children ran around the perimeter of the lake with sticks to guide the boats away from shore.

"Not for me," said Olivia, observing the children at play.

"What's not for you?"

"Children."

"Ah."

"Do you have children, monsieur?"

"No," I lied. At that very moment, I had six grown children somewhere in France. But they all thought I was dead.

"Never been married?"

"No," I lied again. It was a half-truth. I hadn't been married in many years, in at least as many years as Olivia had been alive on this Earth.

"I don't plan to marry, either."

This did not bother me, and I said so. As far as I was concerned, marriage only made a mess of perfectly lovely romances.

"Father wants me to wed a gentleman."

"He is a father. What else could he want for you?"

"He has plans to introduce me to a wealthy doctor in France. We have another house in France. It's where we spend our summers."

"Well, I'm not likely to let you go off and marry this doctor without a fight."

Olivia's eyes met mine. Then she laughed. "You hardly know me."

"Not true."

"What do you know about me?"

"I know you are brave, obstinate, and clever."

"Hmph."

"And your favorite color is yellow."

"How do you know that?"

"Your ribbons."

Olivia raised a gloved hand to stroke the yellow ribbon in her hair. It was the same ribbon she had been wearing at the theater.

"My turn," she said.

"Okay." I opened my arms as if to say, *Give it all you got!*

"You are an old soul," she said. "In a young man's body."

This struck a little too close to home, and I frowned.

"Am I wrong?" she asked.

"No. Please go on."

"You are worldly and well-traveled."

"Yes."

"You are not a pious man."

"What makes you say that?"

"I have never seen you at church."

"That is true. I do not go to church."

"But you believe that God exists?"

"Oh, yes."

"And God has a will for you."

"He does."

"But you feel constantly pulled in the opposite direction."

"How do you know?"

"Because, monsieur," Olivia laughed. "You are like me."

I smiled. She knew me better than any mortal ever had. A cold wind whipped through the park. The sky threatened rain. The children gathered up their boats and ran for cover.

"We should get back," I said. "Before your father notices you are gone."

CHAPTER 22

T HE SNOW ON THE ground was fresh white like the back of
a beluga whale. It banked up against the walls of houses, lay
fresh in the gardens, and clung desperately to the tops of trees. The
world was colorless. London was cold. On occasion, a man would
pass on the street, probably a doctor on his way to some ailing
patient. He would be so completely enveloped in coats and scarves
that I never saw his face.

Certainly, he saw mine framed in the first-story window of my
house in Smithfield Place. The fire blazed brilliantly behind me. I
sat in the seat by the window and watched the snow float down
like cool, white flecks of cloud. I was not put off by the cold this
winter—despite the chill in my bones. My thoughts were kept warm
with wonderings of Olivia.

I had never met a girl so desperately curious, so wonderfully full of
humor, and so patient with all my eccentricities. She never bothered
me about my need to keep an account of my life—my diaries. She
never asked to read them because she knew them to be of a most
private nature. She did not pry into my past—rather, she accepted

that my parents had been distinguished Londoners who had died of cholera when I was only five, leaving me all their estate. I had very little to explain, and I liked that. It was hard to find somebody who did not eventually want to know every detail of my childhood, my youth, and my education. I did not have to fabricate elaborate falsities to satisfy Olivia because she preferred to talk of the future, *our* future.

It was a blissful winter. The snow that fell around us felt like love's very own private shroud, wrapping us in our own fantasies. I paid Olivia a visit almost every day and I always brought her gifts: chocolate from the New World, spices from India, silver from the islands of the Aegean Sea. These artifacts I had collected in my various travels over the last thousand years on Earth. What I appreciated most about Olivia was her fascination with each gift, not for its rareness or worth, but for its history. She was determined to know everything about chocolate, how it had come to Europe from the Americas, how it was manufactured, what its ingredients were. She wanted to know the ancient uses of all the Eastern spices, what their purported powers were, and how they were grown. What was the earliest use of silver? How was it mined? Every gift aroused such unmatched curiosity. She kept a diary of her own and I suspect she recorded each strange gift I had given her with as much detail as I had recorded the habits of field mice in Eden.

I became addicted to the sense of accomplishment I was awarded every time I surprised Olivia with some new trinket from a faraway place. I had exhausted my resources by mid-January, and I had to extend myself if I wanted to continue to surprise and delight Olivia with unusual gifts. It was on January 19, 1661, that I decidedly entered Heaven again for the first time in over a thousand years—for the sole purpose of pleasing Olivia.

London was a mask of white, endless snow. All that could be seen from the rooftop of the church in Charterhouse Yard was a blanket of pure glistening powder. Chimneys coughed gray smoke from invisible holes in the sheet-clean landscape. The streets were nearly impassable, and the only people who managed to get through the snow rode on clomping Clydesdales. There were doctors out and about rushing from home to home. The cold had brought on all sorts of ailments. There were numerous cases of hypothermia and fever. The unfriendly climate agitated arthritic old men and women, and not a single mortal was free of the sniffles.

I trudged through three feet of powder. I wore a coat that might as well have held three other bodies. I had padded myself with undershirts, long underwear, scarves, three layers of socks, and thick boots that made waffle-patterned tracks wherever I marched. I carried nothing. My fingers were wrapped in thin layers of woolskin and then padded with woolen mittens. My face was covered with a large red scarf, save for the tip of my nose, my nostrils, and my eyes. I had on a wool cap. I was unrecognizable beneath the layers of warmth, and I had done such a marvelous job of bundling up that, after five minutes of tromping through the snow, I was wet with perspiration.

I walked two miles like this, discarding at least one scarf along the way, which was icy with sweat from my brow. I had anticipated the journey to be a challenging one, what with the temperature dropping below zero, but I had not anticipated this meeting of extremes, the very cold and the very hot. Outside, where my nose made contact with the environment, I was numb and blue. But inside, underneath the numerous layers, I was on fire. The snow was not easy to manage, and it must have taken me at least an hour to reach the feeble gate off Eliot Vale, because when I got there the sun had already set and the sky was a blanket of stars.

I was so moved by the measure of my discomfort that I did not hesitate to pull the latch on the gate and enter Eden. The gate swung closed with a clatter behind me. There were remnants of snow that had come through the bars of the gate and had formed icy banks on the periphery of the garden. But before me Eden stood completely unmarred by Earth's winter. The lawns and plants glistened from a warm shower that had fallen earlier that day. A warm breeze struck my blue nose with a reassuring gust. The only snow in Eden existed higher in the mountain passes and here at the gate to Earth. The rest of Eden lay in springtime.

I stripped off the many layers I had worn and hung them on the gate to dry. I went forward into the garden cautiously. I did not want to be seen. Nor did I intend to be very long in Heaven. I had one objective. My goal was simple: roses. Roses in the winter were unthinkable in London in 1661. So, I resolved to bring my Olivia roses in January, to defy the laws of nature and present her with a contradiction to tease her unrelenting curiosity.

It had been over a thousand years since I had been there last, and yet I remembered well where Michael had planted the roses. They were still many miles off. I worked my way through Eden very much like a cougar makes its way through the jungle, with swift, invisible ease. I startled a family of shrews, but otherwise, I walked unseen.

The rose bushes stood taller than I had left them. They had stretched their arms maybe two or three feet high. *Is that all a rose bush grows in a thousand years?* I used my hands to break a dozen red rose stems from the thorny trees. My fingers were pricked, even through the woolskin; they bled briefly and healed. These roses were a treat, not only because they were to be delivered in the midst of a snowstorm, but also because they were, of course, the most splendid roses in all of Heaven and Earth. Michael had done well in keeping them, and his expertise, honed over thousands of years, had made these roses more beautiful and more sweet-smelling than any flower ever to grow on Earth.

I wrapped the roses in thin, white wax paper that I had rolled into one of my pockets. The roses were elegant and healthy, and for a minute I felt a pang of guilt for having torn them from their throne in Eden. Surely, Michael would notice them missing and it would perhaps grieve him to see his prized flowers treated so unkindly. But love makes us do funny things, and my guilt was quickly drowned in my thoughts of Olivia.

It was on my way back that I came across God. I stepped so suddenly into a clearing that I did not have time to make myself unseen. He noticed me immediately and called my name as if I had never been gone.

"Lucifer," he said. He was sitting in the shelter of a red, wooden pavilion. Paper lanterns blazed all around him. Before him stood a low table littered with a pasty, molasses-colored substance. He had in his right hand a small blade onto which a small wedge of the substance was stuck like a slice of cheese. He was smiling stupidly. His eyelids were drooping half over his glazed eyes. He looked like a child playing in a sandbox. He was wearing a navy blue *changshan* with gold embroidery. I wondered where he had gotten such a lovely mortal outfit. I also wondered at the sticky substance on the small table.

"Are you drugged?" I asked.

I was astonished at his easy manner. He looked relaxed and sleepy. God sniffed the thin wedge on his blade before slipping it between his lips.

"Try some," he offered. He picked up a small, round wad of the stuff and tossed it at me nonchalantly. I caught it with one hand and looked it over cautiously.

"What is it?" I asked.

God was seated on a bright red cushion. He looked like a sage, but I knew otherwise. I took the cushion opposite him, across the table. He slipped another wedge of the stuff into his mouth before answering me.

"Opium," he laughed. He laughed harder than the word *opium* warranted. I could see he was already far gone. Would he even remember me in the morning?

"Where did you get it?" I asked.

God laughed. All he said was, "It was a gift—from the Far East. But I can make my own now. We have poppies in Eden, you know."

I nodded. What angel had given God human drugs? Maybe it was one of the Fallen—Mephistopheles perhaps.

"You know, they talk to me still. And there are more of them. Millions and millions of humans chatting away. That Jesus fellow made it much harder for me—he seems to have gotten the whole lot of them talking to me."

I nodded. It was true. Christianity had grown exponentially over the last thousand years, and with it, so too had grown the pleas and prayers to God. I could not imagine God's suffering—to have 100 million whispers always in his ear. I did not begrudge him his use of this substance called opium.

"Can you believe how fast they multiply?" God laughed. "Oh, it was a colossal mistake. I lost control of the little bastards. And yet I have to hear about it every time a mother dies or a baby falls ill. I cannot take all their mindless chatter. There must be half a billion of them!"

He was right. When God had created humans, he had started with about a dozen. When they were unleashed upon Earth, with so much space at hand, they began to multiply like rabbits. Now, in 1661, there were perhaps 500 million people on Earth. The numbers of people talking in his ear had increased significantly. Little did either of us realize then how much the population would still grow. In the next 400 years, the human population would go from 500 million to a staggering eight billion. Had God known that then, surely, he would have tried to tear his ears off his head. All those voices would drive anybody mad.

"Like right now." God cackled madly. "This one woman is asking me why I let worms into her cornmeal. Outrageous! Of course I did no such thing. If it was up to me, worms would have stayed here in Eden."

His laughter was frightening. Surely, this was only an effect of the drug. I could sense in every word he uttered an underlying desperation—*Make it stop*, he was saying. Two greasy wax earplugs lay on the table. He had taken them out and perhaps he was enjoying the experience of 500 million voices mixed with the narcotic effects of opium. What a tortured soul, and his could rightfully be called a soul, for it was the first soul. We angels were mere chafings of his soul. Humans were even less; they were the rippled, distorted reflections of his soul. He was life. Everything else was shadows.

And yet, it was the shadows I preferred to this great lump of sobbing misery known as God. He may have been life in its most essential form, but he lacked life as I knew it. He was devoid of joy, devoid of pleasure, devoid of hope and anticipation. He did not have the eccentricities of mortals, or their fear of death. In fact, his supreme immortality made him ungracious. He spat in the face of life because he had never known anything else. Because he could not die, he yearned for death—begged for death. He could not appreciate existence because he did not fear death. Humans were beautiful because they made so much out of their very short lives. They were given so little time, fifty to a hundred years tops. So, they filled every moment with some new task, some new dream. Their fear of death instilled in them a sense of purpose.

God had no such sense of purpose. He had no beginning. He had no end. His life was as vast as the universe. The fear of death may be the one thing that makes life worth living. I admit I have no such fear myself. But in loving humans, in walking among them, I can say I have briefly known what it is to appreciate life. I have loved mortals. They have died. This has given me a sense of purpose. Knowing that the people I care about may at any moment be gone forever supplies me with the sense of gratitude for the life humans share as a mortal race. Living among humans has infused me with the only true life I have ever known—life that inevitably ends.

God begged me to stay with him. I, of course, said no. Did I feel a little bit of remorse leaving him as he was, doped up on opium, laughing at his own cursed fate? Yes, I cared a great deal for my creator. But I had made a promise to myself long ago not to let his sinking ship take me down with him. So, I left him there in the still light of the paper lanterns.

I did not go without offering him some consolation. I took a rose from the dozen. I took a perfect rose and placed it in his hands. He did not look directly at me, nor did he say another word. I think he understood. This was my peace offering. This was my way of saying, *I'm sorry, but you have to let me go.*

We parted. My clothing was nearly dry by the time I reached the gate. I redressed for London's harsh climate. When I stepped into the cold, I realized again why I lived among mortals; it was because the cold gnawed my flesh, the sun burned, the hunger ached, the thirst screamed. It was because every day was a struggle, and nothing can be more satisfying than a struggle.

It was late when I came to Olivia's door. The housekeeper was aghast at the sight of the eleven roses. She fetched Olivia, who came to the door in her nightgown. She saw the precious flowers and shrieked with delight.

"Where did you get these?" she cried. "It cannot be a degree above zero and you've brought me roses!"

She wrapped her arms around my neck, and I must say I was quite pleased with myself. The housekeeper looked on in silent astonishment. I winked.

When the roses had passed hands, Olivia counted them two or three times.

"Eleven," she pondered. "Why eleven?"

I smiled and said nothing.

"Well, this is a riddle," she continued. "First, you bring me a bouquet of roses in the middle of January. And then more strangely, you are one short of a dozen. It must be some kind of puzzle."

"I began with a dozen," I said. "But I gave one away on the way here."

"Did you?" Olivia asked. Her expression was that of such keen curiosity.

"I bet you can't guess who possesses the twelfth rose."

I left Olivia in a state of bewilderment. She was baffled by the mystery of the missing twelfth rose. She proclaimed that she would not be able to sleep until I told her where I had found the roses and to whom I had given the twelfth. I told her she would just have to stay up all night then because a magician never reveals his secrets.

I was in for a surprise myself that night, too. I had a special gift waiting for me when I got home. On my doorstep there was a small leather bag tied with a silver ribbon. I anxiously undid the ribbon and loosened the drawstrings of the pouch. It was dark, so I could not immediately see what was inside. I poured the contents into my cupped hands and reeled back in horror. I had in my possession two soft, bloody human testicles. They were accompanied by a note:

My Lord Satan, Accept these as a token of my devotion. Most esteemed Prince of Darkness, I am forever your humble servant. J.B.

CHAPTER 23

"I T MIGHT HAVE SLIPPED out," Belial said. He was sitting across from me, arms folded on the table. He looked like a dog that had dug up the neighbor's flowerbed—his face was drawn with guilt, and he refused to let his eyes meet mine. His nostrils were wide and dilated.

"Might have slipped out?" I barked incredulously. "*Might have slipped out* that I am Lucifer, Prince of Darkness, Lord of Demons?"

"I was drunk," Belial protested. "Besides, nobody would believe it anyhow."

"Somebody believes it!" I said, heaving the bag of testicles across the room into Belial's lap.

Belial had been at the Red Rooster when he mentioned in passing to an eager audience that his friend, Thomas Ellsworth, was really the Devil incarnate, outcast from Heaven and living among mortals. It had been a good joke then, and everyone had enjoyed a good laugh. But it seemed someone had taken him seriously.

Belial peered into the leather pouch and winced. "Poor fellow," he said.

"How could you possibly have let such a thing slip?" I charged. "It is bad enough to be accused of being a devil, but when you actually are such a thing—I'm going to be crucified, you muttonhead!"

"It will pass, I'm sure," Belial said. "This fellow who calls you Lord is probably bleeding in the streets somewhere." Then he added facetiously, "I doubt he'll have the balls to come around here again."

His attempt at humor only aggravated me further. Normally, when I was found out, I would promptly vanish. I would move locations, change my name, abandon everyone I knew and start over. I refused to live in a world where I was known for who I was. It was too dangerous.

One thing kept me in London: Olivia.

Belial was apologetic. But it was no matter to him. He was not outed as a fallen angel. Testicles had not shown up on the doorstep as a gift to him. If I'd been less of a fool, I'd have left town that very night.

❋

Madam Pomphrey had gone out; the house was quiet. I sat in the parlor with my eyes half closed, amusing myself with thoughts of Olivia, when abruptly the annex bell rang thrice. I was startled and jumped awake at once. I looked at the clock over the mantle. It was half past eight, and I was not expecting any visitors.

I rose cautiously. The chair moaned as would a sleeping lover, saying, *Come back to bed*. I crossed through the dining room and down the stairs to the kitchen, where I was greeted with the stiff smell of ale. The annex door had been bolted twice. Nevertheless, my unexpected visitor jiggled the handle impatiently.

"One moment," I called.

When I opened the door, there stood a stranger, a man. I would later learn that his name was Jacques Bezier. He had three gold teeth, a head of long, dull-brown hair, and, at present, no testicles, or so I would find out. He spoke French, Dutch, and English—though none well—was a child of Paris, abandoned on the steps of Notre Dame at birth, brought up by nuns only to run away and live as a gamin on the streets. He had been abused by the Catholic clergy and had found faith in the one thing his childhood benefactors abhorred: Satan. So it was that he sought me out and presented me with his strange gift.

At least that is how he explained it on our first introduction. He sat across from me in the kitchen, his elbows on his knees, the glass of wine I'd offered him on the wooden worktable, still untouched.

"I was sitting in the pub when I heard some fellow claiming to be the best friend of Satan," Jacques related to me in French.

Jacques had dark pebbles for eyes and a face full of warts no matter which way you looked at him. I assumed he was still living on the street—that the altar boy turned runaway had now turned beggar and thief, not to mention lunatic.

"And I am sure it is you of whom he spoke," he said. "For I have been watching your friend closely for some time now. He led me here."

When I said nothing, he continued. "My Lord, I am your servant. You abandoned God; the way God abandoned us!"

It was incredible how spot-on he was. He might have been the only person who had ever made the very real distinction—I had *abandoned God*. God had not exiled me from Heaven as the story says. It was I who left, willingly. God had begged me to stay. And this half-crazed man was also right on another point. God had abandoned humans. God had given up on mortals long ago.

"All my life I've been wretched," Jacques said. His eyes were hard as stone, and although his voice trembled, he shed no tears. "God has forsaken me."

As if God had anything to do with this poor man's fate. But I nodded.

"There is only one other who I can turn to for mercy." He gave me a look that spoke to all his pain and suffering. "You."

I dared not offer any response for fear of encouraging him further.

Jacques looked at me expectantly. His hands fidgeted nervously, and he plucked absent-mindedly at his whiskers.

"Is my gift not worthy of your Lordship?"

"It is a generous offering," I said. "But I'm afraid you've got the wrong man."

"How can that be?" Jacques shook his head. "I saw you! I saw you go through the gate in Eliot Vale, the one what's always locked. You came out with blooming roses, in the dead of winter. That's how I knew it must be you."

"You followed me?"

"I meant no disrespect."

"Look here!" I was growing increasingly vexed. "I am not Satan."

"Then how do you explain them flowers?"

"None of your business!" I barked.

"Your Lordship," Jacques cried. "If you are unhappy with me, I will make for you another offering to prove my devotion."

Here Jacques lunged for the meat cleaver, which lay on Madam Pomphrey's workbench, and raised it up as if to chop off his own hand.

"Stop!" I yanked the crazed man's arm toward me just as he was bringing the cleaver down on his wrist. The cleaver missed his hand by two inches and made a huge gash in Madam Pomphrey's mahogany tabletop.

"She won't like that," I said.

"Who?" asked Jacques.

"My housekeeper. See how you've ruined her dining table?"

Jacques surveyed the gash in the tabletop. "I meant no disrespect, sir."

"Yes, you keep saying that." I was growing more cross by the minute. I saw that it would be no use trying to persuade this lunatic that I was innocent. He was certain that he had found the Devil, and he was right. So, I decided to try a more transactional approach.

"Jacques," I said. "Please tell me what it is you want?"

"What I need is help getting back on me feet, milord."

"Then let's make a gentlemen's agreement."

"What agreement is that, your Lordship?"

"You must promise me your soul, and I will give you something in return."

"My soul? Yes, yes. Of course you shall have my soul, milord."

"But what shall you ask for in return?"

"Riches! Jewels!"

"And your soul will be forever mine? If I am ever in need, you will come to my aid?"

"Yes, yes! Certainly."

"Then you must do exactly as I say."

"Anything, milord."

"You must share our secret with no one!"

Jacques nodded.

"Come back next Wednesday at this time," I said. "Ring thrice at the back door. I will admit you, and I will give you further instructions."

"Of course, milord."

"You shall have your riches," I said. "Now, get out of my kitchen, before my housekeeper returns."

"Yes, milord. Right away, milord!"

Jacques scrambled out the back door into the night, tipping his hat as he went. I closed the annex door behind him and bolted it twice. Back in the parlor, I collapsed into my chair and covered my face with my hands. What in God's name was I to do? This crazed man had found me out, thanks to Belial's carelessness. And I did not trust him to keep his word. Surely, he would tell others about his Devil's bargain. It was not safe to stay in London any longer.

Then my mind turned to Olivia, and I could not stomach the thought of abandoning her. I had known many loves in my life. But Olivia was my greatest love. She was more than a love. She was an obsession. And I dared not leave her.

But what could I do? Kill this man? Throw his body into the Thames? Surely, nobody would miss him. But to kill this poor half-wit—it seemed cruel. All he wanted was a better life. Perhaps I could send him away. Ship him off to the East Indies—there was money to be made in trade with the East. Mr. Cadwell ran a shipping company. Perhaps that fine gentleman would do me the favor of employing Mr. Bezier on one of his vessels. Yes, let Mr. Bezier set off in search of the wealth and riches he so desired. That would get him out of my hair. If I was lucky, he would die at sea, as so many men did.

I had only to settle the matter with Mr. Cadwell.

❋

Mr. Cadwell was a shrewd businessman, and one easily persuaded by any sum of money, large or small. I promised him 500 pounds to take on Mr. Bezier, claiming the doddering fool was a distant relative fallen on hard times. Mr. Cadwell drew up the contract, and I had only to get Mr. Bezier to sign it.

Wednesday was Madam Pomphrey's night off, and I believed her to be out, when the annex bell rang thrice. I rose from my chair and descended the stairs to the kitchen. There, I was surprised to find

Madam Pomphrey with the door slightly ajar, arguing with someone on the other side.

"My master is indisposed," she was saying. "Now, away with you!"

"Madam Pomphrey," I interrupted. "Who is it?"

Madam Pomphrey looked surprised to see me. "Oh, sir. There's a beggar here what says he knows you."

"Let him in," I said. "He is an old friend."

Madam Pomphrey's eyes went wide. She clearly thought I had misspoken.

"Sir, it's just some feller off the street," she hissed.

"Let him in!" I commanded.

Madam Pomphrey hesitantly opened the door and admitted Jacques Bezier, who was trembling from the cold.

"Come, warm yourself by the fire," I said.

"I'll fetch some tea," said Madam Pomphrey.

"Fine," I said. "But then you must leave us alone to discuss a private matter."

Madam Pomphrey nodded her assent, never once taking her eyes off Jacques Bezier.

Mr. Bezier and I sat quietly as we waited for the tea to be served. Once Madam Pomphrey had excused herself, I withdrew the contract from my pocket and said, "I have secured you employment aboard the *Miranda*. She sets sail for the East Indies tomorrow; she is a trading vessel—spices mostly. Prove yourself useful, and the owner of the ship has agreed to pay you handsomely. But you must work hard and never stray from your purpose. Then, as I have promised, you shall have the wealth and riches you desire."

Mr. Bezier examined the contract closely.

"I can't read, milord."

"No matter. Just make your mark here."

Jacques Bezier marked the space with a thick, black X. I folded up the contract and handed it to him. "Now, take this to Captain Hershey in Blackwall Yard. The *Miranda* leaves at midday tomorrow. You must be on it or else ..." I trailed off.

"Yes, milord. Of course, milord."

CHAPTER 24

THE RAIN WAS COMING down hard outside. It was early March, and Madam Pomphrey was away visiting her ailing mother in Leeds. Incidentally, Dr. Charles Bartlett had also left London on business for a few days. So, Olivia and I had two glorious days alone together. We hid away in the house in Smithfield Place, emerging only once during a break in the storm to stare at the long arc of a rainbow in the sky. Then the rain began again, and we ran back inside and found our way into my big feather bed on the second floor.

"I can't hear your heartbeat," Olivia said, her head resting on my chest.

"Eh?" I murmured. I was drifting off to sleep. I felt her hand slide up my chest and come to rest under my jaw. She pressed two fingers into my neck.

"You have no pulse," she said, sitting up.

"What's that?" My eyes snapped open. I realized my heart had stopped beating, as it was wont to do when I dozed off. It didn't need to beat really. That was just for effect. I could also do without breathing. It was never pleasant. But I could hold my breath for eternity if I had to. I feel the same sense of suffocation a mortal feels, only I don't die. That's the thing about being one of the Fallen: all the feelings are there—the pain, the pleasure, the discomfort—but it can never kill you.

Olivia was pressing her fingers into my jugular with a maddening force, searching for some sign of a heartbeat. I took a deep breath and consciously activated my heart, like striking a match. The blood rushed like the River Fluvius through my veins, warm and comforting.

"Oh! There it is," Olivia gasped, drawing her fingers back in alarm. "I couldn't feel anything and then suddenly it came on like a drum."

"You are fretting over nothing, *mon cheri*. Go to sleep."

"Perhaps the next time my father leaves on business, we can take a trip somewhere."

"Won't the servants notice you are missing," I said drowsily.

"Perhaps," she grinned. "But they wouldn't dare say a word to my father. They are terrified of him."

"Okay," I said.

Olivia smiled and rested her head on my shoulder.

"I love you," she said.

I received a letter from Jacques Bezier a few days later from Porto Seguro. Bezier was on his way to the East Indies aboard the trading vessel *Miranda*. He thanked me profusely for my kindness and generosity in securing him such lucrative employment, and he hoped he could thank me in person one day when he returned to London.

I hoped he would do no such thing. The last thing I needed was Jacques Bezier showing up again at my back door. It was bad enough that Bezier had taken Belial's words in the pub that night to heart. But I had encouraged him. I had bought his soul. At least that's what he thought. What would the gentry of London say if they found out I was peddling souls?

I had heard many stories of pirates pillaging trading ships on the sea route to India, and I hoped desperately that pirates would overtake the *Miranda* and make slaves of everyone aboard. Or better yet, slit their throats.

As it turned out, Bezier was the least of my problems. Thanks to Belial's indiscretion, the cat was already out of the bag.

CHAPTER 25

A T PRECISELY FOUR O'CLOCK on a Tuesday in late March, just as Madam Pomphrey was clearing the parlor table, the bell at the front door rang—once, twice, thrice—as anxiously as any bell can ring.

Madam Pomphrey shot me a look over her shoulder as she went out with the empty sugar bowl. "My hands are full." She pushed through to the kitchen.

I closed the book I was reading and balanced it on the arm of my chair. The front door was off the main hall, which connected the parlor, study, and the dining room. When I opened the door, I was greeted by a most startling sight. Before me stood a woman in a bright pink feathered hat. She wore a red dress with ruffled sleeves and a long flowing tail that looked like it had been dragged through the sewers. Over this she wore a bright orange cape and hood. Her white gloves were stained with mud and torn at the knuckles.

As soon as I opened the door, the woman stepped into the house. It was then that I noticed her feet were bare and her toenails cracked and blistered. She pushed by me in a most agitated state. I was grateful she made her entrance swiftly, for I was fearful of what the neighbors would say if they saw this colorful woman on my stoop.

"Begging your pardon, sir," she said with a voice as thin as wrapping paper. "I shouldn't be so bold as to let myself into your house, sir, without invitation, but I don't want to be seen in the lane, as I've come here with dirty business."

She shuffled down the hall and let herself into the parlor, all the while looking about like a scared alley cat.

"What business is that?" I demanded.

"With all due respect, sir, I take my business only with the master of the house. Twenty-three Smithfield Place, ring thrice and ask for the master of the house. That's wot I was told, sir."

"I am the master of the house, Madam. Now, out with your business, or I'll out with you!"

The strange woman gave me a look of alarm. Her eyes glowed big and wide under the shadow of her feathered hat.

"You're 'im, then?" she said shrilly. "With all due respect, sir, I fancied you much older. Why, you are just a boy!"

She removed her hat and revealed the full craftsmanship of her face. Her cheeks were done over in ruby rouge, thick as paint, like the cheeks of a circus clown. She had jagged yellow teeth stained with lipstick. Mascara was crusting in the corners of her eyes. What was left of her thinning red hair hung limply from her head like wet spaghetti.

She set the feathered hat on the table in the parlor and staked out a place between the coat closet and the china cabinet. There, she paced so vigorously, I thought she might wear a hole in the rug.

"My name is Elizabeth Squires," she began. "Miss Elizabeth Squires, as I've never been married, and from wot I can remember, never had no engagements neither. My mum wasn't much of a lady. She got by selling herself on the street, though she claimed my father was a gentleman because he had gold cufflinks. That's all I know of him. I was raised in the gutters and never knew no goodness in all my life. My friends are beggars, and even they'd poach a bit of bread off me whilst I was sleeping. I've never lived nowhere nice, never dined on fine food, and never had the pleasure of wearing fancy clothes. I don't have a farthing to my name, and I makes my living selling flowers I pinch from fine folks' gardens. Now, I know, sir, you are a man of means, a fine gentleman, but I'm told you might be willing to strike a bargain with a wretched woman such as me."

Here she paused and looked at me expectantly. I had no idea what she was talking about, and when I didn't respond, she continued. "I know it ain't worth much, but I have no use for it no more, seeing as it never done me any good. So, sir, I'm willing to sell it to you in exchange for a better lot in life."

"Sell what?"

"My soul, of course. Ain't that wot you're after?"

I did not reply.

"Hear me, sir. I don't need to be no baroness or nobody fancy, for I'm sure I'd never be able to put on airs like finer folk. But a roof over my head and a bit of cheese and wine now and then wouldn't be so bad. And supposing a bath when I'm dirty. I reckon my soul can buy me that much. If I might be granted these things, sir, I'm sure you would always find a 'umble servant in me."

She finished her speech triumphantly and stopped dead in front of the coat closet. At that very moment, the bell rang again, and I could hear Madam Pomphrey shuffling down the hall to receive this newest caller.

Miss Squires and I locked eyes and listened intently to the voices in the hall. There was Madam Pomphrey with her usual dry greeting. And there was Olivia.

"Dear God!" I exclaimed. "You must hide!"

I sprung across the room and thrust Elizabeth Squires into the coat closet just as Madam Pomphrey entered the parlor.

"Miss Olivia Bartlett to see you," she said.

"Tell her I'm not in."

Olivia must have been standing just outside the parlor door, for she appeared immediately behind Madam Pomphrey. "You would send me away?" she asked, entering the room.

"I'm sorry, Olivia. I am coming down with something. I didn't want you to catch it, too."

"Silly man," Olivia said. "I don't care."

She crossed the room to greet me, and we embraced. All the while, my heart beat wildly in my chest. Suppose that crazy woman in the closet got it into her head to suddenly make herself known. What would Olivia think? What would I say?

"Thomas," Olivia said. "You are pale. Shall we have some tea?"

My voice caught in my throat before I could tell her that I had just had my tea.

"Madam Pomphrey," Olivia said politely. "Would it be too much trouble to have some tea?"

Madam Pomphrey shot me a look of annoyance. I nodded. "Yes, some tea, Madam Pomphrey," and the housekeeper shuffled out to retrieve the wares she had just put away.

As soon as she had left the room, Olivia turned to me and whispered fiercely. "My father is going to Brussels the week following next. I should very much like to take a holiday with you. We have a flat in Paris, and my father will be gone a fortnight. What say you? Shall we go to France?"

I wanted to end the exchange quickly and get Olivia out of the house before Elizabeth Squires came jumping out of the coat closet. So, I said, "Yes, yes. Let's do it. The week after next."

Olivia rose suddenly and crossed to the parlor table, where the pink feathered hat shone like spilled wine on a wedding dress.

"What is this?" Olivia asked, picking up the hat and examining it closely.

"Oh, that's just something of Madam Pomphrey's," I said. "She wears it on her day off. I suppose she must have left it out by mistake."

"You do pay her, don't you? I should think she could afford a nicer—"

Just then, Madam Pomphrey came in with the tea. Olivia blushed and set the hat back on the table.

When the tea was laid out, I said sharply, "I would be grateful if you didn't leave your things lying about, Madam Pomphrey."

The housekeeper lifted her head with a jerk, her face the picture of puzzlement. I nodded in the direction of the hat, and Madam Pomphrey stared at it as if she had seen a ghost. But my loyal housekeeper was always discreet, and with the greatest effort at composure, she went to the hat and with her forefinger and thumb lifted it as if it were a dead mouse. All the while, Olivia looked on, probably still wondering why a well-kept housekeeper would ever own such a mangy hat.

I turned back toward Olivia to say that I thought a holiday in Paris would be nice when I was interrupted by a blood-curdling scream.

Olivia and I whirled around to find Madam Pomphrey standing at the open door to the coat closet with the hat clutched to her breast. Her face was drained of all color.

I never knew whether it was Madam Pomphrey who screamed or Elizabeth Squires. But then the closet door slammed shut, and Madam Pomphrey rushed out of the room, pale as a ghost, still clutching the feathered hat to her breast.

I was certain Olivia must have seen something of Elizabeth Squires in the closet—a finger, a cracked toenail, a rouged cheek—and I was prepared for my world to come crashing down around me. But Olivia simply asked, "What in heaven's name? Is she well?"

"Madam Pomphrey?" I asked. "I don't know. Excuse me a moment."

I found the housekeeper in the kitchen bent over the washbasin, still clutching the pink feathered hat.

"Madam Pomphrey—" I began. But she cut me short with a look that, had I been a mortal, would have killed me on the spot.

"I have always been discreet," she said. "I have tolerated your outlandish friends and have turned a blind eye to your blasphemous talk of God and Satan. But there is only so much this old heart of mine can handle. First there's that strange fellow by the name of Bezier coming 'round, leaving his fingerprints all over the walls. And now a woman in your closet! You should be ashamed, Mr. Ellsworth. If Miss Bartlett were to find out ... or her father! And to think you left Miss Bartlett sitting in the parlor with a prostitute or a madwoman, I don't know which—"

Here I tried to object, but Madam Pomphrey simply silenced me with a flash of her eyes.

"Dear sweet Olivia," she went on. "Alone in that room with a woman in the closet. I should think you would have more honor, sir. Certain enough, you don't attend church, and every so often I say a prayer for you. But you were always honest and fair, or so I was made to think. Now, Mr. Ellsworth, I don't know what you are up to, and you know I never breathe a word about what goes on in this house to nobody. I know how to hold my tongue. I won't be caught spreading gossip that isn't mine to spread. But enough is enough. I cannot keep house for a man who hides women in his closets. With

219

your blessing, sir, I would like to take my last month's pay and be done with this house forever."

It was a reasonable argument and well put. In all the time she had been my housekeeper, I had never heard Madam Pomphrey say so much in one breath. I took out my pocketbook, paid her thrice what she was owed, and never saw Madam Pomphrey or the pink feathered hat again.

Olivia was standing in the parlor when I returned. "What on earth was wrong with her?" she asked when I came in.

"She saw a mouse," I said.

"Has she recovered? She seemed very upset."

"Yes, she is much better."

"Good," she said. Then, "I'm afraid I cannot stay any longer. I promised Father I would translate some old potion book into English for him. I must be off. But please mark your calendar for the week after next. Just think of it! Paris!"

With that, Olivia kissed me on the cheek and let herself out.

When I opened the door to the coat closet, Elizabeth Squires fell out with a squeal.

"Your housekeeper's run off with me hat!" she said. "'Twas my only hat, and I favored it so. She has no right to be taking a poor woman's hat."

Elizabeth Squires was a sorry sight standing there with her fists rolled into tight little balls, defending her claim to an old, worn-out, feathered cap.

"I'll buy you a new hat," I said.

Squires's eyes brightened. All thoughts of her "favored" hat went tumbling out of her head. "I should very much like a new hat," she said. "Seeing as you owes it to me."

Her rumpled form stiffened, and she brushed herself off with the backs of her hands.

"Now that we're squares," she said, "how's about my proposition?"

I put my hand on my chin. "How are you at keeping house?"

CHAPTER 26

E LIZABETH SQUIRES, OR SQUIRES as I took to calling her, proved to be a worthy housekeeper. Having just sold her soul, she was inspired to make the best of her newly acquired lot in life. Perhaps her soul was the only thing she had left to barter—and she wasn't about to waste it. So, she scrubbed the tiles and swept the floors as if she were washing away every vestige of her former life.

She took over Madam Pomphrey's old quarters, but it was a long time before she was comfortable sleeping in a proper bed under a proper roof. At first, she was hesitant to even step into her room. I often caught her pacing up and down the hall outside her door. I don't really think she saw the space as her own; perhaps she felt that by inhabiting it, she might spoil it somehow. Inside her bedroom, she was as tame as a rabbit in a cage. I often looked in to find her sitting at the foot of the bed, staring about the room as if at any moment the walls might cave in.

Squires was eager to adapt to her new surroundings. I gave her some spending money that first day, and she came back with an eclectic assortment of dresses and a single pair of pink slippers; she pranced about the house wearing those slippers as if they were made of rubies. She fancied bright colors and was never once known to wear something drab. She always looked like a gypsy or a rare bird of paradise—she applied rouge liberally, was never caught without a fresh coat of lipstick, and was known to wear the most unusual hats, decorated with flowers and feathers and ribbons and the occasional paper crane. She might easily have been mistaken for an eccentric old aunt if it were not for the standard white apron she wore while she was working.

The first week that she was in my service, she was remarkably obsequious, sometimes saying please and thank you three or four times in a single sentence. She tiptoed about the house like a mouse and set about her work with little objection. She was a different woman that first week: quiet, cautious, obedient. But by the second week, she began to perk up and show a little of that fire she had displayed the day we met.

Pouring the tea one day, she exclaimed, "I never seen such a pretty little cup and never tasted no jasmine tea."

So, I poured her a cup, and we took our tea together.

"You've the nicest manners I ever seen," Squires said. "How'd you come to be so nice?"

"Whatever do you mean?"

"Ain't the Devil supposed to be mean and nasty like?"

"Never call me that again," I said flatly.

"But you is the Devil, ain't you?"

I just shook my head and said, "If you know what's good for you, Squires, you'll hold your tongue."

"Yes, sir." She winked knowingly at me. "It'll be our little secret."

Olivia and I were to go by coach to Brighton, where the ferry would carry us across the English Channel and land us in Le Havre. From there, I had arranged for a coach to take us to Paris, where Olivia's father had a small flat: two bedrooms, one bath, a kitchen, dining room, and library, and a quaint terrace overlooking La Place Royale.

We had intended to go without servants. But as the day of our departure grew nearer, Squires became effusive on the subject of Paris. "Oh, Paris!" she would exclaim as she set the table for supper. "What a lovely holiday! Why, to think I've never been in all my life, and it has always been a dream of mine since I was a little girl."

She insisted on knowing every detail about the flat where we were staying; what kind of flowers grew on the veranda, what sorts of people walked the streets below, what were the colors of the walls, the textures of the linens, the fabrics of the curtains. To every answer I gave, she would sigh deeply and say, "How splendid. What a time you two shall have."

This went on for several days until at last she asked me quite gravely, "But, sir, who's to do the washing and cleaning? Who's to fetch your tea and cook your eggs the way you likes 'em?" And finally: "Two weeks abroad is such a long time. What shall I have to do in this old house all alone by myself? I shall be quite lonely, I shall. What are French housekeepers like? Are they very refined and such?" On and on, until I had no choice but to invite Squires along.

Unlike Madam Pomphrey, Squires had no sense of decorum, no conception of what was proper in polite society, so she didn't question the notion of a single man traveling alone with a young woman. And if anyone did raise objections to a man and woman traveling alone together in Paris, Squires would play the requisite chaperone.

Olivia had since inquired about the disappearance of Madam Pomphrey, which I explained away with a vague lie about her ailing mother in Leeds. Olivia didn't question the matter any further. She rather preferred Squires and called her Auntie from time to time. Squires took very well to the affection and began saying things like, "Olivia, dearie-duck, you mustn't go out without your coat, or you shall catch your death," as if she had been saying such things all her life. She and Olivia got along swimmingly, and it wasn't long before I started to wonder if Elizabeth Squires wasn't in fact a gentler person without a soul.

On the road to Brighton, Squires sat outside the coach next to the driver, and all the long way, Olivia and I could hear her exclaiming, "Look at that lovely garden! I never seen such a quaint little house in all my life! I shall miss England so. Though you know"—all this was directed at the coachman, who never said a word but merely clenched his teeth and hurried the horses along with a lash from his whip—"I ain't never been more than a mile outside o' London. Just look at all that countryside. Just like a painting, it is. What a splendid time we shall have!"

The ferry ride was a different matter. Squires had never set foot on a ship before, and the very idea of crossing all that water made her tremble. On the ride across the Channel, she grew very quiet and still, as if the smallest step could upset the whole boat. As we sailed along, Squires hugged her knees to her chest and closed her eyes tight, for the waves were making her sick. She was not herself again until we set foot on solid ground, at which point she exclaimed, "I don't think I shall ever go back, for I don't think I could be made to board another ferry ever again."

"Oh, Auntie," said Olivia. "You mustn't say such things. We could not possibly return to London without you. You are such a dear creature, and I don't know what Mr. Ellsworth would do without you!"

This seemed to cure Squires of her seasickness. "Quite right you are," she said. "Mr. Ellsworth needs someone wot will look after him."

Here Squires turned to me and said, "Depend upon it, sir, I will brave the voyage home. You will not hear another peep from me." Then Squires yakked the entire coach ride from Le Havre to Paris. I could have strangled her with my own two hands if my dear Olivia had not been so fond of her.

"I am so glad you found Squires," Olivia said when we were alone in the coach together. "She is such a rare bird, and I love her for it. So much better than stuffy old Madam Pomphrey."

Our coachman rode all through the night while Olivia and I slept in the comfort of the cabin and Squires dozed on the driver's box. We reached Paris the following day. Squires carried our luggage up to Olivia's father's flat in La Place Royale and set to work undraping all the furniture. Meanwhile, Olivia and I strolled about the neighborhood, exhausted but in good spirits, for we were alone together at last, in a foreign capital where no one would recognize our faces.

Olivia was fluent in French, as was I, so we had no trouble navigating the crooked, winding streets of the medieval city. Besides, I had lived in Paris for many years in the early part of the century, and I knew the rues and boulevards backwards and forwards, at least those that remained unaltered. Paris was not the city then that it is today. There were pockets of beauty: the Notre-Dame Cathedral, the Gardens at Luxembourg, the Louvre Palace. But there were also large swaths of squalor and decay. It was two hundred years before Haussmann's renovation of Paris, which would see the demolition of many of the crowded medieval neighborhoods that Olivia and I explored that day, and the city was still a sprawling maze of piecemeal tenements and ramshackle hovels.

When we returned to the flat in La Place Royale a few hours later, Squires was preparing supper: pheasant roasted with garlic and potatoes—and the aroma wafted through the house like a midsummer breeze. Olivia and I took our supper in the dining room and then retired to the veranda, where we watched the stars twinkle to life in the darkening sky. It was a chilly April evening, so we wrapped ourselves in wool blankets and huddled together to keep warm.

The following day, we woke late and took our breakfast in bed. Squires had been to the market early that morning and was aflutter with stories of the strange things she had seen: French courtiers with thin-brimmed hats bedecked with feathers; herds of cattle roaming the Rue des Balets; cabarets that served wine *and* bread atop a linen tablecloth; a bitter drink called *coffee*, which a street merchant was hawking in the Rue Saint-Jacques. These were novelties to Squires, who had never set foot outside of London. I was less impressed. I had tasted coffee in the Near East in the fifteenth century. Cabarets had been around for nearly two hundred years. And although Squires expressed shock at the sheer number of cattle in the Rue des Balets, surely she had witnessed herds of cattle roaming the streets of London before.

Olivia, on the other hand, was very kind and listened intently as Squires described the things she had seen. When Squires was out of breath, Olivia said, "Auntie, what an adventure you have had this morning."

"Yes, mistress," she sighed. "I never would have dreamed in all my life that I would live to see such wonders."

"I'm so glad you were able to come with us," said Olivia patiently. "Now, will you fetch us some tea?"

"Certainly, mistress."

Once Squires had gone, Olivia turned to me and said, "She is like a child—full of curiosity."

"She is a silly creature," I said dismissively.

Olivia gave me a jocular shove. "She is a dear."

"Yes," I repeated. "She is a dear."

"Where shall we go today?" Olivia asked.

"Can't we just stay all day in bed?"

Olivia frowned. "We didn't come to Paris to lie in bed."

"Well, what would you have us do?"

"I'd like to visit my aunt's grave," she said. "She is buried outside the Church of the Holy Innocents."

"You know I hate churches," I said. It was true. Churches reminded me of God, and I stayed away from them whenever I could. Cemeteries weren't much better. The thought of all those mortal bodies rotting underground. And the pious drivel written on all the headstones. It unnerved me.

"Then you stay here," said Olivia. "I will go by myself."

"It is dangerous for a woman alone."

"I'll bring Squires."

"Very well," I said. "I will work on my diary while you are out."

Olivia was pleased and promised to return before supper.

But supper came and went, and Olivia did not return. She and Squires had been gone half the day, much more time than was necessary to visit the churchyard of the Holy Innocents. As the evening darkened and I sat alone in the little flat, I started to grow increasingly concerned. Mind you, in those days, there were no phones nor

GPS devices. Inevitably, people got delayed. And without any means of communication, we all had to be much more patient than we are today. But the thought of Olivia and Squires alone in a foreign city after dark made me uneasy. Olivia was never late, so this was particularly unusual for her. Squires was another matter altogether. She could not be depended upon to be on time under the best of circumstances. Still, something seemed off; I could feel it in my gut.

It was after nine when I heard footsteps on the stairs. I flung the front door open to find a distinguished-looking gentleman on the landing. He was clutching Elizabeth Squires by the arm and wielding a long, heavy cane in his free hand. Squires was in bad shape. Her face was bruised, her lips bloody. When she made to speak, the gentleman thwapped her ankles with his stick.

"What's all this?" I demanded.

The gentleman shoved past me into the flat, dragging Squires with him.

The bloody condition of Squires's face sent me into a panic. "Where's Olivia?"

"That is no business of yours—Mr. Ellsworth."

It was then that I recognized the gentleman. It was Dr. Charles Bartlett, Olivia's father, the rightful owner of the flat in which I now stood.

"They intercepted us in the square," sobbed Squires. "I kicked and screamed for 'elp, but the big 'un, he got hold of Mistress Olivia and took her away."

"She is safe," said Dr. Bartlett. "My man is dependable. He will get her home safely."

"I told him wot you are!" cried Squires. "I told him you'd make him pay for this."

"Enough, woman!" barked Dr. Bartlett.

Squires shrank at the sound of his voice.

Dr. Bartlett sniffed the air like a rabid bloodhound. "I see you've made yourself quite at home."

"How did you find us?" I asked.

"This is my house, after all," he said.

"I mean, how did you know we were here?"

"I have spies everywhere," said Dr. Bartlett. "But that is no matter now. Here we are."

"Here we are," I said.

"Miss Squires gave us an earful down in the square," continued Dr. Bartlett. "Was quite persuasive. Said she'd sold her soul. Said you were the Devil."

I shot a glance at Squires, who cast her eyes downward.

"She talks nonsense," I said.

"No," said Dr. Bartlett firmly. "She tells the truth."

"What makes you say that?"

"I told you, I have spies everywhere."

Damn Belial and his big mouth. It seemed all of London had been eavesdropping that night at the Red Rooster. If it weren't for Olivia—weren't for the thought of never seeing her again—I would have turned right then and run from that place, abandoned Squires, abandoned my house in London, and lost myself in Paris, never to be heard from again.

Dr. Bartlett continued. "One word to the magistrate, and I could have you strung up."

"What's stopping you?" I demanded.

"I think we may be of some use to one another."

"How's that?"

"You have something I want," said the doctor. "And I have something you want."

"Go on."

All the while, Squires trembled in a corner of the parlor. I gave her a reassuring nod and stood my ground while Dr. Bartlett circled like a vulture, tapping his cane on the hardwood floor.

Rat-a-tat-tat.

"You want to see my daughter again," he said. "I can grant you that privilege."

I growled through my teeth. "What do you want in return?"

"The Magpie Tree."

The words knocked the wind out of me. I had not thought of the Magpie Tree in what? Four thousand years? The last time I'd seen it, I was a young angel in God's greenhouse, making sketches in my notebook and experimenting on rats. The Magpie Tree, the only immortal tree God ever made. It gave mortal creatures the gift of long life, something any Earthbound doctor would be eager to possess.

But how did this man—so many generations removed from God's garden—know anything about the Magpie Tree?

The doctor seemed to read my mind. "Ancient scriptures tell of a tree whose fruit holds the elixir of life. Some call it the Magpie Tree. It is said to grow in the Garden of Eden. Do you know it?"

"Aye," I said. "I know it."

"Bring me a branch from the Magpie Tree, and you will see your dear Olivia again."

"How do I know you tell the truth?"

"You don't know," he said flatly. "But what choice do you have? You can do as I say or else be condemned to rot in the Tower of London."

I surveyed Dr. Bartlett carefully. His threats did not scare me, for I could have snapped his neck right then and there if I had wished. But what of Olivia? I knew I could not murder her father and hope to retain her love—not in good faith. Nor could I bear to never see her again. I have always favored the path of least resistance, and it seemed that if I did as Dr. Bartlett commanded, I could secure his approval and perhaps win a chance to be with my sweet Olivia once more.

"Very well," I said. "I will bring you a branch from the Magpie Tree."

Squires and I left Paris that night, for we were no longer welcome in Olivia's father's flat. We returned to the house in Smithfield Place, and I immediately wrote to Olivia, hoping to explain all that had transpired between myself and her father that night in La Place

Royale. In my letter I confessed to my being the fallen angel Lucifer, I explained my strange bargain with Elizabeth Squires, and I begged Olivia's forgiveness for not telling her sooner. Whether she would believe me, I did not know. And if she did believe me, would she still have me? After all, what sane woman of the seventeenth century would willfully take Satan for a lover?

CHAPTER 27

MY HAND STAYED A long time on the iron handle of the
gate to Eden. The metal was cold. The gravel crunched
as I shifted my feet nervously. There was a gritty smell, like rust.
I wondered when the last time was that a human had passed
through those gates. I thought it must have been two thousand
years since any mortal hand had been able to turn the latch. I'm
sure countless children had tried to open the gate in their play of
hide and seek, but no mortal would ever enter those gates again.

There was a chill in the night air. I rubbed my gloved hands
together. My breath was like a puff of smoke in the air. If I was
lucky, I wouldn't run into anyone this time. Surely, all the angels
were asleep, and I could duck in and out of Eden before anyone
was the wiser.

The gate creaked like a banshee, and I winced. It was horribly
deafening, and I wondered if I would wake God in his house
many miles away. If he found out that I had taken a branch of
the Magpie Tree, would he come after me? Would he even care?

I carried with me a small hatchet. Otherwise, my hands and pockets were empty. The moment I stepped into the garden, a warm breeze washed over me. I removed my overcoat and gloves and draped them over the gate. The songs of crickets reverberated through the night air, masking my footfalls as I moved stealthily along the wooded trail. Here and there, nocturnal creatures darted across my path. I wondered that these mortal beasts should have it so well in Eden, never wanting for food or water, never suffering from cold or heat. Meanwhile, their brethren on Earth fought epic battles just to live another day. The same went for mortal men, except there were no mortal men left in all of Eden.

And what of my brethren, the angels of Heaven: Michael, Gabriel, Raphael, Uriel, and countless others? Were they still content to spend all their days under God's watchful eye in the garden? I knew not what had become of these subservient Imorti, nor did I very much care. Except for Michael, none of those angels had ever really been a friend. When I lived in God's house, most angels regarded me with jealousy or reverence, but never as a brother. They saw me as separate, God's favorite, and they treated me with detached respect, whether they envied or admired me.

The only angel that had ever treated me as an equal was Michael. I missed him dearly, for he was my first and oldest friend. Without thinking, I took the fork in the trail that would lead me to Michael's little hut in the glade. I did not dare wake him, but I sought some connection to the angel that had advised me all those thousands of years ago.

I was surprised to find that Michael's hut had been transformed. Where once had stood a tumbledown shack now stood a quaint house in the Japanese style of the period, with sliding screen doors and wood-paneled walls. One of the screen doors stood wide open, and inside, Michael slept in a silk kimono on a woven tatami mat on the floor. His breathing was soft and even, and—as is the case with all angels—Michael hadn't aged one day in five thousand years.

The crickets were chirping away, and there was only a sliver of moon, so I was able to approach the house unnoticed. I stood so close now that I could see the smooth contours of Michael's face, his high cheekbones and glossy black hair. I very much wanted to wake him, to tell him I had returned, if only for one night, and to enfold his thin frame in my arms. Here was a friend, someone I had always admired and loved.

But I did not wake him, for my mission was to return to Earth with a branch from the Magpie Tree. Surely, Michael would never approve of my removing such a treasured jewel from God's garden. If I was quick, he would never know it was gone, for the Magpie Tree was immortal, and would regenerate the missing branch before morning.

I turned from the sleeping figure to survey the valley and the forest beyond. A trail wound around the glade and up a steep, arching bridge over the River Fluvius. I followed the trail until I came to the large stone stairway that led up to God's house. Here, I paused to consider the tall white columns and pitched stone roof. They had not changed in all these years. I wondered why God did not update his home as Michael had, in the fashion of the day, but I knew God was not partial to humans, and thus turned his nose up at human ingenuity.

I continued on past God's house, to the sprawling glass conservatory out back. The doors were unlocked. I knew of nothing that locked in all of Eden. Yes, the gateways from Earth to Eden were locked to mortal men, but in the garden, there was nothing to stop man, angel, or beast from going where he pleased.

I entered the greenhouse and was struck by the rich, sulfuric smell of wet earth. It was dark, for the tinted glass obscured most of the moonlight. I felt my way along the rows of herbs and shrubs to the back of the greenhouse, where the Magpie Tree stood in a white porcelain pot. It looked exactly as it had five thousand years ago, with smooth white bark and broad, glossy leaves. The fruit were ripe and welcoming: little purple bulbs of exactly the same size, every one.

The tree stood no more than four feet high and had snaking branches that reached out in every direction. I marveled that there wasn't a single sign of decay in all these years. But what did I expect? The tree was like me—immortal and unchanging. At first, I cringed to think of tearing away a branch of the tree, of marring its exceptional beauty. But I knew well it would restore itself in short order. So, I took my hatchet and with three clean strokes, removed a limb from the tree.

The branch was about the length of my arm and held maybe a dozen of the purple fruit. I hefted it over my shoulder and stood staring at the dismembered tree. Presently, where I had cut the bough from the tree, a new limb emerged, identical to the one I now carried. Satisfied that no one would know the difference, I adjusted my grip on the amputated branch and felt my way along the rows of flowering perennials and budding annuals to the exit, where the door still stood ajar.

When I stepped into the night air, I broke into a run. So far, the garden showed no signs of hostility. Why would it? God had decreed that all of the creatures of the garden should bow to me. That meant even the Imorti. So, if any one of God's loyal angels should try to stop me now, they would find themselves powerless to do so, for I still reigned in Heaven as God had promised. I knew of no reason why that should have changed.

"Tear up whole rows of asphodel," God had said on the day of my creation. "They will be replanted. Michael has been ordered to obey your every wish for all eternity."

Perhaps God could rescind such a promise. But he had not, for—I firmly believed—he still loved me as his greatest creation. Or at least I fancied it was so.

I traced my way back along the winding trail, past Michael's house, to the gate, whose heavy bolt could not stop me leaving that haunted place. I slipped into my overcoat, pulled on my gloves, shouldered the immortal limb of the Magpie Tree, and stepped into the brisk London air.

I did not go immediately to see Olivia's father on Aldersgate Street. It was the middle of the night when I returned to the house in Smithfield Place. In the morning, I sent word by courier that I would be calling that afternoon. The courier returned with a message from Dr. Bartlett.

"Come alone—and bring the branch," it read.

This short missive made me nervous. So, before I left for Aldersgate Street, I told Squires exactly where I was going and when she should expect me back. Then I called on Belial and explained all that had befallen us since our departure for Paris. Belial took the news in stride. He was not at all surprised that I had gone to such great lengths to see Olivia again, but he warned that Dr. Bartlett was unlikely to warm to me, even after I delivered the bough from the Magpie Tree.

"If he thinks you are the Devil—"

"Which I am," I said.

"Which you are—then how do you think he will feel about a courtship between you and his daughter?"

"I don't know," I said. "I don't even know if she'll still have me. But I must see her again. I cannot move on until I know how she feels!"

Was I still cross with Belial for giving away my true identity? Of course. Did I want to expose Belial in retaliation? Yes. But Belial and I had seen darker days together, so I let it go. Belial agreed to come looking for me if I did not return before teatime, and we agreed to leave London together if things went south.

CHAPTER 28

T O TELL THIS NEXT part of my story is to relive one of the most harrowing days of my life. All the way to Aldersgate Street, I was sweating. I both dreaded and anticipated the moment I would see Olivia again. If Dr. Bartlett lived up to his promise, I would have the chance to explain everything to Olivia, and she would be able to make up her own mind about me. I carried the branch from the Magpie Tree over my shoulder and was met with bewildered stares from passersby who wondered why a fine gentleman would be carrying the bough of a plum tree through the streets of London.

Let me start this chapter of my life by explaining one thing: I wasn't thinking straight. In any other lifetime I would have reinvented myself in a faraway land rather than live amongst mortals who knew my true identity. Over the years, tens of thousands of innocent people had been prosecuted for witchcraft all across Europe and the Americas. Clearly, I had lost hold of my senses, for at that very moment in history, witch trials were all the rage in England. But my love for Olivia blinded me. I couldn't see past my nose.

So, when I arrived on Olivia's doorstep, I was more concerned about straightening out the wrinkles in my suit and smoothing down my unruly hair than I was about being outed as a demon.

That was folly.

I rang the bell, hoping it would be Olivia who would be first to answer. The housekeeper, Mrs. Langley, appeared on the threshold holding a broom. If I had been paying attention, I might have noticed that she wielded the broom more like a lance, pointing the blunt end toward my chest. She did not ask my business—that wasn't unusual seeing as I had called many times before, inquiring about Olivia. However, I had never been admitted into the house—I had explicit instructions from Olivia never to enter—nor had I ever come face to face with Dr. Charles Bartlett prior to that fated night in Paris. I had always assumed he was completely oblivious to my relationship with his daughter or else didn't give a damn.

But this time, Mrs. Langley simply said, "Enter," as though she were expecting me.

The Magpie bough scraped the low ceiling of the foyer as I entered, etching a thin line into the wooden paneling and causing one of the ripe plums to fall to the ground. I swiftly scooped up the bulbous fruit and dropped it in my waistcoat pocket.

Mrs. Langley frowned at me. She led me into the parlor, where Dr. Bartlett stood, smoking a cigar and leaning against the fireplace.

"Mr. Ellsworth." He nodded.

"I've kept my end of the bargain," I said, presenting the Magpie bough to Dr. Bartlett.

He stepped forward and examined the branch as though it were an injured animal. Then he took the branch in his hands and inspected it from every angle, running his hand down the length of the bough.

"So you have," he said.

"Well?" I demanded.

Just then, Olivia appeared on the stairs.

"Father—" she began. But when she saw me, she stopped cold.

"Thomas!" she gasped.

"Olivia!"

"Thomas," she cried, tears springing to her eyes. "My father ... I'm so sorry! When I didn't hear from you—"

"Didn't you receive my letter?"

Olivia descended the stairs and crossed the parlor. She fell into my arms.

"What letter?" she asked, burrowing her face into my cravat.

"Enough!" barked Dr. Bartlett.

Olivia and I were so caught up in the moment of our reunion that we did not see all that was happening around us.

"What letter?" Olivia repeated.

"This letter," said Dr. Bartlett, holding up a yellow piece of parchment.

It was then that I noticed the two rough-looking men standing in the shadows at the periphery of the room.

"What is this?" I demanded.

"Father?" Olivia blinked. "Who are these men?"

243

"Mr. Ellsworth has confessed to practicing the dark arts," Dr. Bartlett said curtly. "In this letter he claims to be a demon from Hell. One of the Fallen."

"That's a twisted version of the truth," I said. "Olivia, please, let me explain—"

"It's all here in this letter," said Dr. Bartlett. "Signed and dated the fourteenth of April."

"Yes, but—"

"Apprehend the monster!" said Dr. Bartlett.

The two men pounced. I clutched Olivia instinctively, but one of the men wedged himself between us and pried our clinging bodies apart. Olivia screamed and pounded her fists against the ruffian's back. She might as well have been a feather duster for all the good it did. The men were strong, much stronger than she or I, probably deckhands from the shipyard. They dragged me into the foyer and out the front door.

Olivia tried to follow, but Dr. Bartlett and Mrs. Langley caught hold of her arms and pulled her back into the house. The door slammed and the men continued to carry me down the lane toward Newgate Street. I knew immediately where they were taking me: the prison on the corner of Old Bailey. I put up a fight, but it was no use. Dr. Bartlett had done well in choosing these men, for they carried me between them like a skipping rope, each holding one arm while my heels dragged on the cobblestones.

Several onlookers tagged along, eager to see what all the fuss was about. By the time we reached the prison, a sizable crowd had gathered outside the jailhouse. The constable greeted us at the door as though he had been expecting us. It seemed the doctor had sent word ahead of my arrival, and my accommodations were already prepared. They tossed me into an empty cell in the belly of the prison, where all I could hear were the anguished cries of other inmates and the barking of dogs.

There I sat for what seemed like hours, racking my brain. Surely, Belial would learn of my arrest and come to my rescue. Or Olivia would beg the mercy of her father, and all would be set right in a few days' time. Surely, I had a friend somewhere in London who would vouch for me. But the longer I sat in the dark, the more convinced I became that no one was coming to save me.

There was no chamber pot, so I had to piss in a corner of my cell. The putrid stench of human waste clouded my senses. I could not think properly. I had been naïve. Blind. Of course no man would allow his daughter to consort with the Devil. The doctor had intercepted my letter, had hidden it from Olivia. And now he sought to condemn me with my own words. How could I have been so stupid? Even Belial, who was reckless and foolhardy, would not have signed his name to such a confession.

At long last, the constable came to fetch me. It had to be about three o'clock in the afternoon of the same day. A prison guard dragged me across the street into the neighboring courtroom and placed me in the witness box before two surly judges whose names, they told me, were Sir Edward Altham and Sir James Bromley. The courtroom was full to bursting with eager spectators hungry for blood. They screamed and jeered at me; they threw rotten apples at my head; and only when the bailiff threatened them with his baton did they settle into their seats.

The prosecution was a local magistrate, Mr. Noel Rogers, with whom I was vaguely acquainted, for he too was a member of the Gentlemen's Club at Luxembury. Dr. Bartlett was there as well, sitting quietly in the first row, looking calm and impassive. I tried to spy Olivia in the crowd, but I suspected her father had forbidden her to bear witness to the scene that would play out that day.

It was a speedy trial. The judge asked me to identify myself, and I did so readily, hoping my good name and fortune might buy me some leeway. The magistrate read aloud the letter I had penned to Olivia, which described my fall from Heaven and the Devil's bargain I had made with Elizabeth Squires. Judge Bromley asked if I wanted to say anything in my defense, which of course I did, but my words were quickly drowned out by the angry cries of the mob. When it was clear that any defense I made would not persuade the court, the judges called for quiet in the courtroom, and Mr. Altham read my sentence: death by hanging.

You must understand that I did not fear death—why would I?—but I did fear pain, suffering, and humiliation. If the angry mob realized that hanging wasn't enough to do me in, would they light my body on fire? Drown me in the Thames? I was sure that if they discovered I could not die, they would torture me indefinitely and possibly string me up in the town square to be spit on and debased.

After Judge Altham pronounced my sentence, I thought I would have more time to work out an escape plan. A bribe. A jailbreak. Anything. But the mob was calling for justice to be served that very night, and so I was dragged to Tyburn Square and paraded before the gallows. Before the executioner slipped the burlap sack over my head, I scanned the crowd, looking for anyone who might come to my rescue: Belial, Olivia, Squires. There was not a friendly face anywhere to be seen. The executioner fitted the noose around my neck, the priest mumbled something about forgiveness and God—utter bullshit—and the trapdoor dropped out from under me.

BOOK III: IN HELL

*An apology for the devil: it must be remembered that
we have heard one side of the case. God has written all
the books.*

Samuel Butler

CHAPTER 29

N IGHT. PERPETUAL NIGHT. HAVE you ever opened your
eyes and found that they are still closed? That is the illusion
of true darkness. I thought perhaps I had only tried to open my eyes
and failed. After further review, I discovered, to my dismay, that my
eyes were most certainly open, wide open, and there was no sight.

Had I not been immortal, I might have thought myself blind. But
already the wounds around my neck were healing. I could not be
blind, then. How long had I been in the dark, I did not know. I
remembered the grim stare of the priest. He had promised eternal
salvation if I begged the mercy of God. I couldn't help but smile.
God didn't even know where in the hell I was, and I was pretty sure
he didn't care. Last time I saw God, he had been high on opium,
a therapeutic measure, no doubt. Right now, God was probably
relaxing out in the middle of some lake in Eden with a pipe and a
fishing rod.

Then I heard the last sound I would hear for many years. I did
not recognize it at first: a thud echoing in the darkness above. There
were several more thuds of a similar nature, and with each thud the

darkness around me trembled. My hands and arms were laid across my chest. I lifted my fingers. They were fatigued and responded slowly. I felt around me in the dark. I was met on all sides with the solid impassibility of wooden walls. This was no ordinary bedchamber. This was a funerary box. The rhythmic thud that reverberated above—that was the sound of my burial.

I panicked. I cannot recall what passed through my mind when I realized I was being buried alive. Most people fear being buried alive more than they fear death itself. Few are sentenced to endure such a fate. But none, save I, has ever faced the prospect of eternity in such a state.

I screamed first. I begged and pleaded. What he must have heard, the man laying earth on my grave, I cannot say. Perhaps he kept shoveling to drown out my voice. Perhaps he heard nothing at all. I can only imagine that whoever it was did not pity the Devil laid to rest, for the shovelfuls of dirt continued to fall, no faster, no slower than before—resolutely they came, thud after thud.

I only then thought to free myself. I raised my arms and tried to lift the lid off my casket. But the coffin was sealed. I writhed. I cried. I flung my whole body about like a snake caught in the beak of a hawk.

There was nothing I could do. The Devil, so mighty, descendent of Eden, the one who defied God—I was blamed for the corruption of mankind, yet I could not even loosen the nails on a wooden casket. Freedom was less than ten feet away—ten feet!

I screamed and thrashed until my voice was hoarse and my body was bruised. When my muscles grew too weak to move, I lay panting on the cold wooden slate that was my new bed. I bore the torment of listening to my chance of escape diminish as the thuds of dirt grew fainter and farther away.

There is a Hell. It is being buried alive with no hope of death. And it belongs only to the Imorti.

Humans have it easy. When things get to be too much, your hearts will fail, and you will suffer no more. Your souls will perish, your flesh will deteriorate. The pain is brief.

Not for me. When I thought that I could stand it no more, I found I was still there, awake in the dark like a zombie. I have never yearned for death so fiercely, and I have never known suffering so great. Misery and I took out a lease together in that confounded box. So, Misery was my company for many years.

At first, I held out hope that somebody would come to my rescue. If Belial knew what had become of me, that I lay awake in a box ten feet underground, I had no doubt he would turn up to dig me out. Olivia probably presumed me dead, and perhaps she too was convinced that I was a demon from Hell, so I couldn't expect her to lay flowers on my grave. And Elizabeth Squires—oh, poor Squires. The mob would come for her next; she sold her soul to the Devil. It was all there in the letter. In all likelihood, Squires was already dead. No, my best chance was Belial.

I had no sense of time in the box. I slept. I lay awake listening but hearing nothing. I dreamed fitfully. The box smelled of sawdust at first, but eventually that faded. There was nothing to mark the time, nothing to distinguish night from day. So, I cannot tell you when exactly I gave up hope of ever being found; it could have been days, months, or years later. But eventually I stopped waiting for someone to save me.

There was one moment of pleasure early on, and that was when I discovered the fallen fruit of the Magpie Tree in my waistcoat pocket. It would never spoil, so I held onto it until I could bear the hunger no more, maybe weeks, and then I consumed the sweet plum in a single sitting. And yes, in the beginning, I pissed and shat in the box. There was no way of turning or shifting my body—the confines were too small—so I lay in my filth until eventually it too became a part of me.

By and by, the pissing and the shitting stopped since I no longer drank or ate. My stomach ached, I became delirious from thirst, but still I lived on, withering, weak, and scared. The physical toll was great, but not nearly as great as the psychological toll. Like mortal and immortal creatures everywhere, I could not fathom the thought of being buried alive forever. I could not make sense of what it would mean to spend eternity confined to a box. So, I started to hallucinate, to imagine sights and sounds where there was nothing. I wondered, too, if God could hear my prayers, the way he could hear the prayers of humans. And I prayed, for the first time in my long life, for God to rescue me.

But God did not come. Either he could not hear the prayers of angels, or else he did not care. I did not know. But I prayed for many days and months—maybe years.

I marked time by the few variations I could perceive in my environs. The slow drying of my excrement. The softening and dampening of the wood around me. The appearance of worms, which occasionally burrowed through the cracks in my coffin only to fall on my face or hands or feet. Eventually, the wooden casket became so pliable, that I was sure I could lift the lid without much trouble if it weren't for the weight of the earth above it.

I had some hope of burrowing myself out, but the wooden walls of the coffin proved to be thicker than I expected. For a while, I scratched at the softening mahogany with my lengthening fingernails, thinking that eventually I would break through to the spongy, damp earth. But my fingers bled, and soon I lost all my strength. Without food or water to sustain me, I was a shell of myself. A consciousness with no agency.

I began to imagine my future. Maybe a thousand years would go by, and the casket would decay. But then would I have the strength to dig myself free? Or perhaps some future civilization would exhume my body. Or maybe tens of thousands of years of shifting tectonics would slowly bring me to the surface of the earth. Or bury me deeper below ground. Then, in billions of years, the sun would expand to envelope the Earth, as God had once described, and the planet would become molten liquid. Then I would burn, too. But perhaps somehow, I would be freed. And then what? Would I float forever in the emptiness of space?

A day buried alive is like a lifetime. So, what would a billion years be like? I would surely go mad! There is no such place as Hell. But if there were, it would be a casket ten feet under the ground and eternal life. You have no idea how fortunate you are to be mortal. To have the freedom to die.

CHAPTER 30

I COULDN'T BE SURE if what I was hearing came from inside or outside my head. No doubt, I had heard a good many sounds in the time I spent beneath the earth. Sometimes I thought I heard things that brought me great hope: a voice speaking, the rush of water, or birdcalls. Other times, I heard whispers of a darker nature: the creak of bones, the release of the trapdoor in the floor of the scaffold, the hammering of the coffin lid. So, when I first heard the sound of a shovel, I dismissed it as another of these haunting illusions.

But when the metal spade resounded firmly on the casket lid and shook the whole of my little world, I was awakened to a state of extreme anticipation. I had spent an indeterminable amount of time coming to accept darkness as the horoscope for my eternity. And now? Hope? When the knock of the shovel awakened me from my nightmares, my life ambitions were terrifically altered. Might I see day again?

I was on the verge of calling out to make my presence known, when I realized with sudden terror what would happen if I was discovered in a grave, *still alive*. I would be condemned as a demon and crucified all over again. My mind raced with an intensified anxiety. I had been trapped all these years, and now I was being summoned to contemplate my escape.

I weighed my options. My rescuer was most likely a lawless scoundrel, a graverobber. If I called out, I would be sure to frighten the poor beggar away, and that would be of no great help to either of us.

If I waited until he uncovered the casket, waited until just after he pried open the lid, and then ventured to speak, the fellow would scamper off in terror and I would rise from my prison.

What should I say to properly frighten the young scoundrel away? I wanted to give him a good scare. I didn't want him lingering about to see me crawl out of the pit. Perhaps I would say, "Hello, young rogue, come to tamper with the Devil?" That would send him running.

I waited silently in the dark. I was terrified that somehow the shovel would begin to work in reverse, and I would hear instead the familiar thud of dirt falling back on the coffin. There was no certainty that I would be freed on this day or any other. A thousand scenarios rushed through my mind. Maybe a watchman would come round and scare off the thief before I could be properly released. Perhaps the hole was being made to fit another coffin atop mine to save space in the graveyard. Then I would be buried ten feet underground with a lifeless body hanging over my head. Could it be that the cemetery was being disinterred and all the graves moved to another site? Would I be transported and then buried again?

I put all my cards on the graverobber. I have always had the supremest faith in the lawlessness of man.

The shovel scraped hard and long against the lid of the coffin. I shuddered and trembled in my box. The sound was amplified inside the hollow shell of the casket. Yet each shovelful brought me closer to freedom.

Then I heard footsteps. Someone had crawled into the pit and was walking on the lid of the coffin. He paced the length of the box, stomped a little to see if the wood had rotted any, and then took what must have been a crowbar and proceeded to pry at the edges of the casket. The wood was spongy, and the nails came out more smoothly than they had gone in.

When the first rays of moonlight seeped in through the cracks, I knew it was time to act. I opened my mouth to speak the words I had so carefully thought out. But I had no voice. What came out was a long, parched hiss. The saliva had gone from my mouth. I had not moved my lips or tongue in many years.

The lid was suddenly torn away. Poised above me was a tall, dark figure traced against a silver moon.

"Lucifer," he said. "So, I've found you at last."

CHAPTER 31

I T TOOK TIME FOR my eyes to adjust to the moonlight. I had
never seen anything so brilliant in all my life. Months, years under the earth and not a single ray of hope. If this blinding sensation
was night, then what was day? I coughed and spat. I could not move
at first. Every bone and sinew protested my attempts to rise. I was
helpless, lying still and paralyzed before this man who knew my
name.

"Come on," he said. "We've got to get you out of this ditch. It is
not befitting God's favorite angel."

Only then did I recognize the voice: Mephistopheles.

He reached down and wrapped his arms around my waste. I tried
to speak, but there was no sound. I tried to move, but I was cold,
and my blood was still.

"What day is it?" I managed to hiss.

"July 17 of the year 1665. Don't you worry, Lucifer. Old Mephisto is going to take care of you. Here we go."

He lifted me over his shoulders and climbed nimbly out of the
pit. I drooped and sagged. I was a miserable sight. My clothes were

caked with mud and my hair filled with worms. I had been without sunlight, without fresh air, without food and warmth for four years, three months, and two days. I might have been crying, but there was no water left in my body for tears.

Mephistopheles brought me to an old, trodden-down inn. The innkeeper looked up with alarm when he walked in with me on his shoulders.

"He hasn't got the plague, has he?" she cried.

"No, ma'am," Mephisto said calmly. "Just a friend who has had too much to drink. I'm taking him up to sleep it off."

"Fine, fine," she murmured.

Mephisto laid me on a hard mattress and brought me a glass of water. I drank greedily.

I must have passed out, for when I opened my eyes again, Mephistopheles was at the foot of my bed. He had before him a tray laden with pastries, cheeses, tea, and milk.

"I'm sorry, I would have brought you fruit, but there is none to be found in this dying city. I was lucky to find even these slim pickings."

Slim pickings? These were not slim pickings. What lay before me was a feast. I had not eaten in four years. I lunged for the tray. My stomach churned and ached. Saliva burst forth like geysers and flooded my mouth. I felt the acids in my stomach roiling about like waves in a storm. I swallowed the milk in one gulp. It was like drinking the nectar of Heaven. Nothing had ever tasted so sweet. When I was through with everything else, I sipped the tea slowly and lay back against my pillow.

Mephistopheles sat in a chair and waited for me to finish. "Glad I could be of service," he said.

"How did you find me?" I asked. My voice was no more than a whisper.

"I have been looking for you for many years. I heard that you had gone to London. I came here in search of you. When I arrived, I was told that a man by the name of Thomas Ellsworth had been charged with doing the work of the Devil something like four years ago. He was publicly hanged. His body had been buried in a wooden casket. I asked some of the locals where I might find his grave. A few youngsters remembered well where the Devil had been interred. They took me to an unmarked gravestone in the far corner of the cemetery on Deadman's Place. I paid them each two pence. And then I took up a shovel and began to dig."

"Thank you," I said. "I might have laid there forever."

Mephistopheles said nothing. He poured me another glass of milk from a pitcher.

The curtains were drawn, and the room was dark. Mephistopheles's blond hair and fair skin glowed in the light of a single candle. He was exactly as I remembered him, his disposition at once flirtatious and indifferent. He scratched the side of his nose and looked lazily about the chamber.

"We'll have to be going soon," he said. "We can't stay in London."

"There was a woman," I whispered.

"Olivia Bartlett," Mephistopheles finished. "I know, Lucifer. She is dead."

The words struck me like a sack of bricks. Every cell in my body recoiled, but I did nothing. I simply lay there, helpless and weak. If I had been in a better state, I might have raged, objected, stormed about and broken things. I might have cried in anguish. But I was skeletal and frail. I simply opened my mouth partway and let out every inch of air like a deflating balloon.

"Lucifer," Mephistopheles said calmly. "The plague is on London. Thousands of people are dying every day. The king has fled the city. Shops and businesses are closed. Dead bodies are clogging the gutters of the streets. Olivia Bartlett died of the plague nearly two months ago. Her father left the city. Anybody who can afford to get out is leaving. London has gone to the dogs, Lucifer. And we cannot stay here."

My world was rattled. I wasn't sure I could take the shock. But what choice did I have? I stared glassy-eyed at the flickering candle.

If only I could die.

"Lucifer," Mephistopheles said. "There's no use looking grim. You ought to be glad I pulled you out of that hellhole. Mortals die all the time. What's a plague to us? We have nothing to fear. Now, listen to me. I manage an inn in Brandenburg-Prussia. I have found some of the others like us, the Fallen Imorti. We have assembled there. There are six of us all told. You will make seven. Let me take you there. I will give you food and a place to stay. At least until you are back on your feet."

I closed my eyes and passed out. It was the closest thing to dying that I could manage.

✹

We left London as soon as I was ready for the journey to Branden-burg-Prussia. I had very little packing to do. I returned to my house in Smithfield Place before we set out. It had been burned to the ground, perhaps following my frightful exposure and condemna-tion. I had nothing to show for the five thousand years I had resided on Earth. Everything I owned was reduced to ashes. Belial had long forsaken his house. Perhaps he had been run out of town. He was, after all, an associate of the Devil.

I readied myself for the journey. I had no money. I relied entirely on Mephistopheles. He paid for passage across the English Channel. From there, a coach took us through France and the Low Countries and into what is present-day Germany, where the plague and my years in the grave seemed like a far-off nightmare. The Germanic peoples were friendly when they discovered we spoke their language. I knew a number of languages, including Latin, nearly forgotten by the seventeenth century. I could mimic the accent of the Germans and so I called myself Heinz and became a native of the region.

Mephistopheles was known there as Wolfgang. He managed a small inn in the village of Hölle. The inn was called Das Drachen-lager, *The Dragon's Lair*—an appropriate name for my new home. He had collected a mixed band of fallen angels to tend the bar, clean the rooms, and work the kitchen. There were Azazel, Berith, and Raum, who I had led to Earth. And there were two others who had followed after: Focalor and Marchosias. It was the first time since Mesopotamia that so many fallen had come together and formed a community on Earth.

The angels I recognized from our initial descent from Heaven greeted me heartily. I had been their leader once long ago. Everyone was anxious to know how I had managed all those years buried beneath the earth. I simply replied that I had no choice but to manage them. I warned them against finding themselves in a similar bind.

The inn had a seedy air. Mephistopheles had hired brothel girls to dance on a low, squat stage at the front of the pub. There were back rooms for card games and other private goings-on; there were shady dealings where money was exchanged for personal favors. I had a room above the pub, overlooking the back alley. I was privy to private conversations between gamblers and whores, conversations that drifted up through my window at all hours of the morning.

Mephistopheles quite enjoyed the atmosphere. It was heady and noxious, the way he liked life. He pressed me to try all sorts of drugs and liquors. I was averse to anything that might compromise my awareness. Since being disinterred, I was always on my guard. That ever such a cursed fate should befall me again—I shuddered to think of it. What I experienced in those four years in a coffin gave me at last the appreciation for the life that mortals experience. Humans constantly fear the grave—now, so did I.

I was for a long time silent and withdrawn. The others enjoyed the jubilant lawlessness of the inn. They slept little, drank much, and took to their bed every night two, maybe three women. I kept to myself. I was still reeling from the grave. I had imagined what it might be like to see day again, but little did I realize how profound an effect four years in darkness would have on my spirit. I became anxious in small spaces. I was even more anxious in open spaces. I lashed out any time Mephistopheles called me Lucifer—I did not want to be found out again. Nighttime reminded me of the coffin, and I had fitful dreams where I was stuck again under the lid and the earth was piling on top of me. I could not pass a cemetery without wincing. And because I was so used to holding my breath, I often forgot to breathe. Thus, the effects of those past four years stayed with me for many years to come.

Sometimes, when I was particularly low, my mind would stray to Olivia. I remembered her as I last saw her: with her arms outstretched toward me. Then I imagined her bloated corpse buried in a pit somewhere, infested with worms, not even afforded the decency of a coffin. The plague had claimed thousands of Londoners, and their bodies became unsacred, abject—carriers of the disease—and so they were burned and buried unceremoniously.

I thanked God—and I really thanked God—that Olivia had been spared the unending life I had suffered beneath the earth. At least, I thought, she was dead and not lying awake in a grave somewhere awaiting rescue. I realized then what a gift mortality really was—true, it was mortality that claimed Olivia's life, but it was also mortality that spared her from eternal pain.

✹

I came to Das Drachenlager with nothing. I owed everything to Mephistopheles. He gave me room and board and asked nothing in return. I was grateful. Who is not grateful of the hand that feeds them? He suffered my foul temper with patience. I was, as might be expected, melancholy at first. I did not warm up to the inn for many months. I mostly kept to my room. I did not speak to anyone. My journals and notebooks had all been lost in the fire. So, I started fresh. I picked up pen and paper and began to write again, for the first time in four years.

My hand was shaky at first. It is amazing how quickly one forgets how to hold a pen. My first notes comprised simple lists. First, my regrets: to have kept the truth from Olivia, to have peddled souls, to have taken for granted the freedom to walk where I pleased. My fears: small spaces, graveyards, the dark, my own identity becoming known. The people around me, the fallen angels, the Grigori: Mephistopheles, Azazel, Focalor, and the others. The lists went on for pages and pages. In time, I progressed to full sentences. I wrote about the dingy smell of the inn, the rouged cheeks of the brothel girls, the games of cards played in the back rooms.

As I wrote more and more, a gray cloud began to lift. I began to see where I was—I was stranded in a rundown inn. I was poor. I was dependent, and I was virtually sedentary. I had arrived at the inn on August 6, 1665. It was now November 17, 1666. I had been at the

267

inn for over a year. I realized my situation would not change unless I took some action. I needed money.

I went to Mephistopheles.

"Will you hire me?" I asked.

Mephistopheles looked over his accounting books. He arched his eyebrows skeptically. "Since you've come here, you've been nothing but sullen and dull. I don't know if you'd be very good for business."

"I can wash dishes," I said. "I can sweep floors. I can help with the accounting."

The grandfather clock ticked loudly, so loudly that I could not help but count forty-two seconds before Mephistopheles responded.

"Fine then," he said. "Start with the books." He slid the accounting ledgers across the table.

It should not be forgotten that despite my wretched state of mind, I was still very clever. I had designed the earliest aqueducts. I took one look at the books, and I could see that the inn was losing money. Apparently, Das Drachenlager had done very well at the onset of the plague in London, in April of 1665. Whole families had headed for Brandenburg-Prussia to wait out the Black Death. The inn had been a haven for refugees. But as the plague diminished in London, so had business.

"You're losing money," I said.

Mephistopheles nodded.

"Let me go through these," I said, indicating all the books. "I'll try to work something out."

I would not normally concern myself with the goings-on of a seedy inn. But Mephistopheles was my benefactor. If he lost money, I lost money. I was not about to end up on the streets in mid-winter. We had to make more money, and quickly.

CHAPTER 32

"COME WITH ME, LUCIFER," Mephistopheles said. "Let me show you something."

He took me to his room and closed the door behind us. He went to his bed and lifted the mattress. Tucked between the bed boards was a small wooden box. It was about eight inches on each side and four inches deep. He set the box upon the mattress and removed the lid.

I recognized the contents immediately. They were molasses-colored balls of sticky paste, each about two inches in diameter. The box was only half full. I picked up a ball and examined it under the candlelight. It made me think immediately of God in his garden the last time I had seen him. Mephistopheles saw recognition register on my face. He asked, "You know what this is?"

"Yes," I said. "It's opium."

"Not only opium," Mephistopheles said. "It is blended with tobacco. If it is ground up, it can be smoked. They call it madak."

I pictured God in the light of all those paper lanterns sampling slices of raw madak.

"Where did you get it?" I asked.

"I was in the Far East about eight years ago. I was looking for other Grigori. In part, I was looking for you. Instead, I found this."

"You've made it last, I see."

"I rarely touch the stuff. But it is a wondrous drug. And it hasn't been introduced into Europe yet, at least not to the common people. I see a major business opportunity—if you'll agree to help me."

"What do you want from me?" I asked.

"I need a business partner to help me bring in clientele," Mephisto said. "I have a few well-heeled friends who'd be interested in investing. What say you?"

I considered. What choice did I have? Besides, I had no qualms about making a profit off the drug trade. Whatever humans needed to do to get by was fine by me.

I nodded. "I'm in."

⬡

The first shipment of opium arrived in the Port of Hamburg on April 4, 1667. The ship came out of the North Sea. The water was calm, and the skies were blue and clear—a good omen. Mephistopheles rented out a large warehouse on the wharf. The shipment was placed under lock and key. Berith, Raum, and Focalor kept watch over the warehouse in eight-hour shifts. Mephistopheles and I took up residence in a small, rundown inn in central Hamburg. From there, we conducted our first business transactions.

I had already lined up a number of dealers interested in the new, exotic drug. Mephistopheles and I gave out samples of opium to lure potential buyers to our enterprise. When the shipment arrived, so did our first clients. By the end of the week, we had sold 120 crates. Within a month, we had more than made up for the money we had initially invested in the project.

I got fifteen percent of the cut; Mephistopheles took another fifteen. The rest went into the business and to rewarding our investors. We had our second shipment delivered in late August, but half of the inventory was spoiled by mildew. This put us back a little, but when our third shipment came the following January, Mephistopheles and I were able to relocate to a nicer neighborhood and a modest flat. Our clients were hooked, and we found ourselves busily trying to meet Eastern Europe's demand for opium.

Mephistopheles had an old friend in the shipping business—Johan Steinhaeusser. He was the seedy sort, indebted to Mephisto for some past favor. We did all our shipping through him, and always out of the Port of Hamburg. Within the year, we owned three warehouses along the river that oversaw shipments of opium across the whole of Europe.

Mephisto was loathe to give up Das Drachenlager in Hölle, so we turned the little tavern into an outpost of our cartel, and Mephisto moved back to run the inn, leaving me in charge of the business in Hamburg.

Clientele showed up at Das Drachenlager, ordered the "Oriental Flower Tea" at the bar, and they were shown to an upstairs apartment where they would be greeted by Mephisto and his accounting ledger. Our clients represented a wide range of society: aristocrats from the Spanish and Bavarian Kingdoms, German peasantry, and everything in between. Thanks to Johan Steinhaeusser, there was no limit to where we could ship our wares, and all of Europe got a taste.

I preferred to keep a low profile, so I stayed in Hamburg and managed Berith, Raum, and Focalor, who lived together by the wharf. Mephisto saw the advantage to having someone he could trust on the ground in Hamburg but was not happy to part with me. And although I managed the shipments in and out of Hamburg, I tried to have as little to do with Johan Steinhaeusser as possible, for he was just the kind of untrustworthy character I believed would sell me out for a mark. So, I limited our interactions to brief exchanges regarding orders and payments.

Then one day I was out at the docks overseeing the import of 400 crates to our main warehouse when I noticed a brand-new trading ship with a label painted in bright white paint across the starboard side that read: *Jacques Bezier Shipping Co.* I wondered if this Jacques Bezier was any relation to the Jacques Bezier I had put in the care of Cadwell so many years ago. I hadn't seen or heard from the fellow since before I was buried alive, and I wondered with surprise if he could have come such a long way in the world in such a short time.

I caught the attention of one of the deckhands and inquired further into the nature of the company.

"Yes, sir. This ship belongs to Jacques Bezier. He's got a whole fleet of them based out of Bristol. Seven ships all told. This ship is headed for the East Indies, commissioned by King Charles."

"And where might Mr. Bezier be found these days?" I asked.

"*Sir* Bezier," the young man corrected. "Gone and got himself knighted, he has. Sir Bezier is most like to be found 'round Bristol, where he has a large estate. Eddingfield, it's called. Spends most of his time there now, he does. Gave up the sea. Wanted to settle down. But he still manages the fleet, and he's made quite a living of it."

"I suspect he has," I said.

The deckhand was called back to his task and excused himself politely. I wondered at Bezier's unforeseen success and couldn't help but credit myself for my part in his improved lot.

I dwelled momentarily on the past—I wondered about my friends: Belial, Squires, Bezier. Where had they all gone to? How had I come to this lowly place, working for Mephistopheles, living at his behest, trading drugs? It was a wretched existence. But when Mephisto pulled me from the grave, I had nothing—no money to secure my comfort and not a friend in the world. It was a crooked, unhappy life I led, but the business was lucrative, and in time, I could hope to become a wealthy man. Indeed, I had already amassed a small fortune, and each day added to my lot.

Mephistopheles may have been a dubious employer, but since the sale of our first shipment, he had been paying me my fair share. I had enough money now that I could give up the opium trade and invest in something more up-and-up if I wanted. But the businessman in me saw the profit yet to be made, and I could not bring myself to walk away while the getting was still good. So, I was tied to Mephistopheles by mutual greed.

I thought all this as I stared at the shipping vessel belonging to my old acquaintance, Jacques Bezier. I was startled out of my reverie by the sudden approach of Johan Steinhaeusser.

"Ahoy," he called. "Here's the papers. I took the liberty to calculate the final sum, and it's written there on the bottom of the page."

This was how our exchanges usually went. I took the papers with the inventory listings, the price of each crate, the service fee, et cetera. I examined the papers carefully, saw where Steinhaeusser had overcharged three marks a crate, and sternly pointed out his error.

"Right, sir. Very right. My mistake entirely."

It was often like this—Steinhaeusser was a notorious crook. The amounts were corrected, the payment made, and the date set for the next shipment. It went on like this for two lonesome years, with very little variation except for increasing profits and wider distribution. I became rich again, Das Drachenlager saw some much-needed renovations, and I bought a small townhouse in Hamburg proper where I lived in private. I furnished the little house to my liking—it was an escape from the sordid air of the crumbling tenement where I had been staying up until then. Of course, Mephisto would occasionally come to stay on business, and he would fill the flat with smoke and seedy company. Then my private space became reminiscent of Das Drachenlager. But when Mephisto was away, the place was mine and mine alone.

I often considered buying a larger estate and introducing myself into the society of Hamburg, but I feared being found out again. So, I decided that, when the time came, I would leave the opium business, leave Mephistopheles, and relocate to some faraway place, take up a new name, make proper friends again, live off my fortune, maybe move past Olivia—for I had not been with a man or woman since—and perhaps lead an honest life.

CHAPTER 33

IT WAS AROUND THIS time that I made one of the strangest
friends the Devil can make. It was a day when I had no particular
business at the warehouses, so I was taking a leisurely stroll through
my neighborhood. I was halfway down Meyerstrasse, just in front of
St. Michael's Church, when I perceived Johan Steinhaeusser coming
my way. He had not yet seen me, and I wanted none of the unpleas-
antness of meeting him in the street, so I ducked into St. Michael's
before he could intercept me.

You can imagine how I loathe churches. I am at every turn greeted
with the face of Jesus, who I do not particularly wish to see. And,
of course, I cannot forgive the church its blind reverence for God
and its unfounded disdain for me. But on this occasion, the stuffy
air of St. Michael's was preferable to the sour breath of Johan Steinhaeusser.

I walked the long aisle between the pews. A portrait of Mary
overlooked a small shrine. I was particularly struck by the resemblance of this Mary to the real woman I had known. I had seen
many depictions of Mary, but none of them ever came so close to

the real thing as this one. I stood admiring the portrait for some time, recollecting an age long past, when I was startled by the sudden appearance of a figure beside me.

"Beautiful, is she not? I believe it is the most magnificent portrayal of the Virgin Mary I have ever laid my eyes upon. And to think I have just yesterday come into possession of it."

The man who spoke stood no taller than my chest. He was frail and gray and wore the uniform of a pastor. He smiled amiably and shook my hand with both his tiny hands.

"I am Pastor Konstantin," he said in German. "I have just arrived in Hamburg and will be the new pastor of Saint Michael's. Very pleased to meet you. I am sorry if you came to see Pastor Weber; he just left for Berlin this morning. He has taken a position there, and I do not imagine he will have much occasion to return to Hamburg. As I always say, 'If you don't like where you are, then get up and go.' And that's exactly what Pastor Weber did. He up and went. Was it Pastor Weber you came to see?"

"No," I replied. "I saw that construction had begun for a new bell tower, and I came in to see how it was getting along. I have never been inside Saint Michael's before."

"Ah," said Pastor Konstantin. "Then you are not a member of the congregation. I see. Welcome, welcome. I must have sounded quite silly going on about Pastor Weber—I just assumed ... Well, I'm new here, and I have only just seen the inside of Saint Michael's myself. It is a beautiful church, no doubt, and I am very lucky because I hear Hamburg is a very decent sort of place. How do you find it?"

"I daresay it suits me quite well. And I imagine it will be all the better when construction on the bell tower is completed."

"Ah, yes. The bell tower. It has just begun to go up, and already there is sawdust in the pews. It shall be the tallest in Hamburg. One hundred meters. Ships will see it from miles away."

"Certainly," I agreed.

"Oh, but what a racket all the construction will cause. When visitors come to see the church, their eyes will be distracted by all the mess. But I shouldn't mind all that. Vanity is pointless in cases such as these. Let the sawdust rain down on the congregation—so long as the pews are filled, I am quite happy."

At this point in our conversation, I was eager to quit the place, for, however cordial Pastor Konstantin may have been, I did not think it wise to be consorting with a religious man—a pastor. I remembered the noose around my neck, and I was certain that all pastors everywhere would be glad to see me buried alive again.

I was on the verge of taking my leave when Pastor Konstantin said, "You look a strong man. Perhaps you could lend me a hand. A new desk just arrived this morning, and the handlers set it in the wrong corner of my study. I should very much prefer to sit by the window when I work. I like to look out on the street when I compose my sermons. Would it be asking too much to borrow you for a few minutes? I think together we will be able to move it to its proper place."

I assented. Pastor Konstantin led me into the rear of the church, where he kept his private quarters. It was a small apartment off the main church—a kitchen, a study, and a single bedroom. For the most part, it was bare. There were various crates—packed and unpacked—lying about. It was clear that Pastor Konstantin had just arrived and was in a hurry to be situated before Sunday's mass.

Together, we moved the desk from one corner of the study to another. It wasn't so heavy, but tiny Pastor Konstantin struggled with it every inch of the way. When the deed was done, I was given such a flood of unnecessary thanks, that I struggled not to laugh. "It was nothing."

"It was a huge help to me. Quite well done. Quite well done, indeed. Now, I shall be much happier when I write. I thank you more than you can imagine, Mister—" He stopped and looked very puzzled. "Now, I've forgotten your name."

"I never gave it," I said. "I am Henry Morgan." I made up the name on the spot, not wishing to form any lasting relationship with this pious mortal.

"An Englishman!" Pastor Konstantin exclaimed. "But you speak German so very fluently. I should never have guessed." A pause. "Mr. Morgan," he continued. "Might I beg your assistance again—a week from tomorrow? The rest of my furniture is due to arrive from Heidelberg. I do not trust it will be situated entirely to my liking, and I should very much appreciate a set of strong arms to help me move things about. Might you be able to come again? I would be ever so grateful. I have no one else to ask, you see."

It wasn't in me to refuse this pleading old man, so I agreed to return the following Tuesday.

I then took my leave only to realize an hour had passed since I had spotted Johan Steinhaeusser on the street. Never in my life had I spent so much time in a church. But Pastor Konstantin seemed harmless—there had been no mention of God or Jesus, and Mary had only come up as a topic of beauty. I resolved to no longer be afraid of churches, or at least to be no longer afraid of St. Michael's.

✸

I returned there the following Tuesday, and sure enough, all was exactly as Pastor Konstantin had predicted. The furniture was in such disarray that I had to pick my path between chairs and side tables just to reach the study. Pastor Konstantin called from the bedroom. "Herr Morgan, is that you? I do believe I am trapped. I do not know how it happened—the furniture arrived all at once, and I have been stuck back here since the handlers left. Would you be so kind?"

I moved a wardrobe away from the window, and out popped Pastor Konstantin. He smiled to see me and took my hand graciously.

"I wondered what would become of me if you did not come. But I had a feeling you would be true to your word. And sure enough, here you are! Shall we set immediately to work? There is such a lot to be done today."

Two hours we spent arranging and rearranging the furniture to suit Pastor Konstantin's fancy. Every so often, the pastor asked my opinion on the placement of a chair or a lamp, and I spoke my mind freely. The good man's even temper and warm humor put me in good spirits, and the afternoon passed easily away. When all was done, Pastor Konstantin put on a pot of tea and implored that I should stay and have a cup. There was no reason for me to object. I was so desperate for good company myself, and I quite enjoyed the familiar and easy manner of the old man.

We discussed small things over tea: the weather in Hamburg, the booming spice trade, the construction of the bell tower—and never once did he inquire into my personal business. I was grateful. What he suspected of my dealings, I do not know. But he was perfectly natural around me, like a kindly grandfather. I was warmed by his generous spirit, and I promised to return the following Tuesday for tea.

I took my tea with him nearly every Tuesday thereafter. Whenever I was unable to join him, Pastor Konstantin asked no questions. He simply nodded and said, "Next week, then." If he noticed that I did not attend mass on Sundays, he never said anything about it. Our conversations never strayed to talk of God. We kept our exchanges simple and took comfort in the little silences between us.

Pastor Konstantin may have had some suspicions about my line of work, for I let it slip that I was in the trading business—still, he never showed me anything but absolute respect and amiable trust.

Our Tuesdays were pleasantly spent, and the months passed away. When Mephistopheles was in town, I said nothing of Pastor Konstantin. And, of course, I told Pastor Konstantin nothing of Mephistopheles.

One day, while we were taking our tea in the pastor's study, we came to the subject of the bell tower again, which was coming along nicely, but had recently experienced some minor setbacks. In early spring, the construction had been put off for nearly a month due to foul weather, and recently it had been discovered that the costs would be greater than expected, which would further delay construction until the church raised a considerable sum. The work had been abandoned for the present, and what remained was the skeleton of a tower without a proper spire. The whole thing was encased in a jungle of creaky scaffolding that clung precariously to the side of the tower like vines.

In the meantime, the stairwell and some part of the clock had been installed, and a great set of bells for the belfry sat neatly at the back of the church under a tarpaulin. These were all of great curiosity to Pastor Konstantin. He wondered about the stairwell. It was said to be safe to climb, but Pastor Konstantin had not ventured to do so, since he was all alone and did not dare risk getting stranded in the scaffolding.

"Why don't we climb it together," he suggested. "I should feel much more at ease if I were to have a friend with me. I'm sure I would like to see how it looks inside—and the view from the top. Mr. Morgan, how would you like to accompany me up the new tower?"

"I would like that very much." I admit I was curious to see how the construction was coming along. I always did have an interest in architecture, ever since I had invented the arch in Mesopotamia, and

I wanted to see what kinds of modern methods were being employed in the building of this new tower.

We set off at once to scale the tower. The stairwell was a long, winding thing that spun upward into darkness. Pastor Konstantin took some candles from the altar, and together we began our climb.

The stairwell was sturdy, and I was not in the least afraid of its giving way beneath us. But Pastor Konstantin was less confident; he never ceased to exclaim "Oh, dear!" or "Oh, my!" whenever a step would creak. When we had gone some fifty or sixty steps, the world opened up around us. There we were encased in scaffolding, only the frame of the building to protect us, like birds in a cage. The whole of Hamburg was below us. The sun was setting over the horizon, and lamps sparkled throughout the city.

The stairwell wound up for a long time above us, 140 steps all told. So, we climbed in the twilight, and the ground dropped further and further below. I led the way and charged onward, unafraid, while Pastor Konstantin climbed more cautiously. When we would lose sight of each other, he would call up to me, "Herr Morgan?" In answer, I would call back, "Still here."

It was in this way that I reached the observation deck well before he did. It could hardly be called a "deck" at this stage. It was more a crisscross of wooden boards and iron poles. Here, there were no walls, and I could easily step out onto the scaffolding and peer below. It was a 100-meter drop to the cobblestone street.

What surprised me most was that the central bell had already been strung up in the rafters. I suppose this one had gone up before all the others because it weighed two tons and would be impossible to install after the walls were fitted. A cord hung from the great bell. When Pastor Konstantin joined me on the observation deck, we agreed to try the bell together. He stepped back nervously and plugged his ears with his fingers while I yanked hard on the cord.

The bell rang out loudly, and although we were expecting it, we jumped when the gong sounded.

"It appears you have a bell to ring before Sunday services," I said.

"Oh, yes." Pastor Konstantin nodded. "But I daresay I shall never come up here to ring it. I fear it will not get much use until the tower is complete—it is much too dangerous to be wandering around this place alone, and at my age. Why, who's to say a great wind won't come along and blow the whole thing to pieces? Yes, that bell will just have to wait until the tower is absolutely secure."

We remained to enjoy the view for as long as Pastor Konstantin's nerves would permit. Then we descended the tower together. The closer we came to firm ground, the more verbose Pastor Konstantin became.

"That was quite an adventure. Yes, quite an adventure, indeed! To think we stood 100 meters above ground. And with no walls or railings. Only old planks of wood under our feet. I feel quite brave. It was very much what I should think flying feels like, there being no walls and nothing to grab onto. I don't think I have been up that high before. Yes, it was exciting, but I don't think I'll ever have the nerve to do it again. It is fortunate that you agreed to accompany me, or I should never have seen it. Yes, an adventure of grand proportions!"

I found myself giddy as well—there is such a rush that comes from standing at great heights with all of mortality at your feet. One false step and it is ended—for a human at least.

I left Pastor Konstantin in the best of spirits—both of us were quite pleased with ourselves for daring such a feat—and it was determined that I should join him again for tea the following Tuesday.

CHAPTER 34

M EPHISTOPHELES CAME TO TOWN a few weeks later to settle a few affairs with Johan Steinhaeusser, and as was his
custom in those days, he made himself a guest in my house during
his stay. On such occasions, Mephisto slept on the floor, but today
he was making a fuss about it. We had just arrived home from the
pub, where we had had too much to drink.

"You wouldn't have me sleep on the floor again, would you?" he
asked.

He smoothed the cotton sheets on my bed with his pale white
fingers. I did not answer.

"Eh, Lucifer?"

"Don't call me Lucifer," I mumbled.

I went to the liquor cabinet and poured myself a whiskey.

"Aren't you going to ask me what I'd like to drink?" Mephisto
begged.

I fumbled with the bottle and splashed whiskey down the front
of my tunic. I went to the kitchen, took a rag from the wash bin, and
dabbed the wet spots on my shirt.

"Vodka," he called after me. "With a splash of orange juice."

"I don't have orange juice," I said.

"Then just make me whatever you're having," Mephisto said with a shrug.

I poured him a whiskey and shoved the glass into his hand. He took a sip and grinned.

"Lucifer, are you trying to get me drunk?"

"You're already drunk."

Mephisto took another swig of whiskey and shuddered. I was sitting across from him in a chair. He motioned that I should join him on the bed. I shook my head no. He patted the mattress invitingly and smiled mischievously.

"I'll stay right where I am," I said.

"Suit yourself," he said. "More bed for me."

He stretched himself out across the full length of the mattress and made a point of reminding me that if I didn't join him on the bed, I'd be sleeping on the floor. I changed the subject.

"How's business back in Hölle?" I asked.

"Oh, you know. The same." Mephisto sounded irritated.

"How are sales?" I continued.

"Come now, Lucifer. You're no fun at all. I don't want to talk about business."

"Then why did you come all the way up here?" I growled.

Mephisto downed the last of his whiskey and set the glass on the floor.

"Oh, you know," he said. He made room on the bed and raised his eyebrows at me. "I missed you, that's all."

"You know I don't feel that way about you."

"Anymore," Mephisto finished.

"It was a long time ago that we lay under the Tree of Knowledge," I said. "We are not the people we were then."

Mephisto snorted. "Must you always be so rational? You never just let things happen. You're thinking too much about it. Why don't you just lie down next to me? Just lie next to me. That's all. Nothing funny."

"No, Mephisto."

"You've hardly touched your whiskey. You need to drink up, Lucifer. Pour me another, will you?"

I poured the second glass all the way up to the brim. Mephisto drank it greedily.

"You were always such a thinker," Mephisto rambled on. "Always figuring, analyzing, wondering. You never let go. Never really."

"Mephisto, we've had this discussion a hundred times before."

I couldn't bring myself to look at him. Instead, I fixed him a third whiskey.

Mephisto sat up as I handed him the drink. His face was red and hot. He grabbed my wrists. His hands were clammy and cold.

"Do you not find me attractive?" he asked.

"Don't do this right now," I said. "You're drunk."

I pried his fingers loose and shoved the whiskey into his hands. He drank it absentmindedly. His eyes were on the floor.

"Once I had your admiration," he mumbled. "Once, so very, very long ago. You came to me every day under the tree. Never once did you forget. And I pretended to be indifferent. I pretended I did not notice you. But I've loved you ever since that first day you found me there. And sometimes when you thought I was asleep, I was really just lying there thinking of you. Did you know that, Lucifer? I knew you were drawing me while you thought I was sleeping. You adored me."

"I was young, then," I said. "You took advantage of me."

Mephistopheles raised his head. His eyes were icy blue.

"God damn you!" he cried. He splashed the rest of his drink all over the front of his trousers. The glass fell out of his hands and rolled across the floor until it hit the toe of my boot. Mephistopheles threw his arms up in the air and then buried his face in my pillow. There he sniveled and sobbed until he fell asleep.

I took the glasses to the kitchen. I had hardly touched my drink. I poured the remains into a basin and rinsed out the glasses with soap and water. I tidied up the rest of the flat until I could feel my eyelids becoming heavy. Then I went over and nudged Mephistopheles.

"Alright, out," I said.

Mephistopheles was too drunk to protest. He rolled onto the floor. I gave him a blanket and a pillow. He curled up like a child next to the hearth and fell quickly into a deep slumber.

It must have been four in the morning. The fire was dying, and the apartment was cold. I crawled into bed and pulled the covers up over my head. I could hear Pastor Konstantin's voice in my dreams. *If you don't like where you are, then get up and go.*

⬡

It could only have been a few hours before the noise of traffic on the street woke me from a fitful sleep. I rose quietly and tiptoed around Mephistopheles's prostrate body. He was passed out hugging his knees and drooling all over my pillow. In the daylight he looked harmless—like a child.

I left him lying on the floor and went down to the docks to oversee an incoming shipment. It was a frosty, clear morning. There were icy white patches on the roofs of houses. Spots of blue rime coated the leaves and branches of the trees.

I was just turning onto Hyde Row when I beheld a sight that stopped me dead in my tracks.

All along the wharf, ships that had arrived overnight were unloading their freight. At the very end of the wharf there was a sharp-looking two-mast schooner. The deckhands had just harnessed the boat to the pier, and a steady stream of elegantly dressed passengers flowed down a ramp onto the dock. In the midst of the din, I perceived a face that struck me as very familiar. I had to squint to see. It was then that I recognized Olivia Bartlett.

At first, I told myself that I must be mistaken, that Olivia was long dead, and this woman was just some stranger that happened to look very much like Olivia. But moments later I saw something that vanquished every doubt. At the foot of the loading ramp stood Dr. Charles Bartlett. He was directing the transport of a very large cage on wheels. Four or five deckhands were handling the cage with great care. It was only once the cage had landed safely on the dock, after the deckhands had disbursed, that I could see what it contained. Reaching through the bars like the fingers of a great octopus were the branches of a Magpie Tree.

By the time I realized the full magnitude of the situation, Olivia and her father were already advancing down the wharf in my direction. I turned on my heel and bolted down Hyde Row. Just as I thought I had made my escape, I ran directly into Johan Steinhaeusser.

"Where are you headed in such a hurry?" he scoffed.

"I have an urgent appointment, and I'm very late."

He grabbed my forearm violently. "If you think you're going to run off before I get my money, then you've got another thing coming."

I glanced over my shoulder. Olivia and her father were not far behind and advancing rapidly.

"It will have to wait until next week," I muttered.

Johan yanked me so close I could smell the whiskey on his breath. "What are you playing at, Heinz?"

I could hear Olivia's voice now.

"I don't see why we have to cart that thing around, Father. People will stare."

I kept my back toward them and fumbled about in my jacket for my pocketbook. They were so close now that I doubted I would remain unnoticed.

"What do I care if people stare?" Dr. Bartlett grumbled. "People are always going to stare. What they think has nothing to do with me."

"Yes, Father," Olivia said sullenly. She was so near that it sounded as if she were talking directly into my ear. I caught a whiff of her old perfume, and I couldn't resist getting a quick look at her. I glanced briefly over my shoulder.

She happened to turn toward me at the very same moment. I gulped. When she saw me, her face went white. Her eyes rolled back in her head, and she collapsed against a barrel. Several men that were working along the dock rushed to Olivia's aide. Dr. Bartlett's attention was entirely on Olivia. He hadn't seen me. He jabbed his walking stick on the wooden planks of the pier and cried out orders to the passersby.

"Stand back," he commanded. "Give her air. She needs space."

I quickly pulled a handful of notes from my pocketbook and shoved them into Johan's hands.

"That should be enough," I said.

"Don't you want to check the condition of the freight?" he asked.

"No. Just take the money."

A crowd had gathered around Olivia, and I used the opportunity to slip unseen down a side alley. I ran all the way to my flat. I could think of nothing but Olivia. And for the first time since I had been pulled from the grave, I felt alive.

⬤

My first business after the incident at the harbor was with Mephistopheles. I stormed into the flat, making as much noise as I could manage, hoping to wake him. He was exactly as I had left him: curled in a fetal position on the floor, drool running down his chin. I pressed the toe of my boot into his ribcage and gave a push. He started angrily and moaned.

"Get up," I ordered.

"What's wrong?" He rolled onto his hands and knees and coughed onto the floor. I gave him another jab with my boot.

"Get up and face me, you coward," I said.

"Lucifer, what has gotten into you?"

"You told me she was dead," I hissed.

Mephistopheles clambered to his feet. He was unsteady and had to prop himself against the bedpost. He wiped the long blond hair out of his face and stared at me with his cobalt eyes.

"What are you talking about?" he hissed.

I walked right up to him. My face was so close to his that I could feel his putrid breath on my skin.

"You told me Olivia Bartlett died of the plague." Spit issued from my mouth like gunfire.

Mephistopheles wiped his face and sneered. "And you believed me. You always were gullible."

"Why would you do that?" I asked. "Why would you lie to me?"

Mephistopheles pushed past me and crossed to the kitchen. He took a glass from the cabinet and filled it with water from the large pitcher. After he drank half the glass, he splashed the rest on his face.

"Because," he said.

"Because what?"

"Because you wouldn't have come with me otherwise," he burst. "Because there was no other way for me to be with you. You would never have agreed to come to Das Drachenlager if you had known she was still alive."

He was shaking now. His face was so pale I could see the green and blue veins in his temples.

He slammed the glass down and said, "I've spent the last two thousand years looking for you. I searched all over the world. I went to Asia, Africa, even to the Americas. Every time I caught some hint of your trail, it faded into nothingness. I talked to hundreds of people who had known you once. And it always came to nothing. You were so good at covering your tracks, so good at hiding. I was always a few years too late. Then you were condemned and buried, and you couldn't run anymore. I finally caught up with you."

The morning light streaming through the window shone on his face, and he had to squint to see me.

"Do you really think I was going to let some mortal girl take you away from me?" he asked. "When I dug you up, you were so weak and helpless. You needed me."

"You can't keep me to yourself," I said. "Olivia is here. In town. I saw her this morning."

Mephistopheles let out an embittered laugh. "Aren't you forgetting her father?" he asked. "If he finds out you're back—I don't even want to think about the kind of torture he'll subject you to next."

"Get out," I said. "Get out of here. You are the lowest of angels. And most unworthy of men. Why God made you, I'll never know."

Mephistopheles lunged at me, and I thought for a moment he was going to strike. But he simply fell to his knees and threw his arms around my legs.

"Don't leave me," he said. "You are the only person I have ever loved."

"Don't touch me!" I pushed him away. "Get out of my sight! You have never been a friend to me."

Mephistopheles stood. His body sagged and swayed. I turned him around by the shoulders and led him to the door. He clutched onto my arm and wailed. It was a sorry scene but there was not an ounce of pity left for him in my heart. I shoved him out the door and slammed it shut in his face.

I did not know what Mephistopheles would do next. He could throw himself off a bridge, he could cut his wrists for all I cared, but unfortunately, he would never die.

Two days later, I received a letter from him. He was back at Das Drachenlager. The letter was purely business. Not a hint of what had passed between us appeared in his message.

> *Thieves looted the inn while I was away. Fortunately, nothing of value was taken. Only fourteen marks from the bar and a few casks of our finest wine. In other news, a large shipment arrived today. The crates were in bad condition and nearly a quarter of the goods were spoiled. Expecting an account of the inventory by next Wednesday and a summary of expenses by the end of the month.*

CHAPTER 35

I T WASN'T HARD TO find out where Olivia and her father were staying. Dr. Bartlett was a renowned physician; naturally, many people knew his address. It only took a few inquiries at the local tavern to glean that the doctor and his daughter had taken a house on Düsternstrasse, not far from St. Michael's Church.

I wondered if Olivia still loved me. Or had she come to her senses—had she cast all feelings for me aside, as any woman in her right mind would have done after all that we had been through. After all, Olivia now knew I was the Devil—or perhaps some other demon in service of the Devil—I wasn't quite sure what she believed. I suspected she had never read my letter in full, since her father had turned it over to the magistrate as evidence of my wickedness. Therefore, she had never heard my side of the story. All she knew was what her father had told her. And if I knew anything about her father, I knew he would have done and said all in his power to poison her against me.

But now she knew I was alive—she had seen me with her own two eyes down at the docks. What she would do with that information,

I did not know. How she felt seeing me all these years later, I could not tell. Whether she wanted anything more to do with me, I could only guess. But I knew I had to find out. I had to see Olivia one more time, to speak to her, to explain myself. I had to find out whether there was any love left in her heart for me.

It was late November, and the opium trade consumed my life. My days were occupied managing shipments in and out of Hamburg. There were hardly enough daylight hours to visit all the warehouses, pay all the distributors, and update the inventory. That Tuesday I sent word to Pastor Konstantin that I would have to skip our regular teatime. I was determined to visit the house on Düsternstrasse to get a glimpse of my beloved Olivia.

It was easy to conceal my face since it was so cold. I wrapped my nose and chin in a thick scarf and pulled the hood of my cloak low over my eyes. A light snow fell outside, but the temperature had not dropped enough for the snow to stick, so the city was a labyrinth of muddy puddles and slippery cobblestones. I pulled on heavy boots and set out in the direction of Düsternstrasse around midday, when a short break in the snowfall made it easier to navigate the streets. There were coaches in the lane for hire, but I chose to walk the short distance between my flat and the house on Düsternstrasse so as not to attract too much attention. I feared Dr. Bartlett would notice a coach pulling up in front of his house, and since only fine gentlemen had the means to hire coaches in the winter, it would likely cause a stir.

Although I was well-disguised, I didn't want to be caught loitering in front of the doctor's house. I crossed the street and strode briskly along as though I had some important business in the direction of Herrengraben. The snow began to fall again, heavier now. Just as I was passing opposite the house on Düsternstrasse, the front door opened, and a woman stepped into the swirling snow. She carried a covered basket and wore a long green cape and hood. It was unmistakably my Olivia, and to my great relief, she was alone.

She hurried down the lane toward Herrengraben. The snow was coming down in thick sheets now, and Olivia was moving quickly, as if dogs were nipping at her heels. I hailed a coach and directed the driver to catch up with the lady in the green cape. When finally the coach pulled up beside Olivia, I threw back my hood and parted the carriage curtains.

"Olivia!" I called.

She stopped midstride and turned, startled.

"Olivia! Get in!"

She stared at me in utter astonishment. I swung the carriage door open and held out my hand. Olivia stood frozen like an ice sculpture. Then, to my great surprise, she took my hand and stepped onto the runner. I quickly pulled her inside and closed the carriage door.

"Where to?" cried the driver in German.

I looked at Olivia questioningly.

"Hullstrasse," she said. "Number eighteen."

The coach lurched into motion, and Olivia was pitched into my arms. There she stayed, her face pressed into my collar. We rode in silence for some time, my arms wrapped around her shoulders, her breath ragged and warm against my chest. I watched as the little flakes of snow on her cape dissolved and disappeared.

When at last she spoke, her voice was soft and low. "Father said you were dead."

"Yes," I replied. "I promise to explain."

Olivia sat back. Her face was wet with tears. "What took you so long to find me?"

"I thought the plague had taken you," I said. "It was mere chance that our paths crossed all these years later in this foreign place."

"I have been the wretchedest of creatures these eight years without you," she whispered. "Father has kept me under lock and key. He only lets me out of the house to make calls on patients when he is too busy to go himself."

Just then, the carriage pulled up in front of number eighteen Hullstrasse. We were pressed for time. I needed to take action now. Clasping Olivia's hands in my own, I begged, "Will you run away with me?"

Olivia didn't even bat an eye. "Yes."

In that moment, I felt as though I could walk through fire. Every part of me seemed to awaken to a new purpose.

"Then we must find another time to talk in private—to plan."

"My father is unpredictable." Olivia shook her head. "I cannot say when I shall be permitted to leave the house unsupervised again."

"Tell him you are going to confess."

"Confess?"

"Yes," I said. "Tell him you have decided to ask God for forgiveness."

"Father will want to come with me," she said. Then, upon reflection, she added, "I will put something in his tea."

Olivia pulled back the cover of her basket to reveal a collection of herbs and potions. She removed a bottle of clear liquid and held it up to the light. Scribbled on the bottle in black ink were the words *oleum dulce vitrioli*—sweet oil of vitriol.

"It should put him to sleep for a few hours," she said.

"Good," I said. "In three weeks' time, you must meet me at Saint Michael's Church. That will give me time to work out the necessary arrangements."

Olivia looked anxiously over her shoulder. "Herr Schneider is expecting me."

"I will wait for you in the belfry at Saint Michael's," I said, kissing her soft cheek. "Midday."

When she stepped out of the carriage, a part of my heart went with her. But there was another feeling, too. A feeling of hope. For the first time in many years, I was alive.

✹

I wrote Mephistopheles to say I needed a holiday, that I would return in time for Christmas. I would leave instructions for Berith, Raum, and Focalor. They would manage shipping, warehousing, and inventory while I was gone.

I didn't wait for a reply.

I also sent word to Pastor Konstantin to beg forgiveness for my prolonged absence, but not to worry about my welfare, for I was on holiday. Then I penned a quick letter to Jacques Bezier at his estate in Bristol. I told him to expect a visit from an old friend, that I had a favor to ask. I signed my erstwhile name, "Thomas Ellsworth." The letter was posted straightaway. The next day, I booked passage to London on the *Mariner*.

I spent three miserable days at sea. It was another day by coach to Eddingfield, where I finally planned to collect on the Devil's bargain I had made so long ago.

CHAPTER 36

THE HOME OF SIR Jacques Bezier was a large, stately thing overlooking the River Severn from atop a great hill in the countryside just outside of Bristol. The carriage brought me up the long drive, past great rows of ferns and elm. Deer roamed the grounds and grazed in the snow-laden meadows. I bumped along in the carriage with curtains drawn wide open and breathed in the scent of pines and wet earth.

You can only imagine my surprise when I first beheld the Bezier estate. Jacques Bezier had been penniless, pathetic, and poor when he arrived on my doorstep some eight years ago. He had barely been able to hold a job as a lowly crewman on the *Miranda*. Now, he was the proud owner of England's most profitable shipping company and the lord of an inestimable manor.

The carriage pulled up in front of the house, and the footman helped me out. I was grudgingly received by a manservant with a lazy eye—the sort of fellow that gives the impression of being eternally unhappy. He growled as he said, "This way," and he ushered me through a set of doors and down a long hall to a blue velvet sitting room.

"Sir Bezier will be with you presently," he said, and left me standing alone. The blue chamber was extravagantly ornate. Only a man who had once had nothing and now had everything would decorate a room in such excess. I marveled at the draperies and rugs. There were oil paintings and statues and busts. Artifacts of every origin—flatware from the Far East, ceramic jugs from Egypt, Spanish gold—lay scattered about the room without respect for taste or style. I paced the perimeter of the room and fingered the trinkets. There was an old sea compass and a beaten ship log—both worn and weather-stained. I was just gazing through a long, wooden periscope when the door opened again and in walked the lazy-eyed manservant and his master.

"Milord!" cried Jacques Bezier. "You look a right seafaring man. I will have your portrait drawn, and you shall wear a captain's hat and hold the periscope as you have just done. Then perhaps you will pass for a man of the sea, and I will give you a ship of your own."

We shook hands vigorously.

"Jacques, you scoundrel. Knighted! Sir, I would never have believed it, not in all my life. But here you are! Look at you."

"Yes, milord. You lived up to your part of the bargain. I have been around the world and have brought His Majesty treasures from every corner of the Earth. Spices from India, gold from the Americas, ivory from Africa. I have sailed the seven seas, and moreover, I have sailed back again."

"Have you?" I exclaimed. "Then you have seen more than I—I must admit—for I was never much disposed to sailing."

"Weak in the knees, ay? Can't handle the motion of the sea? Well, many a great man, sturdy and strong as he may be on land, hangs his head overboard when the ship starts swaying. Why, King Charles is known to get a little seasick from time to time."

At that very moment, the manservant reentered the parlor with the tea. He laid it out on a low table, and I was obliged to sit and enjoy "some of the finest tea in all the Empire." Jacques dumped several spoonfuls of sugar into his cup and added enough cream to turn the tea milky white. He had grown more robust since I had last seen him. His once famished frame was now ripe and plump with all the excesses of good living.

"When your letter came, I was delighted," he said. Tea dripped down his moustache onto his chin. "I hadn't heard from you in eight years, and I thought you'd returned to the fiery depths from whence you came. A journey to the East Indies and then to the Americas took me away from London for six years. And when I returned, you were vanished. I thought it no wonder since the plague had chased away many of my former acquaintances, and those who had not been scared away by disease were made homeless by the Great Fire. I inquired after you but found very troubling and contradictory reports. Some said you'd been run out of town. Others said you was dead and buried. I could not discern truth from commonplace gossip. I searched in vain until at last I found record of your death. It said you was charged with heresy and witchcraft and executed on

April 15, 1661. I went to the place where you'd been buried and found the grave open and the coffin empty. It was all a great mystery to me. From there, I could find nothing more. After many months I gave up the search in vain. Now, my Lord! Pray tell me all what happened. And omit nothing, for I am desperate to know the truth once and for all!"

I explained the strange circumstances of my trial and execution, from Olivia to Dr. Bartlett to the Magpie Tree to the noose around my neck. Then me waking up in the darkness of a funerary box. To the best of my abilities, I described the agony I experienced those four long years in the grave. The recollection and recitation of the facts caused me a great deal of heartache, and I paused many times during the telling of my story to steady my voice.

When I came to the part where Mephistopheles rescued me from the grave, Jacques interjected, "Ah, had I only come sooner, I might have been the first to find you buried there. And I would have lifted you out of your misery and taken you here to Eddingfield where you could be looked after properly. I envy Mephistopheles the chance of rendering you such a noble service."

"Had it only been you instead of Mephistopheles," I growled. I could not mask the fury in my voice. Jacques leaned forward intently as if to encourage me to go on.

So, I told him everything, beginning with the disheartening report of Olivia's death. I described my years of solitude at the inn and how I finally came out of my stupor to get in on the opium trade, which, subsequently, made me very rich.

"But all the money in the world hasn't made me happy," I finished. "I am just as miserable as ever because I have no friends to speak of, no love, and I am financially bound to a man I loathe."

Here Jacques erupted with, "If I had known, I would have offered all the services a man can give. I am indebted to you. There is nothing I have which you cannot rightly claim as your own—nothing I couldn't spare."

I gave Jacques my most sincere thanks and assured him he did not owe me anything—that he had made an honest living for himself.

"Bah!" he laughed. "If you call pillaging and plundering honest. Most of my fortune is the spoils of colonization. Do not call me honest. I loathe the word."

Just then, we were interrupted by a startled cry. I turned toward the parlor door just in time to see Elizabeth Squires come flying into the room, arms spread open, with the broadest and sincerest of smiles. I was startled and amazed to see her, and it took me some time to regain my composure. I stood to greet her, and she dropped to the floor and hugged my knees.

"It is you!" she exclaimed. "I thought the letter were written in your hand, but I was 'fraid it were a trick, see. I warned Master Bezier. I said, 'It could be the magistrate come to collect on account of us sellin' our souls.' But Master Bezier, he said he owed you his life, and he were willing to take the risk. And here you are!"

She hugged my legs harder and pressed her cheek against my trousers. She was crying and her tears made dark stains on my pant legs.

SATAN'S DIARY

I was struck with such sudden sentiment that I began to weep. To be surrounded by such unlikely and unexpected family after being so long alone—it was more than my calloused heart could bear. I was all rapture and excitement.

"How is this possible?" I cried. "Two of my old comrades in the same house!"

Jacques explained. "After I left your empty grave in London, I returned to Bristol where I manage a shipyard. It was there that Squires hunted me down." "I was all aflutter when I saw Master Bezier," Squires interjected. "I thought I'd found 'im at last, but he was turned such a fine gentleman that he hardly matched your description."

"My description?" I asked.

"Oh!" said Squires. "I've forgotten an important detail! I paid a scribe to read your diaries, you see, after you disappeared, hoping to find a clue to your whereabouts. Besides for Miss Olivia, sir, I didn't know who else to turn to. So, when the scribe got to the part about Master Bezier, a man from London who sold 'is soul like me, I said to meself, 'Squires, keep a lookout for that fellow.'"

"And she did," finished Bezier.

"Cost me a pretty penny to 'ave all them pages read," said Squires. "Scribe said he didn't do no Devil's work, so it cost me double, it did."

"I was at the fish market in Bristol when she found me," Jacques went on. "She introduced herself as the woman who had kept

309

milord's house in London. I thought it most urgent that we should speak to learn what'd become of you."

"Master Bezier weren't hard to find," Squires said proudly. "His name was on every ship in Bristol 'arbor."

"And so it was that you two were acquainted," I finished.

"Yes! Yes!" cried Squires. "And now you have come back to us. What a joyous day!"

"But pray tell me, Squires," I said. "What on earth were you doing in Bristol? And what became of my diaries?"

"Oh, sir," Squires said. "Has Master Bezier not told you?" Squires flushed with anxious excitement. "It broke my heart to leave London, sir. I protested, I did, and begged Master Wellington"—here she was referring to Belial—"to wait just another quarter of an hour. But he was so fierce with me and bid me to get into the carriage at once. I grabbed everything I thought you might need, all your diaries, seeing as all you ever did were write in 'em, and left that house forever. I am so sorry, sir, but we could not wait for you a moment longer."

"I don't follow you, Squires," I said. "Why did you leave with Mr. Wellington? You will have to start at the very beginning."

"Oh, yes, of course," Squires said. She smoothed her apron with the backs of her hands and brushed a strand of wavy red hair behind her ear. "It was April 15 back in the year 1661. I was at the house as usual. You'd gone off to see that horrid man who accosted me in Paris. I had just finished polishing the silver when the clock on the mantle chimed the five o'clock hour. It was at that very moment that

Master Wellington burst into the house in a sweat. Pale as a ghost, he was. I never saw him look so ill. I begged him to sit, but he wouldn't hear of it. He had just come from the Rooster where he had received a very distressing report from one of the local drunks.

"'They're coming to crucify us,' he says to me. 'Somebody's ratted us out and now they'll be after us with torches and pitchforks.' 'A witch hunt,' he called it. I grew very faint and shook all over, for I knew I was a Devil's minion. But Master Wellington steadied me with his hand and said, 'Pack your trunk, Squires. I have ordered a carriage to convey us to Bristol. It waits just outside.'

"'But what of Master Thomas?' I asked. We agreed we must wait until your return. I was sure you would be back before supper. But when you did not come, Master Wellington grew very restless. He said that it were only a matter of time. If we did not leave straightaway, it would be too late. They were coming with torches to burn down the house and kill us both.

"I'm so sorry, Master Thomas, but we couldn't wait any longer. The mob could be heard all the way from Charterhouse Yard. It was only moments after midnight that we was seated safely in the carriage and all sounds were drowned out by the galloping 'orses. It is no doubt we would have been dead if we had waited even five minutes longer, for looking back we could see flames and smoke rising from the 'ouse."

"I am glad that Wellington had the good sense to have a carriage ready," I said. "You are very lucky, indeed. But do not let me interrupt you. Please, Squires, tell what happened next."

"We arrived in Bristol early next morning. Neither of us had slept, and we were sick with weariness and grief. Master Wellington found us lodgings at a dodgy inn. I was afraid to be alone, and so Master Wellington, the kind sir, he sat with me until I fell asleep. When I awoke that evening, he was gone. He had left no trace save an envelope containing a large sum of money and a brief note."

Here Squires produced a worn piece of yellow parchment from the drawer of a bureau.

"You'll have to read it for me," she said, handing me the note. "Seeing as I can't read none."

"'Dear Ms. Squires, I am grieved to be leaving you now in the midst of all that has happened. But it must be so. I have left you £500, which should be sufficient money to sustain a modest but comfortable living for some years. Yours, Myles Wellington.'"

"Right!" said Squires excitedly. "I never seen so much money in all me life. I settled down right there in Bristol, same inn and everything. Then one day out on the 'arbor I see them ships. I don't read none, but I 'eard someone say them were Bezier's ships, and so I went to find 'im."

"We traded tales," said Bezier. "But couldn't get any closer to finding you."

"But Master Bezier is such a gentleman. He says, 'Eliza,' for that's wot he calls me. He says, 'Eliza, we are both indebted to Mr. Ellsworth, so why don't you come on and join the staff at me estate?'"

"So, you did," I said.

"Best job I ever 'ad—except, of course, working for you, Master Ellsworth."

One thing was still on my mind. "Where are my diaries?"

"Oh, them," said Squires. "They're put away upstairs with a few of your things. Would you like me to fetch them for you?"

"No, no," I said. "Please don't bother. If you don't mind, Jacques, I would like to leave my diaries in your care for now. They are precious to me, and I do believe they are safer here at Eddingfield than anywhere else."

"Anything for milord."

"That brings me to my purpose," I said. "I have come with a very special request."

"I am at your service, now until I die," said Bezier. "I'm sure Eliza feels much the same."

"Yes, rightly I do," said Squires.

I cleared my throat. "I need a ship."

CHAPTER 37

I STAYED ON AT Eddingfield a few days more to make all the necessary arrangements with Bezier. He took me down to the docks to see the ship he had chosen for me. The vessel was a seventy-seven-foot schooner called the *Reaper*, his very best. Despite my protestations, Bezier volunteered to come out of retirement to captain the ship—"Anything for milord." But he needed time to settle his affairs at Eddingfield, so he urged me to go on ahead to Hamburg, where I was to rendezvous with Olivia. Bezier would follow a week later and arrive in the Port of Hamburg by Christmas Eve.

"Sooner, if the conditions are fair," he promised.

I told him to send word when he docked and gave him my address. Then I bid farewell to the old goat and retraced my steps back to Hamburg.

On the third Tuesday after my first encounter with Olivia, I made my way to St. Michael's Church. I was happier than I had been in ages, and I felt as though nothing could dampen my spirits. But before I reached the church, Johan Steinhaeusser caught up with me to complain of Focalor's handling of the most recent shipment. Apparently, Focalor—who went by Meiers in those days—had not reserved enough space in the warehouses to store the entire shipment and was demanding that Johan keep the extra forty-seven crates aboard his ship until space cleared up.

"Meiers is an imbecile," complained Johan. "Does he think ships sit around in port all day and have nothing else to do? I swear, I will have the crew throw all forty-seven crates overboard if they are not removed tonight."

"I'll see to it," I said. My mind was elsewhere, on Olivia, getting to Olivia, seeing Olivia.

"What will you do about Meiers?" Johan demanded.

"I'll talk to him."

Johan slouched off looking like I hadn't quite given him the response he was looking for. Perhaps he was hoping I would share in his rage—and in another time I would have—but I couldn't help but feel as if the whole business of shipping and storing opium weren't my problem anymore. I had to remind myself to stay engaged in the trade, at least until Bezier arrived, or else somebody might start to suspect I was up to something and call in Mephistopheles.

It was nearly noon when I arrived at the church. I knew that Pastor Konstantin would be in the confessional box administering penance, as he was from ten to two every weekday, and I wanted to avoid him. Avoid any questions. As I slipped past the confessional booth and heard the low murmur of voices beyond the curtain, I felt some remorse at the thought of leaving Pastor Konstantin so precipitously. But what could I do? Tell him I was Satan on the run? No. I kept my head down and wound my way around the pews to the bell tower off the west end of the nave.

Construction on the steeple was nearly finished. Still, it was encased in treacherous scaffolding that shuddered and swayed with every breath of wind, and the guardrails had yet to be installed in the belfry. Otherwise, it proved to be quite complete.

When I reached the top of the tower, the world opened up. Hamburg lay plainly exposed in every direction. The weather had been fair of late, but little patches of fallen snow had accumulated in the shade of the four support pillars. The air was frigid at this altitude, but the belfry seemed like the only place in the church that could offer any privacy given Pastor Konstantin's fear of heights.

The views from here were spectacular. To the south lay the River Elbe and the port. The tall masts of the ships collectively looked like a vast forest of barren trees stretching across the water. The spires of St. Nicholas, St. Peter, St. James, and the Duomo pierced the sky in the east. The north and west were mostly undeveloped landscapes speckled with smallholdings and cattle farms. Hamburg had never looked so beautiful. I wondered if I would miss it after I was gone.

"Thomas?"

I nearly jumped out of my skin at the sound of Olivia's voice. She emerged from the stairwell, sweat beading on her forehead. She wore the same green cape as before. I didn't remember the cape from our time in London. But a lot of things had happened in the intervening years; we had so much to tell one another. I was bursting with things I wanted to say.

Once I recovered from the surprise, I pulled Olivia into a long embrace. She melted into my arms, and we stood holding each other with the icy wind gusting all about us. Olivia's body felt warm and safe. We could have been standing at the South Pole, and I would have felt warm with her at my side.

When we finally came apart, she said, "I've imagined this moment many times. But never did I truly think it would come to pass."

"So, you still love me?" I asked.

"I've never stopped loving you."

"But ... don't you know what I am?"

"Your letter was printed in the papers. I know the whole story."

"And you are not afraid?"

"I do not know how I feel. At first, I was angry. I wanted nothing more to do with you. But as the years went on, I found my thoughts returning to you time and time again. Even if you are who you say you are, you are the person I fell in love with."

"It will not be easy to share a life with me."

"It would be harder without you."

I embraced Olivia again, this time lifting her off the ground. When I set her back on her feet, she spoke hurriedly. "We must be quick. Father is asleep, and I don't know how long the effects of the tonic will last."

"Soon we will have all the time in the world."

"Yes," she said. "Now, tell me. Where are we going that my father will not be able to track us down?"

"America."

"America?"

"We will start over. In the colonies."

"But my papers," Olivia said. "Any passenger ship will need to see my papers. There will be a record. My father has spies everywhere. He will find us, even in America."

"That's why I have arranged for a private vessel to take us there. We can cast ashore anywhere we please. No one will know where we've landed. It will be as if we vanished."

"Do you know how to sail?"

"No," I said. "But I have hired a captain that is very discreet."

"I don't trust anyone. My father will pay any sum to find me."

"You can trust this man," I said. "He is independently wealthy and greatly indebted to me."

"What'll we do about money?"

"I have money."

"Do you know anyone in the colonies?"

"No."

Olivia thought for a moment. "Nor do I."

"We shall be free to do as we please."

Olivia furrowed her brow as if trying to root out some small detail I had overlooked.

"I will have to leave all my things behind," she said finally.

"I will buy you new things."

"What excuse will I give? Father will not readily let me leave the house unchaperoned."

"The *Reaper* will arrive by Christmas Eve. You will say you wish to attend the midnight mass at Saint Michael's, and we will meet here in the belfry. Then we will go together to the port and set sail that very night."

"What if Father wants to attend mass as well?"

"Put some tonic in his tea," I said. "He will sleep right through it."

Olivia nodded and then smiled softly. "You have thought of everything."

I stayed in the tower until I could see the small speck that was Olivia making her way down Krayenkamp toward Düsternstrasse. Then I descended the stairs two steps at a time, feeling like I could fly. When I entered the nave, I took caution not to run into Pastor Konstantin. But he was still in the confessional booth. A woman was just leaving. I quickly made my way past the pews to the church doors. But then something stopped me.

Pastor Konstantin had been a friend. My only friend. I owed him at least an explanation. I needn't tell him where I was going, but I felt the urge to be honest.

I turned and considered my options carefully. Then I traced my way back to the confessional and slipped into the shriving pew.

319

"My dear Pastor," I said. "I have a confession."

"Proceed."

Pastor Konstantin was a blur behind the screen. I wondered if he recognized my voice. Could he see my face? I was struck by how much I felt I needed to say to this man.

"I am running away," I said. "I am leaving everything and everyone I know behind."

"Go on." Pastor Konstantin's voice was gentle.

"I am running away with a woman. A woman whom I love. But I am leaving a dear friend without saying goodbye."

Pastor Konstantin said nothing.

My eyes welled with tears. I was struck by how much emotion I felt.

"I must depart in secret. No one can know where I am going, for there is a man who would have me killed if he knew where to find me."

"I see," said Pastor Konstantin.

"So, I must leave my friend without warning—for his own protection. But I am eternally grateful for his friendship."

Pastor Konstantin paused. "I am sure he is eternally grateful for yours as well."

I smiled and wiped the tears from my eyes.

Pastor Konstantin continued. "Dost thou believe that my forgiveness is God's forgiveness?"

I cringed at the sound of God's name, but for the sake of simplicity, I said, "Yes."

"As thou believest, so be it done unto thee. And by the command of our Lord Jesus Christ, I forgive thee thy sins, in the name of the Father and of the Son and of the Holy Spirit. Amen."

The mention of Jesus made my blood go cold. But I said what was expected of me, perhaps for the first time in my long life.

"Amen."

"Go in peace," said Pastor Konstantin.

CHAPTER 38

O N THE MORNING OF Christmas Eve, I was full of anticipation. My stomach was in knots; I had not felt so alive,
so human, in a very long time. The anxious feeling was not always
pleasant, but it was a *feeling*, which I desperately craved after so
many years living like the walking dead.

I packed several trunks with the things I would need in the New
World: clothes, jewelry, my most recent journals, and some of the
finer things I had collected over the past few years. I lined my coat
with paper notes that would pass for currency in the New World,
and I weighted the pockets with Spanish dollars, which I heard were
popular in America. I had to be judicious about what I chose to take
on my person: a dram of red wine, a dagger, and a small box of madak
tucked away in a satchel. The rest of the supplies that we would need
to survive the journey to America were already aboard the ship.

I set the luggage by the door and hung my coat and satchel on
the rack. At noon, I received a note from Bezier via courier that the
Reaper had docked in the Port of Hamburg the previous evening.
Thank god the ship made it safely to harbor—and on time, I thought;

I was more than a little relieved. I sent the trunks ahead with the courier and spent the rest of the afternoon pacing up and down my apartment floor, trying to think of anything I might have missed.

Midnight was such a long way off. I had my supper at four: leftover pheasant roasted with saffron followed by gouda cheese and sliced apple. I drank more red wine than I could stomach out of sheer nervousness and vomited in my chamber pot. My head was spinning when somebody rapped loudly on my door. At first, I thought I was hearing things, but then the rapping came again.

It was half past ten, and I was not expecting anyone. I panicked and immediately convinced myself that the courier had returned with bad news: the weather was too foul to set sail or perhaps Olivia could not get away from her father.

I opened the door expecting the worst, but nothing could have prepared me for what waited outside.

"Good tidings, Lucifer!"

"Mephistopheles! What are you doing here?" My voice was high and thin.

"I came to celebrate the Christmas holiday with my dear friend and business partner. Are you surprised? Let me in, will you? It's freezing out here." Mephistopheles brushed past me, carrying with him a bottle of vintage champagne.

I closed the door, feeling all my hope slip away.

"Going somewhere?" Mephistopheles asked, noting the satchel hanging by the door.

"No," I said. "Just haven't unpacked from my holiday."

"Hm," sniffed Mephisto. "So, where did you go? You didn't say in your letter."

"I took a trip to England," I said.

"Back to the place where you were hanged and buried alive? Doesn't sound like a holiday to me."

"No, it wasn't really," I said.

"Well, you're back now," said Mephistopheles. "That is what matters."

There was no way I was going to let Mephistopheles ruin my life again. He had been a sore on my bottom since he had rescued me from the grave. And although I owed him my life, I could not forgive him his lies.

"I can't celebrate with you tonight," I said abruptly.

"Why ever not? You have somewhere else to be?" asked Mephisto.

"I'm not feeling well," I said.

"Well, maybe that's because you're drunk." Mephisto turned up his nose at the sight of my soiled chamber pot. "Maybe you just need to sleep it off."

He plopped down on my narrow bed. "Come to bed."

"No!" I said. "You really are a fool!"

Mephisto stared up at the ceiling and laughed. "One day, Lucifer, you will see that there is no one in the mortal world that can truly satisfy your needs. Mortals are nothing, mere shadows of beings. We are the Imorti, and we must stick together."

I glanced at the clock over the fireplace. It was quarter to eleven. I wanted to be at the church by half past so that I would be sure to intercept Olivia.

"What are you so anxious about?" asked Mephisto.

"I need to clear my head," I said. "Walk off the booze."

Mephisto rose and reached for his coat. "Then let's walk."

"No. Alone."

Mephisto eyed me suspiciously but never ceased smiling.

"Very well," he said. "We will have a little celebration when you return."

Mephisto watched my moves very closely. I would have to leave the satchel. What choice did I have? I couldn't very well pick it up on the way out without giving away my true purpose. I tried to look casual as I slipped my jacket on, but the Spanish dollars jangled loudly in my pockets, again arousing the suspicion of Mephistopheles.

"Lucifer," he said with a sly smile. "Are you gambling?"

I started to deny the accusation, but then I decided to try a different approach.

"Yes," I said. "You are perceptive, Mephistopheles. I have a game of dice down at the tavern for which I am late."

"Hah! I knew you were up to something," said Mephisto. "Well, I find dice exceedingly boring. I'll sit this one out."

"You weren't invited." I couldn't help myself. Mephisto was getting on my last nerve. Then, with my coat pockets rattling, I swept out of the apartment.

I half expected Mephistopheles to follow me, so I took a circuitous route, past the tavern, through the park, and then south again toward the church. Nobody seemed to be trailing me, so it was with relief that I came upon St. Michael's at half past eleven. Worshippers wishing to honor God on this most holy of nights were pouring in the front doors.

When I entered the church, I kept close to the walls. There must have been a thousand candles burning inside. The light was dazzling. Pastor Konstantin would be in the rectory preparing for mass, but nevertheless, I didn't want to chance being seen. I stayed tucked away in the crowd and made my way through the nave to the bell tower.

Here there were a few torches burning in the walls, but the stairwell was dark. I started to climb. The low murmur of the churchgoers faded as I ascended the stairs. When I finally reached the belfry, the light of the moon shone brightly enough for me to see clearly all around. The platform was empty, and the air was still and quiet. I tightened my cloak about my shoulders and waited.

It must have been quarter to midnight. I gazed long and hard at the masts of the ships in port, wondering which one was the *Reaper*. A sudden gust of wind swept through the belfry, whipping up my overcoat and ruffling my hair. A good omen. We would need the wind tonight if we intended to make a speedy getaway. I didn't know much about sailing, but I suspected the easterly breezes would hasten our westward escape.

The fall of footsteps on the stairs roused me from my reverie. I turned just in time to see a figure rise from the dark.

"Mr. Ellsworth."

Dr. Bartlett stood before me with a flintlock pistol pointed at my head.

I stepped back, but there was nowhere for me to go. Dr. Bartlett stood between me and the stairwell. All around us the scaffolding creaked and moaned in the breeze.

"Where is Olivia?" I demanded. "What are you doing here?"

"Olivia is at home where she belongs," said the doctor. "She told me about your little plan."

"Why would Olivia tell you anything?" I spat.

"You think she loves you?"

"I know she does."

"Then why did she give you up?" The doctor smiled and arched his eyebrows.

"What have you done with her?"

"That is no longer your concern. Olivia stays with me, and you will burn in Hell."

He cocked the pistol and took aim.

"You cannot kill me," I said, stepping toward the doctor, hoping to threaten him.

"No," said the doctor, standing his ground. "But I can put a hole in your head the size of a shilling. My men are on their way now. You have no choice but to do as I say."

I may have been immortal, but a bullet through my brain would quickly immobilize me. No doubt I would lose consciousness. And I didn't want to wake up ten feet underground again; the mere memory of those years in the grave was enough to make me rethink my strategy.

"Don't shoot," I said. "I will go with you willingly."

"I highly doubt that."

The doctor's trigger finger twitched. I braced myself for impact. Then a figure leaped from the stairwell and gave the doctor a firm push. There was a bright flash as the gun went off. I felt the impact of the bullet in my shoulder, and I fell back against a column in a daze. The doctor stumbled sideways, tripped over the edge of the tower, and landed hard on the wooden scaffolding. The planks gave way beneath his weight, and the doctor fell through the decking and out of sight.

The bells of St. Nicholas rang the midnight hour, marking the advent of the Christmas holiday and the start of midnight mass. Pastor Konstantin rushed to my side, his ceremonial robes billowing in the wind. My wound was bleeding, but I did not feel especially hurt. I said so to Pastor Konstantin, and with his help, I rose to my feet and peered over the edge of the tower. The doctor had crashed through three levels of scaffolding and now lay moaning on the wooden planks below.

"You must go," said the pastor. "Before more men arrive."

"How did you know I'd be here?"

"I didn't. I came to ring the midnight hour."

"But your fear of heights?"

"It was God's will."

I clasped Pastor Konstantin's hands in my own. "Thank you."

"Go!" he said.

I descended the stairs and emerged in the nave, where people were still milling about, finding their seats, awaiting the arrival of Pastor Konstantin, wholly unaware of all that was happening 100 meters above their heads. I tried to look calm as I pushed my way upstream. Blood had soaked through my torn overcoat, but the darkness of the wool masked the extent of the damage. Once I was outside, I started in at a full sprint, up Krayenkamp toward Düsternstrasse. The streets were empty, and the windows were dark. All the townsfolk were already asleep or else at church. When I came to the house on Düsternstrasse, I banged on the front door.

"Who is there?" came a voice from inside. She spoke in German.

"My name is Ellsworth," I said. "I've come for Miss Bartlett."

"At this hour?" she exclaimed.

"Her father has had an accident."

The door creaked open slowly, and a timid chambermaid peered at me in the light of a stout candle. I didn't have time to explain myself to this stranger, so I shoved past her and ascended the stairs. Several doors opened off the second-story landing. It was easy enough to find Olivia's chamber. A candle burned at her bedside. Olivia lay delirious on the bed. When she saw me, she said, "Thomas?"

"Yes," I said. "It's me."

She gazed at me in bewilderment. Her pupils were dilated, and she glistened like a porcelain doll.

"What did your father give you?" I demanded.

She shook her head and retched.

"No matter," I said. "Come with me."

I tried to help her to her feet, but when it became clear she could not stand, I heaved her over my shoulder and carried her out onto the landing. Olivia's hands and feet dangled helplessly as I descended the stairs.

"Get the door," I barked at the chambermaid.

The girl ran ahead and opened the front door. I took care not to bump Olivia's head on the way out. The lane was empty. Patches of snow sparkled like stars in the light of the full moon. I trudged down the street toward the docks. It must have been half past midnight now, and Bezier would be starting to worry. But I didn't want any trouble with the locals, so I kept to the least trafficked streets and took the long way down to the riverfront.

I recognized the *Reaper* immediately, but I could see no sign of Bezier. Behind me, I heard a cry and, looking over my shoulder, discerned a small party of men a quarter mile off hastening down the wharf.

The ship bobbed at the end of a long quay. I set off at once down the pier, but just as I came to the ramp leading up to the foredeck, a cloaked figure stepped into my path, pointing a longsword at my chest.

I stopped cold.

"Liar!" It was Mephistopheles. He held the longsword with both hands and pressed the tip of the blade into my diaphragm.

"Let me through," I said.

"You thought you would simply slip away unnoticed," he sneered.

Then it occurred to me. I had left the note from Bezier on my writing desk. A foolish mistake.

"Get out of my way, Mephistopheles."

My shoulder ached from where I had been shot. Mephistopheles eyed the bloody stain on my coat and said, "What have you gotten yourself into this time?"

"What do you care?"

"I do care," he said.

"Then you'll let me through."

Mephistopheles jabbed the sword into my chest, piercing my tunic and drawing blood. "Take me with you."

"Absolutely not."

Mephistopheles shifted the sword so that it was pointing at Olivia's limp frame. "You will take me with you or else the girl dies."

I tried to back away, but Mephisto followed me, keeping the sword trained on Olivia.

There was another cry from down the wharf. The men were closer now. They had spotted us and were signaling loudly to one another.

"They will burn you at the stake," said Mephistopheles.

"Then you will burn with me."

Mephistopheles grinned.

"You need me, Lucifer."

"No," I said.

Mephistopheles advanced. The men were closing in behind me.

"I love you, Lucifer," he said.

I was preparing to throw myself into the Elbe when Jacques Bezier appeared out of the shadows shouldering a large, wooden barrel. He brought it down with a crash on Mephistopheles's head. The sword clattered to the deck, and Mephistopheles lay unmoving on the ground. Blood trickled from his ears.

"Come, milord!" cried Bezier.

I climbed onto the ship. Bezier followed, raising the gangplank behind him. I laid Olivia on the deck and loosened the ropes binding us to the dock. Shots rang out. The men were firing on us. Bezier shouted orders. I followed his commands. The sails went up in a flurry, and the ship lurched away from the pier.

CHAPTER 39

WE WERE SIX DAYS at sea before Olivia was well enough to stand on her own. She climbed the ladder to the main deck and stood with me looking out at the empty horizon. The skies were remarkably clear for December, and the winds were in our favor. The *Reaper* sliced through the water like the slick blade of a guillotine.

"Are you hungry, dove?" Squires appeared at Olivia's side.

"No, thank you, Auntie."

Squires had somehow convinced Bezier to bring her along on the voyage to the New World. "I just can't bear to sit 'round this big old house for months all by myself," she'd said. So, Bezier relented and took her aboard. On the night of our escape, Squires was on lookout duty when Mephistopheles appeared on the dock. Squires alerted Bezier, who bid her to hide belowdecks. Then Bezier watched from the shadows until he had a clear shot at Mephistopheles.

"Heard his head crack wide open, I did!" he said later.

Mephistopheles would recover. Even now, he was probably plotting his revenge. But that didn't matter. Even Jacques Bezier didn't know where we were to drop anchor; the New World was a big place, and I suspected it would be a long time before Mephistopheles caught up to us.

My wound healed, too. The bullet that had lodged itself in my clavicle slowly resurfaced, and I was finally able to remove it with a set of pliers. There was not even a scar to mark where the bullet had gone in.

Olivia was very sick for some time. Her father had coerced the truth out of her using a mix of henbane, mangrove, and deadly nightshade. Any one of those poisons could have easily killed her; that she managed to survive the night was a miracle. Thankfully, as the days wore on, it seemed more and more likely that she would not suffer any lasting damage.

On the seventh day, Olivia had an appetite again. She had yet to inquire about all that had transpired on the night of our escape. She had been too ill to speak at length about anything. But halfway through a lunch of bread and cheese, she asked flatly, "What happened to my father?"

"I don't know," I said. "He was alive last I saw him."

Olivia nodded. "He'll never give up."

We were two months at sea before we reached the island of San Salvador. We sailed another two weeks up the coast, searching for a friendly port. During this time, I shared much of my life story with Olivia—more than I had ever shared with anyone in my long existence.

How did she take it?

Hard to say. She hardly said anything about it. I wondered if she thought I was making it all up. But for the most part, she treated me as she always had. She didn't ask lots of questions, and for the duration of the journey, she kept steering the conversation back to the present—where would we go, how would we live?

She did say something once that struck me as funny.

"I'm relieved there's no Hell."

"Me, too," I said. "A dreadful human invention."

"I always figured that's where I'd end up," she said.

"Hell?"

"Yes."

"But you won't end up anywhere," I said. "How do you feel about that?"

"Much better than an eternity in Hell," she said.

"True."

Then she frowned. "What will become of you?"

"I will go on," I said. "I always do."

And I did. I would have other loves, other heartbreaks, other adventures, other misfortunes. But I never loved another woman as much as I loved Olivia. And when she died, I mourned a long time. Then I moved west.

But that's another diary.

POSTLUDE

❧

I SAW GOD TWO months ago. I was in the UK for the Basingstoke Kite Festival. Basingstoke is just over fifty miles out of central London. I took a Lyft into the city the day after the festival and walked the bank of the Thames from Westminster Abbey to the National Maritime Museum. The yachts on the Thames bobbed like the heads of old ladies nodding off to sleep.

London is very much now as it was in the seventeenth century. It has put on a new face, undergone a sort of plastic surgery characteristic of the twenty-first century. The buildings have been retrofitted, restructured, and replaced. But underneath it all, London still smells of chamber pots and dry rot.

I made my way past the National Maritime Museum, down Park Row, through Greenwich Park, up Duke Humphrey Road, and into Eliot Vale. There is a small alley off Eliot that goes mostly unnoticed. Silverstone is what they call it now, although it has been known by many names. The buildings here have escaped the glossy highlights and fashionable manicures of recent decades. I was glad of such a familiar sight. Brick buildings huddled together against the wind.

Empty windows, empty windowsills. The road was cobblestone. There was an old smell. It reminded me of Olivia. The only people in the alley were down-on-their-luck beggars and panhandlers. I threw a few pounds into a McDonald's cup, and a woman flashed me a toothless smile.

I told myself not to come up this way. But Basingstoke is hardly more than an hour's drive out of London. I could not resist a look at the gate. I made myself the promise not to go in. I planned only to stand outside for a while and take in the scent of eternity, maybe even peek through the bars. What was behind that gate? Heaven. There in Silverstone Alley stood the entrance to Eden: the garden where I was born. I had vanquished myself from that place long ago, but it was hard to keep away. One is inexplicably tied to the womb. And Eden is my womb. So it was that I found myself standing on the cobblestones of Silverstone Alley.

The gate stood as I had left it. The wrought iron bars creaked and moaned like the poor beggars in the street. The place was overlaid with a misty light. The sun never shone directly upon this place. The gravel at my feet was moist, and the air was chilly. If I had stood there a hundred years, I wonder if I would have ever seen a human soul take notice of the old gate. People passed on the street wrapped in their shawls, but none took their eyes off the cobblestones long enough to see the entrance to Eden. Tall hedges flanked the gate on either side. Had the way been clear, I might have been able to walk the whole perimeter of the place in a hundred paces or less. The leaves on the hedges drooped and the gate sagged—the garden might have passed easily for a small graveyard, perhaps belonging to some family in the neighboring brick apartments. Or perhaps it was invisible, because it was shielded forever from mortal eyes, ever since that day the Serpent seduced the man.

I wrapped my fingers around the rungs of the gate and pressed my nose and chin between the bars. There was nothing to see beyond but a light gray fog. I was disappointed. I had hoped to find the gardens in their splendor laid out before me like a picnic on the beach. But God had done well in shielding Eden from prying eyes.

I don't pretend that it was an accident—my hand found the latch. I am immortal, after all, and I can still open doors into Heaven if I like. The gate swung back. I stepped inside and the mist parted like the Red Sea.

The Garden of Eden stood before me. Sweeping lawns, swaying willows beside swan-filled ponds. Trimmed hedges, rows of flowers. Narrow walks lined with wooden benches. The names of the species of plants were engraved on little plaques: crocus, amaryllis, aster, chrysanthemum daisy, freesia, and larkspur. The plaques were a new addition to the garden. Decidedly modern. Across the pond, sprinklers poked their heads out of the ground like gophers and showered the lawn. A small technological advancement. Perhaps Silverstone Alley had escaped the tides of change, but the Garden of Eden had certainly undergone a facelift.

I heard a sudden rumble, the pull of a chain, and a motor starting up. I ducked behind a hedge and slinked cautiously toward the sound. When I crested a small hill, I noticed the form of an angel moving across the lawn. He was pushing a lawn mower before him. He was dressed in a workman's overalls and had over his ears a pair of muffs. I watched him closely as he wound his way around the perimeter of the lawn. He worked diligently and seemed to be humming to himself. When he had come round and was within twenty or thirty feet of where I crouched behind the shrubs, I recognized his face: Michael, guardian of Eden. Only he did not carry a sword and sheath as so many legends told. Rather, he wielded a green deck-side discharge lawn mower and a pair of hedge clippers. He was bobbing his head rhythmically. Occasionally, he mouthed a few words to himself.

"Michael," I cried out.

He did not hear me. He turned the mower around and headed again in the opposite direction. I ran across the lawn and threw my arms around his shoulders. I felt a jolt of surprise run through his body. Then his face turned and saw mine and his expression turned from shock to joy.

He shut down the motor, yanked off the earmuffs, and pulled from his ears two small earbuds that I only then noticed were synched with an iPhone at his hip.

"Look at you," I said. "A lawn mower? What happened to the silver scissors? And what's with the music?"

"Ah," Michael sighed. "Eternity in this garden can start to eat away at you." His words rolled off his tongue like marmalade—the sound of his voice was familiar and reassuring. "I've been listening to Harry Styles to pass the time."

"I see things have changed," I said.

"It's been what, four decades?"

"Five since we last spoke. Have you heard? The humans call you the Guardian of Eden."

"Bah," Michael spat. "I'm merely a humble gardener."

"They also say you carry a sword."

"No, sir. Just these here clippers. What brings you to Eden, old friend?"

"I was at a kite festival in Basingstoke and thought I'd pop in."

"That's good, that's good." Michael glanced at his iPhone. "We'd better be getting off this lawn," he said. "The sprinklers will be coming on any minute, and I have to get the mower back to the shed."

We moved onto a narrow paved road. Michael pushed the lawn mower before him like a baby carriage. We rolled up to a tin shed. Michael lifted the sliding garage door and tucked the mower away inside.

"Are you thinking of paying God a visit?" Michael asked. "I'm sure he wouldn't mind. Been in a good mood lately. He's just down the road. At the sixteenth hole by now I should think. I'll take you to him."

Before I could object, Michael hopped into the driver's seat of an electric golf cart with multi-terrain tires and a sunroof. He flicked the engine on and pulled onto the road.

"Get in," he said.

I slid reluctantly into the passenger seat. I was nervous. It had been over a hundred years since we'd spoken, God and me. It is like that with us. We can go centuries without seeing one another. And yet no matter how many eternities we put between us, we find ourselves inevitably intertwined in the myths and legends of mortals. He is Good, and I am Evil. And we are incomplete without one another.

The cart buzzed down the asphalt road and over a little concrete bridge that spanned the Fluvius. Michael peered ahead, serene as always. Hardly more than two words passed between us.

About a mile out we came upon God's fifty-two-acre golf course, complete with recreation center and gym.

"He had the rainforest torn out. It took me nearly two years to get the thing complete, with a host of thirty-six angels, eleven bulldozers, and countless sprinkler heads. We had some fellow on Earth draw up the plans."

I marveled at God's newest creation.

"It's what he wanted," Michael shrugged. "Eighteen holes, a lounge and bar, an Olympic-sized pool, Jacuzzi, recreational room, seventy-inch flat-screen plasma TV, gym and showers, and a classy little Armenian café. He's been spending all his time out here nowadays."

The golf cart rode smoothly over the hills, past sand traps and long fairways. The holes were marked with bright orange flags: thirteen, fourteen, fifteen. And there he was, poised at the tee of the sixteenth hole, exactly as Michael had predicted. He was wearing white slacks and a matching sports coat. He had dyed his hair. The speckles of gray were gone.

We came up behind him. His personal golf cart stood off to the side. God was practicing his swing, and he didn't turn to see us approach.

"He's got earplugs in," said Michael. "Helps him concentrate."

I nodded. Michael pulled the cart onto the lawn and parked just downwind of the tee. We waited patiently until God had hit the ball up the fairway before speaking.

"My Lord," Michael called, trudging up the hill to where God stood. "My Lord, you have a visitor."

I followed closely behind, hiding as best I could in Michael's shadow. God removed the two yellow earplugs. He peered at us, the sun in his eyes. Except for his dyed hair, he looked the same—only he was smiling, looking relaxed.

Then he truly saw me for the first time.

"Lucifer," he said. "Have you really come?"

"Aye," I said. "I have. I was in Basingstoke for a kite festival and, well ... I just kind of ended up here." I smiled sheepishly and shrugged. "Look at your hair!"

"Do you like it?" God asked. "L'Oréal for men."

"It looks fine."

It looked like a midlife crisis.

"Well, this is a pleasant surprise. It's been a while. What's new? You look great. Really great."

He was talking so fast I thought he might hyperventilate.

"I'm doing well," I said. "I have a place in Berkeley. I work near the university. Scraping by as always."

"Why don't we go back to the bar and get something to drink? You ride with me, Lucifer. Michael will follow behind us."

So it was that I got to ride shotgun in God's very own golf cart. I was special. I was Lucifer, bringer of the light. Even after God in all his glory had come crashing down, even after he had been unmasked and demystified, even after I'd been privy to his darkest thoughts, I couldn't help but feel honored to ride shotgun in his cart.

At the bar, Michael poured us both a drink. God sipped happily away. I suffered my drink more slowly.

"How do you like the clubhouse? Did Michael tell you about the plasma TV?"

"Yes," I said. "He also told me about the pool and gym. Very nice."

"I've been trying to mix things up around here. My therapist says it's the only way I'll be able to move past some of my old issues."

"You're seeing a shrink," I said in surprise.

"Yeah. Once a week. She's really great. Mortal gal in London. I go in every Tuesday for my appointment. She's pretty cool with the whole God thing. She has me on this medication: Paxil. It's an antidepressant. Works wonders."

I smiled. So, mighty God had condescended to visit the lowly human world at last. He had been so opposed to the whole idea of walking among the humans, and now he was immersed in their world—taking their medications, seeking their advice.

God had placed the two yellow earplugs on a coaster at the end of the bar. He had been wearing earplugs since 29 AD. I wondered how the voices in his head were getting along. The human voices—praying, pleading, hoping. God saw me eying the earplugs. He chuckled.

"I hardly need them anymore," he said. "There are some eight billion humans now—I'd have thought they'd be driving me mad with their incessant prayers. But you'd be surprised. People don't talk to me as much as they used to—not nearly as much as before. It's great!"

I knew the Pope wouldn't think it so great. But it made God happy. The twenty-first century had produced a new breed of people—a people less hungry for God. The idea of talking to God had become archaic. Prayers were no longer compulsory. Humans were defining a new faith; it was called science.

"I'm really pleased to see you so happy," I said.

"One hundred years of psychoanalysis will do that to you," he said.

"What convinced you to go down there?"

"You did." He took a sip of bourbon. "You said humans were a wondrous race. That I should try living amongst them for a while."

"I don't remember saying that."

"You did. I didn't listen. Then one day I popped over to Earth for a quick visit. That's another story. But what I saw boggled my mind. Why, the humans are more inventive than even I!"

"Come on," I said. "They still don't know all the secrets you know."

"No, but they have such good ideas. I mean, look at this place." God indicated the bar, the lounge, the flat-screen television.

"They're destroying the Earth with all their good ideas," I said.

"Never mind that! I'll make a new Earth."

I laughed. God was still crazy after all these years. I finished off my drink.

"It's good to see you again," I said, rising to leave. "Really good."

God gripped my wrist tightly. "Maybe I'll come down and see you some time?"

Did I really want to renew my friendship with God? Was I ready to let him back into my life? Five thousand years after I'd left him, I still felt something powerful in his presence. Something like love. I was nervous. Giddy. God wanted to see *me*.

"Sure," I said. "You're always welcome to crash on my couch."

I made my way back to Basingstoke, imbued with a sense of ease that I had not felt since my earliest days in Eden. Maybe God and I could coexist, after all. We had once shared a bed. Surely, we could share a universe.

A NOTE FROM THE AUTHOR

If you enjoyed *Satan's Diary*, please take the time to visit Amazon and Goodreads to rate this book. Hearing from readers like you is the best part of putting a book out in the world. If you are interested in joining my author newsletter, in which I announce deals, giveaways, and other noteworthy news, please visit www.booleanop.com and request to be added. And check out my other titles.

Novels & Novellas:
Do Not Resuscitate
The Maiden Voyage of the Destiny Unknown
Cuckoo Cuckoo
The Secret Order of the Scepter & Gavel

Short stories:
The Button
Three Wishes: And Other Stories
The Misshapen

ABOUT THE AUTHOR

NICHOLAS PONTICELLO is an educator and writer in Los Angeles, California. He graduated from the University of California, Berkeley, with degrees in mathematics and astrophysics and later earned his master's degree in education from the University of Pennsylvania. Mr. Ponticello is interested in exploring the intersection of science, sustainability, mental health, and education and hopes to encourage more systems thinking and sustainability-themed curricula at the secondary school level.

**For more titles by this author, please visit
www.booleanop.com.**

Made in the USA
Las Vegas, NV
20 June 2025

23866752R00208